To Michael Caesàr and Michael Spender

HELL

Steve Ellis, a Senior Lecturer in English at the University of Birmingham, was born and brought up in York, and studied in Florence as part of his doctorate for London University. His frustration as a student with existing translations of Dante spurred a long-lasting desire to translate it himself. His critical works include *Dante and English Poetry: Shelley to T.S.Eliot* and a study of Eliot's *Four Quartets*. A major Gregory Award winner, he has also published two books of poetry, *Home and Away* and *West Pathway*.

BY STEVE ELLIS

Poetry

Home And Away
West Pathway

Criticism

Dante And English Poetry:
Shelley To T.S.Eliot
The English Eliot:
Design, Language And Landscape
In The Four Quartets

Translation

Hell

Dante Alighieri

HELL

TRANSLATED, ANNOTATED,
AND INTRODUCED BY
Steve Ellis

VINTAGE

Published by Vintage 1995

2 4 6 8 10 9 7 5 3 1

Copyright © Steve Ellis 1994

The right of Steve Ellis to be identified as the author of
this work has been asserted by him in accordance with
the Copyright, Designs and Patents Act, 1988

First published in Great Britain by
Chatto & Windus Ltd, 1994

Vintage
Random House, 20 Vauxhall Bridge Road, London SW1V 2SA

Random House Australia (Pty) Limited
20 Alfred Street, Milsons Point, Sydney
New South Wales 2061, Australia

Random House New Zealand Limited
18 Poland Road, Glenfield,
Auckland 10, New Zealand

Random House South Africa (Pty) Limited
PO Box 337, Bergvlei, South Africa

Random House UK Limited Reg. No. 954009

A CIP catalogue record for this book
is available from the British Library

ISBN 0 09 947671 1

Papers used by Random House UK Ltd are natural,
recyclable products made from wood grown in sustain-
able forests. The manufacturing processes conform to
the environmental regulations of the country of origin

Printed and bound in Great Britain by
The Guernsey Press Co. Ltd., Guernsey, Channel Islands

Contents

Acknowledgements

I could not have produced this translation without the assistance, support and distraction provided by many people, above all by my wife Joanna Porter and our children, and by our two families. I should also like to thank many colleagues (too many to mention by name) at the University of Birmingham, above all Tom Davis, who designed and laid out the pages of this book. Also Bob and Moira Taylor, in whose house in Wandsworth this translation was begun, John C. Barnes, A. S. Byatt and Ron Taylor, as well as my original teachers of Dante, John Lindon, Prue Shaw, John Took. Much gratitude is due to Jenny Uglow and Jonathan Burnham at Chatto, and to Jeff Fisher for his cover. There are many more who have made life manageable, or have encouraged me, over the period this work has taken, and to two of these I dedicate it; I must thank finally Mary Gallagher, the indispensable support of the last seven years.

Introduction

1 Translating Dante

This new translation of the *Inferno* aims at reproducing important features of Dante's style which it seems to me previous versions have obscured and misrepresented. It is first of all a colloquial version, in the type of diction, grammatical construction and speech rhythms it uses throughout, and in this it tries to recapture some of the vigour and directness of Dante's original. In the famous letter to Can Grande, lord of Verona, Dante explains how the language he uses in the poem befits its status as a 'Comedy', that is a work beginning in the horrors of Hell and ending in the joys of Paradise, for, as opposed to the high style of tragedy, comedy employs a style that is 'unstudied and lowly, as being in the vulgar tongue, in which even women-folk hold their talk'. Although the authenticity of this letter has sometimes been questioned, it is generally accepted as an accurate description of Dante's purpose and method in the *Comedy*. *Hell* in particular, the first of the three parts of the poem, abounds in striking idiomatic expressions, vivid homely details and comparisons, and dialect terms and phrases, not only from Dante's native Florence but from other Italian regions as well. Previous translations have not really brought out this popular emphasis and indeed have tended to convert a lively and fast-flowing original into something much more plodding, formal and prolix, keeping Dante, as a venerated 'classic', safely within the purlieus of the academy. During the 1970s and 1980s some attempt has been made, if not to recapture Dante's vigour, at least to simplify the language of translation to a kind of plainness that might go some way towards reproducing his 'unstudied and lowly' style; but here again the result has often been a de-energising of Dante (understated long-windedness replacing stately long-windedness) that must have been fatal for the attention of countless readers. One must make an honourable exception here of Dorothy L. Sayers's version of the *Inferno* (1949), which, whatever its faults, does aim at conveying Dante's energy and spiritedness. Of course, this popular emphasis can go too far, and nothing dates more quickly than contemporary slang and modern notions of medieval quaintness, as Sayers's version now shows. Dante's poem not only has an affiliation with the language of the street but also with the language of epic tradition, with Virgil's *Aeneid*, Statius's *Thebaid*, Ovid's *Metamorphoses*. In what follows I have tried not to exclude these competing claims, but keeping a modern reader interested in a medieval Italian poem of over 4,800 lines has meant, for me, using primarily the language of the 1980s and 1990s.

There is a regional dimension here as well: the fact that Dante's poem used a specifically Florentine speech and language, that is, a dialect, has allowed me to draw on my own native Yorkshire background. But I have not wanted to push this to excess: in fact I have rejected the use of individual dialect words and expressions and drawn rather on this background for the basic speech-tones which are employed; indeed some readers may be unaware of this 'northern' input, and it will fall very differently on different ears. For me however this translation is bonded within a particular speech-community, and my objection to other available versions of the poem might be summed up in the belief that they employ no particular language at all: rather an odd mix of the bookish and the self-consciously demotic, a strange hybrid that lives nowhere off the page (nor frequently indeed even on the page).

Many readers will want to know immediately about the 'problem' of *terza rima*, and I can reply equally immediately that I have simply ignored it. The familiar complaint that English simply cannot reproduce the abundance of Italian rhymes might be brought forward here, and yet I doubt that it is convincing. Suffice to say that, in my own poetry, I have always found the handling of rhyme difficult, whereas there are many accomplished rhymesters among my contemporaries: if Tony Harrison, say, turned his attention to Dante we might have a successful *terza rima* version, and Sayers's version (which, along with H. F. Cary's, is the only one I can enjoy reading), uses rhyme. Dante's rhyme scheme of course provides a marvellous musical bonding that not only structures the text but also provides a fluent linkage leading the reader briskly forwards; if *terza rima* is dispensed with then some other means of stimulating readerly momentum must be found. One of the features I have been especially keen to reproduce is Dante's concision and economy, his ability to compress much meaning into a few words, and I hope readers will find that my attempts to avoid unnecessary padding are an aid to narrative fluency. I not only hope that my translation will be found readable, but also that it will be found more accurate than others, for Dante's meaning is often muffled or unwarrantably supplemented by the relative verboseness other translations adopt. I have wanted to be faithful (as far as possible) to both style and meaning; the only 'liberties' I have taken are with punctuation, often introducing a comma for Dante's full stop in the interests of keeping the verse moving. It makes little sense, if you jettison Dante's rhyme scheme, to keep slavishly (as some translations do) to his punctuation, and at times I have used longer verse sentences to make up for the problems with linkage that the absence of rhyme creates. I have tried to avoid making a thing of stops and starts. And although my translation is in free verse, I have attempted to impose formal constraints upon it by regularising line length and the number of words and stresses per line.

How best to annotate Dante might itself provide enough material and debate for the entire Introduction. Even though I have aimed at keeping the annotations to a minimum, they are still fairly substantial, and I hope that readers will find them of most use in their present position, on the same page as the text. There is the danger that the reader will be continually distracted by them and I would suggest that each canto be read straight through, without interruption, before the notes are used. Often Dante himself will provide all the information needed to answer some earlier problems and puzzles in his text; the notes are mainly there to provide supplementary historical and cultural information. Readers of Dante in the original will realise that the page lay-out of this translation is based on Natalino Sapegno's celebrated edition of the *Comedy* (2nd edn, 1968); Sapegno has generally been my Bible where controversial issues of interpretation relating to Dante's text have arisen, though other editions and commentaries have been consulted, as the notes make clear.

2 Dante's Life and Works

Dante's writings are heavily autobiographical, and most of our knowledge about his life comes from them, though it is supplemented by a famous *Life* written by Boccaccio and a few other accounts and documents. In the *Paradise* (XXII, 115) Dante tells us that he was born under the sign of Gemini (21 May–21 June), and we can work out the year, 1265, from various places in his writings, as at the beginning of *Hell*. His family seem to have been small landholders, settled for several generations in Florence, who eked out their income through money-lending; as a young man Dante received a good education at various convent schools in the city, and may or may not have owed his early training in rhetoric and in classical literature to Brunetto Latini, whom he meets and salutes as his teacher in *Hell*, canto XV (see notes to ll. 30, 84). The main works of Dante's youth are the sonnets, *ballate* and *canzoni* that he collected together in the early 1290s and to which he added a prose commentary, entitling the whole the *Vita nuova* (*New Life*); this famously recounts his first encounter with Beatrice at the end of his ninth year, going on to describe the course of his love for her, her early death (in 1290), and his final vow to write a major work about her (which became the *Divine Comedy*). Its importance as a poetic document is recognised in *Purgatory*, canto XXIV, where Dante has his poetic predecessor Bonagiunta da Lucca coin the famous term 'dolce stil nuovo' ('sweet new style') to sum up the *Vita nuova*'s innovatory quality. Dante wrote the first of the sonnets preserved in the *Vita nuova* when he was eighteen; the whole book is a fervent, mystical and esoteric working of the *fin amour* tradition into a Christian context in which Beatrice becomes the vehicle of divine grace and of Dante's salvation, roles which she will resume in the *Comedy*, where her allegorical function is manifest (see note to *Hell*, II, 70). As a book full of enigmas, visions and arcane symbolism, and one addressed to a circle of fellow-poets and initiates, it is well calculated to appeal to later circles of initiates like the Pre-Raphaelite Brotherhood, with whom for the English reader it probably remains most closely associated (D. G. Rossetti's own translation can still be recommended).

The *Vita nuova* is not in any sense a 'realist' narrative; Dante never reveals Beatrice's historical identity or identifies the city in which it is set, nor does he give us any contemporary detail or context that is not part of his symbolical plan. It was left to later writers like Boccaccio to begin the romantic novelisation of Dante's book, and to tell us that Beatrice was a member of the Portinari family and was later married to Simone di Geri de' Bardi, thus inviting us to speculate on all sorts of personal and domestic details that Dante was not concerned with. The raging nineteenth-century rejection of Beatrice as an allegorical invention now seems more to emphasise the Victorian cult of 'manly' love for a womanly woman than to inform us about Dante's book; certainly I can now take Beatrice as a convention of some kind without feeling that I am impugning Dante's sense or his sensuality. Of his life beyond Beatrice in the 1280s the *Vita nuova* tells us nothing; nothing, for example, about one of the best-known dates in the early biographies, 1289 and the battle of Campaldino, when the Florentine Guelphs defeated the Ghibelline forces headed by Arezzo, and where Dante served in the Florentine cavalry (see the opening of *Hell*, XXII and note).

The Guelph–Ghibelline struggle raged throughout Italy during Dante's lifetime. The latter party represented the claims of the German emperors in Italy and was mainly identified with the feudal aristocracy; the Guelphs pressed the claims for independence of the various Italian cities and communes, recruited from the lesser gentry and the mercantile classes, and looked to the Pope for support. In 1260 the Tuscan Ghibellines won a great victory at Montaperti near Siena, but their subsequent control of Florence was short-lived; the Pope called on the French crown for assistance, which led to the decisive defeat of the Emperor Frederick II's son Manfred by Charles of Anjou at Benevento in southern Italy in 1266. Charles assisted the Florentine Guelphs to take over their city in 1267 and enact fierce revenge on the Ghibellines. The story of these years is given in *Hell*, canto X, where Dante meets the soul of the great Ghibelline leader at Montaperti, Farinata degli Uberti, who died in 1264. After the Guelph ascendency in 1267 Florence enjoyed some decades of relative stability and commercial expansion, largely through its banking, usury and wool trades, but although Dante himself belonged to a Guelph family he looks back on this period in the *Comedy* with a good deal of misgiving; in cantos XV and XVI of *Hell* he laments the decadence that has overtaken Florence with the quick money that can now be made there, and the accompanying influx of undesirables (see especially XVI, 73 and note). Throughout the *Comedy* Dante's nostalgia for a Florentine society of probity, discipline and aristocratic civility is recurrently contrasted with the commercial boom city it has become. Many of the figures he meets in Hell in fact seemed to exemplify the former, so that part of Dante's painful education is the discovery that they too are damned (see, for example, VI, 79 and note).

After completing the *Vita nuova* in the early 1290s Dante's philosophical studies began in earnest, leading to his immersion in writers like Boethius, Cicero and Aristotle, and to his writing *canzoni* on ethical and philosophical themes. By the mid-1290s he was also involving himself in the government of Florence, and council records report his participation on several occasions. By 1300 he had been elected one of the six priors who governed Florence for periods of two months (15 June–15 August in his case), and during his governorship the recent party feuding between the so-called Black and White

Guelphs, which originated in nearby Pistoia, came to a head. Dante was a signatory to the decree of exile against the leaders of both parties, a decree that was eventually to lead to the Blacks' intriguing with Pope Boniface VIII and to their triumphant return to the city, assisted by the forces of the French king's brother, Charles of Valois (these events form the background to *Hell*, canto VI). When the Blacks resumed control, Dante, who belonged to the White party, was away on an embassy from Florence which had been sent to treat with Boniface VIII, and in a decree of 27 January 1302 he was charged with corruption while in government, and penalised by a fine, two years' exile, and disqualification from future office (see further the note to XXI, 2). Dante's refusal to meet these conditions led to a second proclamation of 10 March in which he was condemned with fourteen others to be burned at the stake *in absentia*; after he had set out on the embassy of 1301 he never returned to Florence again.

The last twenty years of Dante's life were years of exile in various Italian courts and cities, in which he produced the *Divine Comedy* and also a great deal of other writing. At first Dante seems to have joined in the Whites' schemes to return to Florence, but he quickly fell out with these, as *Hell*, XV, 71 and especially *Paradise*, XVII, 61–9 indicate. This last passage is part of a famous speech by Dante's ancestor Cacciaguida in which Dante's exile is described, and its hardships: 'You'll find how salty it tastes,/other people's bread, how hard it is/going up, down, other people's stairs' (*Paradise*, XVII, 58–60). Cacciaguida 'predicts' that Dante's first refuge will be with the della Scala family, lords of Verona, and anticipates in particular the munificence of Can Grande della Scala, who was Dante's patron after 1314. In between we learn from the concluding lines of *Purgatory*, canto VIII, that Dante was received by the Malaspina family, lords of Lunigiana, around 1306, and we know that his final refuge, from 1317, was in Ravenna with Guido Novello, count of Polenta, on a mission for whom he died on 13 or 14 September 1321. He is buried at Ravenna, in spite of many subsequent Florentine attempts to get his bones returned to his native city.

In the early years of exile, from about 1304 onwards, Dante was at work on two prose treatises, the *De vulgari eloquentia* and the *Convivio*. The former is a search for a quintessential, 'standard' Italian that might underlie all the various tongues and dialects spoken throughout Italy, an Italian appropriate to a regal court if Italy actually had a political and administrative centre. Dante concludes that such an Italian language is available in the work of the poets (i.e., himself and his contemporaries) who epitomise the cultural efflorescence of late thirteenth-century Italy. The *De vulgari* is both a study in poetics and an adumbration of political unity for Italy, set, however, against the dark background of the real state of affairs, where even in the same city people can speak two different dialects, as if in token of the prevailing civil discord. The *Convivio* (or *Banquet*) is Dante's longest prose work, written deliberately for a wider audience (and hence in Italian) who may not have the time or means actually to sit themselves at the table of Philosophy, but who may benefit from receiving some of the crumbs from the banquet, which Dante is intent on passing to them. A deeply autobiographical work, written partly with the intention of repairing Dante's reputation after the political calamities that have befallen him, it includes at the outset a picture of the poet in exile, 'wandering as a pilgrim, almost a beggar, through nearly every part to which our language extends . . . like a ship without sail or steering, brought to all sorts of ports and harbours and shores by the dry wind that wretched poverty breathes' (I, iii, 4–5). The *Convivio* was a planned fifteen-book work, taking the form of commentaries on fourteen of Dante's own *canzoni*; concerned with purely philosophical ideals of human behaviour and virtue, it follows a humanist programme that is enormously indebted to Aristotle and that excludes from consideration specifically Christian ideas about grace and redemption. Also, like the *De vulgari*, it frequently eulogises Virgil's *Aeneid*; if in the Latin treatise Virgil's poem is upheld as a poetic and stylistic exemplar, in the *Convivio* Dante is more concerned with treating its hero, Aeneas, as a model of humanist virtue, and with praising the Roman Empire as a divinely ordained political institution, ideas that will feed powerfully into the *Divine Comedy* itself.

The *Convivio* was broken off unfinished, after four books, and it is frequently surmised that it was the gathering momentum of the *Comedy* that led Dante to abandon his other projects. We do not know exactly when the poem was begun, and there is a theory that the early cantos at least date from before Dante's exile (see notes to *Hell*, VIII, 1 and VI, 70), but most commentators would see the entire poem as a post-exile work. Dante's belief in the Empire as institution is displayed not only in the *Convivio* but also in the series of letters he wrote in support of the Emperor Henry VII's expedition into Italy, to claim imperial lordship over the peninsula, between 1310 and 1313, letters of encouragement to Henry himself, to the rulers of Italy calling on them to accept Henry, and specifically to Florence, fulminating against its resistance to the imperial claim. Henry unsuccessfully laid siege to Florence in the autumn of 1312, and was to die the following year near Siena, and with him died Dante's hopes of the imperial restoration. It was during or after Henry's campaign that Dante wrote his political treatise *Monarchia*, in which he claims that the Roman Empire was ordained by God as the optimum system of rule, and the only one capable of controlling the internecine feuds of the Italian peninsula; the ideal of Empire and Papacy working hand-in-hand, controlling humanity's temporal and spiritual welfare respectively, is developed at length here and underpins the entire scheme of the *Divine Comedy*, testifying to the passionate symmetry of Dante's imagination.

Enough has been said to indicate how Dante's life and writings are inextricably entangled, and how that life itself could be seen as having 'the quality of art', in W. B. Yeats's phrase. Yet on some personal matters Dante's works are curiously silent: on his marriage and family, for example. We do not know precisely when he married Gemma di Manetto Donati, but we do know they had at least three children who were incriminated in Florence's charges against him, and who may have shared part of his exile (two of them, Pietro and Jacopo, later wrote commentaries on the *Comedy*). In

1315 Florence repealed this exile, and the sentence of death, but only upon Dante meeting certain conditions, which he refused to do; a letter to an unnamed friend exists in which he rejects these scornfully. We might leave the final encomium of Dante, and description of his hardships, to a well-known passage from Boccaccio's *Life*:

Studying generally requires privacy, the absence of worry and a calm state of mind . . . But instead of this seclusion and quiet, Dante, practically from the beginning of his life to the day of his death, experienced fierce and intolerable feelings of love, a wife, family and public responsibilities, exile and poverty.

And Boccaccio's judgement as to how Dante would have fared without these impediments is emphatic: 'io direi che egli fosse in terra divenuto uno iddio', he would have become a god on earth.

3 The *Divine Comedy*

Hell is the first of the three parts of the *Divine Comedy*, and is followed by *Purgatory*, in which Dante, still accompanied by Virgil, climbs the mountain of purgation and is reunited with Beatrice in the earthly paradise on its summit, and by *Paradise*, where Beatrice escorts Dante through the ten spheres of Heaven and towards a concluding vision of God. The entire poem (which Dante himself simply entitled the *Comedy*, the epithet 'Divine' being a sixteenth-century addition) consists of one hundred cantos, with canto I being an introduction to the whole, so that each part can be sub-divided into thirty-three units (there is obvious numerological symbolism here, relating to such things as the age of Christ at his death and to the fact that what Dante calls the 'perfect number' in the *Vita nuova* (XXIX, I), i.e., 10, is multiplied by itself to give the whole). Here I intend to make some very brief comments on *Hell*, preferring that the reader should proceed quickly to the poem itself, and given that the notes accompanying the text provide sufficiently comprehensive information.

The poem opens famously with the pilgrim lost in the 'dark wood', generally taken to represent Dante's mid-life crisis in which his earlier contact with God, through the intermediary of Beatrice, has been exchanged for a fruitless immersion in the secular: local politics, civil strife, even the over-absorption in classical learning and literature. Yet this classical heritage itself richly informs the poem; Virgil is sent by Beatrice to rescue Dante by showing him the workings of the divine plan in the afterlife; many of the details of Hell are taken over from the classical Hades; the ethical categorisation itself is Aristotelian, rather than specifically Christian. Thus Virgil will explain in canto XI how the major division into 'upper' and 'lower' Hell, the latter entered by Virgil and Dante through the gates of the city of Dis in canto IX, is based on Aristotle's distinction between sins of incontinence and of malice. Indeed, many readers new to Dante may be surprised at the relative absence of 'theology' in *Hell*, and at the concentration on secular politics that informs much of it.

Canto XI is a good example of Dante's marvellous powers of clear and concentrated exposition, and might be set beside other notable instances of this, such as the description of the old man of Crete and of the arrangement of the rivers of Hell in canto XIV, and of the lay-out of the eighth circle, Malebolge, at the beginning of canto XVIII. As well as the celebrated graphic realism of cantos like XXI and XXVIII–XXX, these passages of technical exposition have their own brilliance and their own challenges for the translator, which can be as gratifying as reproducing Dante's more vibrant passages. I have not included in my commentary any 'maps' or diagrams of Hell, preferring to leave it to the reader's imagination to construct the place from information Dante himself provides. As we go deeper into Hell, the scenes become more violent, vivid and disgusting, though as early as canto VI we have a foretaste of such things in the gluttons, wallowing in the rain-drenched mire. Cantos I–V might seem a little slow-moving in parts, with the expository matter of cantos I–II and the description of Limbo in IV, but these emphasise by contrast the frenzy and drama we are about to embark on, beginning with the episode of Paolo and Francesca in canto V.

From the beginning of the journey proper, in canto II, to the final encounter with Lucifer, canto XXXIV, twenty-four hours elapse, and during that journey Dante provides time references and topographical measurements which contribute to the sense of verisimilitude that invests this supernatural vision with such everyday power. One wonders how much Dante's attention to the details of time and place has contributed to a work like Joyce's *Ulysses*; and more, how much what Auerbach called the 'well-nigh incomprehensible miracle' of Dante's language and of his realism is the founding voice of modern literature.

Further Reading

Most of Dante's works other than the *Comedy* are also available in English translation. Apart from D. G. Rossetti's translation of the *Vita nuova*, there are modern versions by Barbara Reynolds (Penguin Classics 1969) and Mark Musa (OUP 1992). Dante's *Letters* have been translated by Paget Toynbee (Clarendon, 1920), and the *De vulgari* as *Literature in the Vernacular* by Sally Purcell (Carcanet, 1981). There are several Victorian or more modern versions of the *Convivio* and the *Monarchia*.

The English commentaries on *Hell* which I have found particularly helpful are those accompanying Dorothy L. Sayers's translation (Penguin, 1949), and Mark Musa's (Penguin, 1984). See also Charles H. Singleton's *Commentary* (Princeton University Press, 1970). Boccaccio's *Life* (he also wrote a commentary on part of *Hell*) can be found in *The Early Lives of Dante*, trans. Philip H. Wicksteed (Chatto & Windus 1907).

Modern criticism in English on Dante and his work includes George Holmes, *Dante* (Past Masters, OUP, 1980), Robin Kirkpatrick, *Dante: the Divine Comedy* (Landmarks of World Literature, CUP, 1987), Marguerite Mills Chiarenza, *The Divine Comedy* (Twayne Masterwork Studies, Twayne, Boston, 1989). A full account of his life and work is in William Anderson, *Dante the Maker* (Routledge & Kegan Paul, 1980). More detailed studies include Kenelm Foster, *The Two Dantes and Other Studies* (Darton, Longman and Todd, 1977), Patrick Boyde, *Dante Philomythes and Philosopher* (CUP, 1981) and Alison Morgan, *Dante and the Medieval Other World* (CUP, 1990). The forthcoming volume on *Hell* in the *California Lectura Dantis*, ed. Allen Mandelbaum and Anthony Oldcorn (California University Press), promises to be very useful. See also chapter 8 of Erich Auerbach, *Mimesis*, trans. Willard Trask (Princeton University Press, 1953). Dante's influence on some later writers is explored in my *Dante and English Poetry: Shelley to T. S. Eliot* (CUP, 1983); further information about the present translation can be found in my forthcoming article, 'Translating Dante into the 1990s', in *Dante and the Twentieth Century*, ed. John C. Barnes and Ursula Fanning (Dublin: Irish Academic Press).

HELL

CANTO ONE

Halfway through our trek in life
  I found myself in this dark wood,
  miles away from the right road.   3
It's no easy thing to talk about,
  this place, so dire and dismal
  I'm terrified just remembering it!   6
Death itself can hardly be worse;
  but since I got some good there
  I'll talk about the bad as well.   9
I can't say how I wandered in,
  I was in such a heavy slumber
  the moment I left the right way.   12
But then I reached rising ground
  where this wood came to an end
  that had so horrified my heart,   15
and I looked up: the hill top

1 **Halfway** etc: at thirty-five years of age, half of the Biblical 'three-score years and ten' (Psalms, 90: 10). The poem is set in the year 1300 (Dante was born in 1265), near the beginning of spring (see later in this canto, ll. 37–40). In XXI, 112–14 we are told that Dante's journey to the afterlife begins exactly 1266 years after Christ's death, which serves to fix the descent into Hell as occurring on Good Friday 1300, the day that dawns at l. 37. Dante leaves Hell on Easter Sunday, in a symbolic concordance with Christ's death and resurrection.

2 **this dark wood**: the symbolic wood of Dante's own sense of sin and spiritual travail, and more generally the benighted state of a whole civilisation gone astray, the remedy for which will be outlined in the political and religious teaching of the *Comedy*.

13 **rising ground**: the hill Dante comes to represents the virtuous life, illuminated by the sun (l. 17) of God's grace.

already wore that planet's rays
18   that light up the paths of men.
So my fear thawed out a little
that had iced over my heart
21   on this night of such misery.
I was like a weary swimmer
getting from the sea onto shore,
24   gazing back at the huge waves;
so my spirit was still escaping
as it went back over that stretch
27   no one ever comes through alive.
Now I rested for a moment,
then on up that lonely slope
30   with the firm foot always lower.
And here, just at the beginning,
there was a spotted animal
33   like a leopard, racing about,
who wouldn't get away from me:
in fact, he impeded me so much
36   I often turned round to return.
It was right at the start of day,
the sun rising with those stars
39   he'd risen with the first time
God started all this beauty going,
so they seemed like good omens,

27 **no one ever** etc: the wood of sin leads to the death of damnation; so few survive it that Dante can be permitted his hyperbole here: the hill on the far side of it is 'lonely' (l. 29).

30 **with the firm foot** etc: the line has caused much controversy. The simplest explanation is that Dante's weight tends to be backwards rather than forwards in the climb, indicating the difficulty and even reluctance involved in the arduous ascent to virtue.

33 **like a leopard**: the Italian is 'lonza' rather than 'leopardo', but it's clear that an animal like a leopard, if not identical with it, is meant. It symbolises lust, as the lion and wolf we're about to meet represent pride and greed for possessions, this latter in particular being the root cause of the world's corruption in Dante's eyes (l. 51). Again, we are meant to see the animals as having a much wider social import than as sins specific to Dante.

38 **the sun rising** etc: the sun was thought to have been in the first sign of the zodiac, Aries (21 March–21 April) at the Creation.

2

the hour and sweet season, against 42
this beast with the brilliant skin.
   But they couldn't stop my panic
when I found a lion there too, 45
and he came for me, I thought,
   his head high, mad with hunger,
so even the air seemed terrified. 48
Next a wolf, greediness itself
   oozing from her famished body,
the cause of hurt to so many – 51
well, this one upset me so much
   just from the fear of her look,
I gave the hill up completely. 54
I was like him that likes to win,
   but then the time to lose comes
and all his thoughts turn sour; 57
so this animal that never rests
   pushed me backwards, bit by bit,
to where the sunshine's silent. 60
Now as I plummeted downwards
   a figure rose before my eyes,
hoarse from long silence, it seemed. 63
When I saw him in this wasteland
   I shouted out, 'Have pity on me,
whatever you are, man or ghost!' 66
He says, 'Not man, though I was:
   my parents came from Lombardy,
both born at Mantua; I was born 69

63 **hoarse from long silence:** Virgil is best understood at this point as representing allegorically the voice of reason and human wisdom, which hasn't spoken to Dante for a long time; hence his situation.
67 **He says** etc: The figure is Virgil, symbol of wisdom, reason and human learning, and author, in the *Aeneid*, of an epic poem that the *Comedy* pays tribute to and emulates.

The imperialist politics of Virgil's poem are the inspiration for Dante's own world-view, both in this present work and in his treatise *Monarchia*; Virgil's own account of the underworld in *Aeneid* VI, and his reputation in the Middle Ages as a prophet of Christianity, supplement his qualifications to be Dante's guide. The humanistic heritage is thus co-opted here into medieval Catholicism.

sub Julio, even though it was late,
then I lived under good Augustus
72   when our sham gods lied to us.
I was a poet; I sang of him,
Anchises' son, that noble Trojan
75   who left the proud, burning city.
But you, why sink under again?
Why not climb this gorgeous hill,
78   this road to perfect happiness?'
'You're not that Virgil, that spring
where all the river of style rises?'
81   I ask this, awe all over my face.
'O light, O glory of every poet,
may my devotion benefit me now,
84   and all my studying of your book.
You're my master, and my author,
only source of that noble style
87   that's helped me to some honour.
You see this beast that stops me:
O mighty poet, help me with her,
90   she makes all my pulses tremble.'
'You'll have to go another way,'
he says, watching while I cried,
93   'if you want to leave this waste:
this creature you're hollering at,
she lets no one past her, rather
96   she'll hound him till he's dead;
and her nature's one so monstrous
she'll never fill her greedy guts,

70 **sub Julio** etc: in the time of Julius
Caesar, though before he came to
power (Virgil was born in 70 BC).
Caesar was assassinated in 44 BC, so
Virgil was born too late to enjoy his
patronage.
74 **Anchises'** son: Aeneas, whose
flight from Troy and founding of the
Roman state form the matter of
the *Aeneid*.

86 **that noble style:** in the *De vulgari*
(II, iv, 5–8) Dante discusses the
'tragic' style of poetry, that most
elevated in subject and construction,
and which is suited to works that
deal with arms, love and virtue. The
philosophical and love poetry he'd
written before 1300 would then fall
into the same general category as the
Aeneid.

after she eats she's hungriest.   99
Yet she never lacks for husbands
and never will – until the Dog
comes, who'll hunt her to death.   102
He won't chase gold or territory
but wisdom and love and virtue;
he'll be born into felt swaddling.   105
He'll rescue this prostrate Italy
that the wounded fell for, Turnus,
the maid Camilla, Euryalus, Nisus.   108
He'll chase her through every city
till she's hunted back into hell,
where she was till malice freed her.   111
So now I say, for your own good
you follow me, and I'll lead you
out of here, and through eternity;   114
you'll hear some grisly screaming,
you'll see ancient ghosts in tears
howling over their second death,   117

101 **the Dog**: this famous prophecy of the wolf's pursuit and death has never been satisfactorily explained, the two most favoured identities for the Dog being probably the Emperor Henry VII and Can Grande della Scala, ruler of Verona from 1308 to 1329 and a patron of Dante's. Dante purposely leaves the identity undisclosed, and he may indeed have had no specific individual in mind; the following lines suggest however a religious rather than secular leader, one who would cleanse the church of its covetousness, a recurring complaint in the poem.

104 **but wisdom** etc: the three attributes of the Trinity (the Son, Holy Ghost, Father respectively).

105 **he'll be born** etc: another much-disputed line. The Italian, 'tra feltro e feltro', has sometimes been thought to indicate a geographical location for the Dog's birth, between Feltre (in the Veneto) and Montefeltro (Romagna). The literal reading 'between felt and felt' seems preferable – i.e., the Dog will be born into low estate (felt would make a rough, coarse swaddling) or even brought up by the Franciscans.

107 **Turnus** etc: Dante records figures killed on both sides in the conquest of Latium (lower Italy, including the region where Rome was subsequently founded) by the Trojans. Turnus, leader of the Rutilians, was killed by Aeneas himself (*Aen.*, XII, 697–952), Camilla was the daughter of the king of the Volscians and died in battle (*Aen.*, XI), while Euryalus and Nisus were Trojans killed fighting the Volscians (IX, 179–445).

117 **second death**: probably referring to the state of damnation itself.

but you'll see contented spirits too
in their fires, who hope to come,
120   when they can, to the blessed.
But if you want to visit these,
there's one better than me for it:
123   I'll leave you to her when I go,
because that Emperor ruling above,
well, I rebelled against his law,
126   so he won't let me lead you in.
Emperor everywhere, king there:
that's his capital and his throne;
129   to be summoned there is ecstasy!'
I tell him, 'Poet, I ask you now
by this God you didn't know of,
132   so I escape this evil and worse,
that you take me where you've said,
so I can see St Peter's gates
135   and those you paint in such pain.'
Then off he went, and I follow.

118 **contented spirits too**: the souls experiencing the torments not of Hell but of Purgatory, from which they'll eventually be released.

122 **one better**: Beatrice (see Introduction). As he explains in the following lines, Virgil was a 'rebel' to God's law, in so far as the religion of his civilisation was pagan (see further IV, 25–42); allegorically, Paradise can only be entered through the grace of Revelation (represented by Beatrice), not through human reason alone.

134 **St Peter's gates**: the obvious meaning of the gates of Paradise is more likely, rather than the gate on Mount Purgatory guarded by the angel appointed by Peter (*Purg.*, IX, 76ff.).

CANTO TWO

The day was dying, the dark air
  took every creature on the earth
  from its labour, leaving only me   3
to prepare myself for the battle
  of that journey, and its miseries,
  that the memory's going to show.   6
Now muses, and my genius, help:
  O mind that scribbled what I saw,
  this is where you show your worth.   9
And so I began: 'Poet and leader,
  make sure I'm really up to it
  before entrusting me to eternity.   12
You say yourself Silvius's father
  went there, still in the flesh,
  actually alive to the afterlife.   15
But if the enemy of every evil
  was good to him, having in mind

---

7 **Now muses** etc: canto 1 has formed a prologue to the entire *Comedy*, and it is rather here with this invocation for assistance in describing the infernal journey that *Hell* proper begins (similar invocations occur near the beginnings of *Purgatory* and of *Paradise*). The poet's summoning of both internal and external powers in the quest to describe Hell reflects the pilgrim's need of reassurance on the threshold of the journey itself.

13 **Silvius's father:** Aeneas, whose journey to the underworld in *Aeneid* VI involved the meeting with his father Anchises, who prophesied his son's part in founding the future glory of Rome (see ll. 25–7). The idea is maintained in the speech that follows that the classical Roman Empire, however much an ideal of secular government to Dante, was a preliminary to something more important in the founding of the Papacy.

7

18   the who and what that followed,
it seems just to anyone with sense:
he was chosen in highest heaven
21   as father of Rome and Empire,
both set up, to speak the truth,
as foundation of the holy place
24   where St Peter's successors sit.
This visit you celebrated for him,
it gave news that led him onward
27   to his triumph, to papal power.
And later the chosen vessel went
to collect comfort for that faith
30   that opens the way to salvation.
But me, why me? Who allows it?
I'm neither Aeneas nor St Paul:
33   no one, me included, thinks I am.
So if I let myself go further
I'm worried it will all be folly:
36   you're wise, you know my meaning.'
Someone who refuses what he wants
and changes the more he thinks,
39   so the original idea disappears;
that was me in this darkened place,
thinking away all the enterprise
42   that was so lively at the outset.
'If I've understood you properly,'
the ghost of the great man said,
45   'your soul is sunk by cowardice;
this is always mankind's affliction,
so that they spurn good projects
48   and shy like beasts from shadows.
But so you can slip these worries
hear why I came, what I heard

---

28 **the chosen vessel:** St Paul (Acts, 9: 15), who recounts being 'caught up into paradise' in 2 Corinthians 12: 2–4. Extended accounts of Paul's journeys to the afterlife circulated in the Middle Ages. Dante's reference to two such celebrated predecessors as Aeneas and Paul serves to enhance the status of his own divine mission and the teaching it affords.

to trigger off my grief for you.   51
There I was, suspended in Limbo:
a blessed, lovely lady calls me,
one whose orders I begged for.   54
Her eyes outshone all the stars
and her soft and serious voice
was like listening to an angel's: 57
"O noble-hearted Mantuan soul
whose fame still fills the world
and will last for just as long,   60
that friend to me, not fortune,
he's held up on the empty slope
and turns back round in fear;   63
I worry he's already so astray
that I come to his aid too late,
from what I hear up in heaven.   66
But go, and with your poet's speech
and whatever he needs to escape,
help him, so I can be at ease.   69
Beatrice I am, who sends you;
love makes me speak, sending me
from where I burn to be back.   72
When I've returned to our lord
I'll praise you to him often."
Then she was silent. I spoke: 75

52 **suspended in Limbo**: we are to visit Limbo in canto IV; there the souls of virtuous pagans are 'suspended' (IV, 33–45), outside both the joys of Heaven and the pains of Hell.

61 **that friend** etc: one who loves me disinterestedly, not for any advantage from fortune which he hopes to get out of it. The alternative meaning is that fortune, unlike Beatrice (who is speaking), is no friend to Dante: an indication of the suffering Dante has gone through.

66 **from what I hear** etc: we'll be informed what this is later, in Lucy's words to Beatrice (ll. 103–8).

70 **Beatrice**: her allegorical significance as revelation (see note to I, 122), or that science that studies the things of revelation (theology), is suffused throughout this canto with the evocation of her as Dante had already presented her in the New Life; that is, as a Christianised version of the beauteous lady of fin amour tradition, invested with dolce stil nuovo imagery.

9

"Lady of virtues, by which alone
humanity excels all that's inside
78   the heaven with the smallest arc,
I love your instructions so much
I'd feel backwards if I'd begun
81   already; you needn't ask again.
But tell me, how don't you fear
dropping down here, to this core,
84   from those spaces you so desire?"
"Since you want to know so much
I'll tell you quickly," she said,
87   "why it's no worry coming here.
One should only fear those things
that can actually do you harm,
90   others no, they're not fearful.
I've been made so by God's grace
that your pains can't touch me,
93   these blazing fires can't hurt.
A noble lady sorrows in heaven
at this hindrance I send you to,
96   enough to break its iron decree;
and she called St Lucy, told her
how her devotee needed her now,
99   recommending him to her care,

78 **the heaven** etc: the orbit of the moon, which in the geocentric system is the first of the heavens circling the earth. All things within this orbit (i.e., all mortal creatures on earth) are surpassed by humanity in so far as it possesses virtue.

83 **this core:** Hell, at the centre of the earth and therefore of the universe, and circumscribed in contrast to the heavenly 'spaces' (l. 84) Beatrice normally inhabits.

93 **these blazing fires:** a generic reference to the flames of Hell, torments that exist outside Limbo itself.

94 **A noble lady:** the Virgin Mary, transmitter of Divine Grace to Dante, and an intermediary capable of appeasing the severe justice of Heaven (l. 96).

97 **St Lucy:** Lucy, whose name derives from 'lux' (light) represents Illuminating Grace, though the precise allegorical significance of the three ladies in this canto has been explained in a number of ways. That Dante was Lucy's 'devotee' (l. 98) possibly refers to the eye trouble he tells us about in the *Convivio*, since Lucy was the patron saint of the weak-sighted.

and Lucy, foe to anything cruel,
she came to where I sat down
with Rachel, the ancient of days.   102
'Beatrice,' she says, 'praise of God,
succour this one who loved you so
and left the crowd through you.   105
Can't you hear agony in his cry?
Don't you see death bully him,
that flood more vast than the sea?'   108
No one on earth was ever so fast
to fly from evil or to win good
as I was, after these words,   111
and I swept from my holy throne
to put trust in your noble speech
that honours you, and all listeners."   114
After she'd told me these things
her bright eyes turned to tears
which increased my hurry here;   117
so I came just as she wanted,
to rescue you from that animal
on the fair hill's direct ascent.   120
So now what? Why, why dither,
why feed your heart with fears?
Where's your go, your passion,   123
since three holy ladies like these
plead for you in heaven's court,
and I promised you bliss before?'   126
Like flowers all bent and huddled
in cold nights, at the sun's touch
shoot up and out on their stems,   129
so I aroused my jaded spirits
and the fire ran into my heart

102 **Rachel:** one of Jacob's two wives, commonly representative of the contemplative life, hence her proximity to Beatrice.
105 **and left** etc: through the distinction of his earlier poetry in praise of Beatrice and through the ennobling effect of his love for her.
108 **that flood:** cf. 1, 22–7.
126 **and I promised:** referring to 1, 112–29, culminating in the bliss of Heaven.

132   and I spoke, raring to be off:
   'O tender heart that rescued me!
   and you, how good to obey her
135   as soon as you heard the truth!
   You've sparked my wish so much
   to go, with what you tell me,
138   that I'm back to my first idea.
   On then, we're both of one mind,
   you leader, instructor and master.'
141   So I spoke; with him in front
   I started that deep, craggy path.

CANTO THREE

THROUGH ME TO THE CITY OF PAIN,
  THROUGH ME TO ETERNAL AGONY,
  THROUGH ME TO THE LOST TRIBES.   3
JUSTICE MOVED MY MIGHTY MAKER:
  THE DIVINE POWER CREATED ME,
  ALMIGHTY WISDOM, LOVE SUPREME.   6
BEFORE I WAS WAS NO CREATION
  IF NOT ETERNAL, ETERNAL AS ME.
  SHED ALL HOPE, YOU WHO ENTER.   9
This message in bleak characters
  I saw, inscribed above a gateway.
  'Master,' I said, 'what tough words.'   12
But understanding me, he replies,
  'Here any doubts must be dropped,
  any cowardice has to die now.   15
We've arrived where I told you,
  where you'd see spirits in agony,
  losers of the intelligence's good.'   18
And then he takes my hand in his
  and looks serene, so comforted

---

1 THROUGH ME etc: the sudden, dramatic opening of this canto, taking us straight to Hell proper, is in marked contrast to the courteous interchange of Beatrice and Virgil that forms the bulk of canto II.

5 THE DIVINE POWER etc: power, wisdom and love, the attributes of Father, Son and Holy Ghost respectively, all entered into the creation of Hell.

6 BEFORE I WAS etc: Hell was created when Lucifer fell from Heaven (see canto XXXIV, 121–6) after the rebellion of the angels; it thus preceded the creation of mortal life on earth.

18 the intelligence's good: or God, in his identification with supreme truth.

21   I'm led inside to these mysteries.
        Here sighs and sobs and screams
        echo through the starless night,
24   and have me in tears at first:
        strange cries and awful language,
        moans of pain or anger, voices
27   shrill or faint, sounds of blows,
        they all make a great confusion
        whirling in the changeless dark,
30   like sand swept up in a storm.
        And as the horror circles my head
        I ask, 'Master, what's all this?
33   Who are they, so sunk in pain?'
        He tells me, 'This miserable state,
        it's for the sad souls who lived
36   without blame, without praise.
        They're mixed with that evil pack
        of angels, not faithful to God,
39   not rebels, but all for themselves.
        Heaven banishes them its beauty,
        but they're not down in deep hell
42   since guilt might glory in them.'
        I ask, 'Master, what's up with them,
        that they make such awful groans?'
45   He says, 'I'll explain very quickly.

22 **Here sighs** etc: here as in many
places in this canto the description of
Hell is indebted to that in the *Aeneid*,
where the tumult of groans, oaths
and blows is described, and its un-
nerving effect on Aeneas; see *Aeneid*,
VI, 557ff.

36 **without blame** etc: Dante's alloc-
ating these wretched 'neutrals' to a
kind of antechamber on this side of
the river Acheron (l. 71) seems largely
his own invention. His disdain for
them contrasts with the reverence he
will show later for some of the

damned, who in T. S. Eliot's words
'preserve any degree of beauty or
grandeur that ever rightly pertained
to them, and this intensifies and also
justifies their damnation'.

37 **that evil pack** etc: the idea of the
neutral angels has its source in popular tradition, rather than in the Bible
or in patristic writing.

42 **since guilt** etc: the rebel angels
could gloat over those who ended up
with the same punishment as themselves, even though they didn't join
in the rebellion.

They haven't any hopes of death,
    and this life's so low, obscure,
    they've envy of all other states.   48
They've left no records on earth;
    mercy and justice disdain them;
    they're not worth words: look, pass.'   51
Then I looked, and saw a flag
    that circled around so rapidly
    it seemed granted no repose;   54
and behind, such a long trooping
    of people, I'd never have known
    that death had undone so many.   57
Some of them I could recognise,
    including the soul of that coward
    who made the great abdication.   60
Then I understood immediately
    that here was that pathetic crew,
    loathed by God and his enemies.   63
These nonentities, who never lived,
    they were naked now, pestered
    by followings of flies and wasps   66

46 **They haven't** etc: that is, no
hopes of the spiritual death of damnation itself. Cf. I, 117.

50 **mercy and justice** etc: the neutrals are neither pitied nor judged, in
that they're excluded from both
Heaven and Hell. We learn later that
the damned are eager to take up their
place in the scheme of divine justice
(ll. 124–6).

52 **a flag** etc: the *contrapasso*, or
symbolic concordance of punishment
with sin, which obtains throughout
Hell, is emphasised here: the multitud-
inous neutrals took up no cause for
good or evil on earth and now have
an eternity of chasing behind a flag.

59 **the soul** etc: most of Dante's
early commentators identify this fig-

ure as Pope Celestine V, who abdicated in 1294 after five months in
office, and thus allowed Boniface
VIII to succeed him. Dante's attacks
on Boniface as simonist (canto XIX,
52ff.) and political intriguer (XXVII,
90ff.) are repeated at several points
in the *Comedy*; one should also note
the part he played in Dante's own
political fortunes (see VI, 60–70, and
notes). Though Boniface's temporal
ambitions exemplified the corruption of the Church in Dante's eyes, it
seems unlikely that Celestine is here
being blamed on account of giving
them scope; a more likely candidate is
Pontius Pilate, who abdicated responsi-
bility when Christ was brought before
him (Matthew 27: 1–26).

biting the blood from their faces:
blood, tears, trickled to their feet
69   where vile worms lapped it all up.
Now I looked past them, and saw
the near bank of a great river
72   with souls on it; 'Master,' I say,
'tell me about these: what impulse
makes them so keen to cross over,
75   as far as this light lets me see?'
He says, 'You'll know soon enough
when our steps come to a stop
78   by the woeful river of Acheron.'
Then I looked down chastened,
worrying my talk annoyed him,
81   and kept quiet until the river.
And here a boat shoots towards us
with an old, grey-haired pilot
84   crying, 'Damn you, you sinners!
Don't look for any heaven here:
I'm taking you over to the dark,
87   to your eternal furnace, or freezer.
And you over there, still alive,
get away from these dead ones.'
90   But when he sees I won't move
he says, 'Other paths, other gates
will take you to a different shore;
93   your voyage is on a lighter ship.'
But my leader: 'Charon, don't fret:
this is wished where there's power
96   for any wish, so say no more.'

---

78 **Acheron:** river on the threshold
of the underworld found in both Virgil and Homer. Dante further takes
from classical tradition the figure of
Charon, the infernal ferryman (l. 82ff.);
see *Aeneid*, VI, 298–304.
91 **Other paths** etc: Dante explains
in canto II of *Purgatory* how souls

who are saved gather at death at the
mouth of the river Tiber and are
taken by a swift ship to the island-
mountain of Purgatory.
95 **this is wished** etc: Virgil uses a
formula which he will repeat at other
obstructions (e.g. V, 22–4) and which
immediately silences opposition.

Then his shaggy mouth was silent,
   that ferryman of the black mire
   with fiery rings round his eyes.   99
But those souls, exhausted, naked,
   their colour goes and teeth grind
   when they hear his awful words;   102
they curse God and their parents,
   humanity, the place, time, occasion
   of their births, and their ancestors'.   105
And now they all draw together,
   sobbing loudly, on that evil shore
   awaiting all who don't fear God.   108
The devil Charon, his eyes embers,
   he marshals and gathers them all,
   his oar smacking any who delay.   111
As in autumn leaves come away
   one after another, till the branch
   sees all its dress on the ground,   114
so with this bad stock of Adam,
   jumping from the bank one by one
   at a sign, like birds are lured.   117
Then they go on the dark water,
   and before they've landed yonder
   another flock gathers over here.   120
'My son,' says my kind master now,
   'all those who die in God's anger,
   they converge here from every land: 123
and they're eager to sail across
   because divine justice pricks them,

---

101 **teeth grind** etc: cf. 'the wailing
and gnashing of teeth' described in
Matthew 14: 42.
103 **they curse God** etc: echoes the
Biblical curses in Job 3 and Jeremiah
20: 14–18.
112 **As in autumn** etc: the comparison derives directly from the description of the crowds flocking towards

Charon's boat in *Aeneid*, VI, 309–10:
'quam multa in silvis autumni frigore
primo / lapsa cadunt folia . . .'
124 **and they're eager** etc: the desire
of the damned to take up their place
within the scheme of God's justice
highlights the wretchedness of the
stranded neutrals, described earlier
in the canto (see especially l. 48).

126   so their fear turns to yearning.
But good souls never come this way;
and so, if Charon moans at you
129   you see now what his words mean.'
He finished, and that dark region
shook so much, remembrance of it
132   still makes me sweat with fright.
The sad earth belched out wind,
then a flash of crimson lightning
135   knocked out all of my senses,
and I fell as if seized by sleep.

133 **The sad earth** etc: earthquakes and tremors were felt to be caused at this time by the release of vapours trapped in the earth.

CANTO FOUR

A loud thundering in my ears
  broke this deep sleep, and I jump
  like someone woken up by force;   3
and now that my sight was back
  I was up, looking round hard
  to know the place I'd come to.   6
Truly, I found myself on the edge
  of that profound pit of pain,
  that reservoir of endless tears.   9
So dark, deep and obscure it was
  I strained to see the bottom,
  but I couldn't make out a thing.   12
'Down we go to the blind world,'
  said the poet, deadly pale now:
  'I'll be first, you come second.'   15
But noticing his colour I said,
  'How will I do, if you're afraid,
  you comforter of all my doubts?'   18
He says, 'The torture of the people
  in there, this paints my face –
  you see my pity, not my fear.   21
On we go, we've a long journey.'
  So it was he settled our entry

---

1 **A loud thundering**: presumably the aftermath of the commotion described at the end of the previous canto.
7 **Truly** etc: Dante affirms that he is now on the other bank of the Acheron, and has crossed the river in some mysterious way which is not disclosed to the reader.

24   into the first circle of the abyss.
         And here our hearing told us
              there were no screams, only sighs,
27   an eternal rippling of the air,
         sadness without any bodily pain
              that they felt, all the big crowds
30   of children and women and men.
         My good master says, 'Don't you ask
              about them, these ghosts you see?
33   Before going on, you must know
         these didn't sin; but their virtues
              weren't enough without baptism,
36   that key to the faith you hold.
         And those preceding Christianity,
              they didn't love God as is due,
39   and I too belong with these.
         Defective through no other fault
              we're lost, and only punished
42   in living with hopeless desires.'
         I felt heart-sick on hearing him,
              since I knew illustrious people
45   were there, adrift in that Limbo.
         'Lord and master, please inform me,'
              I began, wanting to be sure now
48   beyond any possibility of error,
         'have any here ever won salvation

24 **the first circle:** Limbo, the place as Virgil goes on to explain where the souls of virtuous non-Christians go, with those of unbaptised infants. Their punishment is a desire for God that has no hope of fulfilment (l. 42).
38 **as is due:** others preceding Christianity (like the Hebrews of the Old Testament) did love God 'as is due', and were saved from Limbo as Virgil goes on to explain.
46 **Lord and master:** Dante's affirmation of Virgil's importance to him here takes on an added poignancy after what we've just heard of the limitations of those living outside Christianity. The entire canto reads as a tribute to human reason, with its achievements in art and knowledge, as well as a statement about its limits.
49 **have any here** etc: Dante's desire for confirmation of Christ's Harrowing of Hell may be motivated by the fact that the episode had an apocryphal, rather than biblical, basis (aside from an obscure passage in 1 Peter 3: 18–20).

by their own worth or another's?'
He saw what I was driving at   51
and said, 'I'd recently come here
when I saw this champion arrive,
crowned with the sign of victory.   54
The soul of our very first father
he got out, his son Abel's, Noah's,
Moses the obedient lawgiver's;   57
the patriarch Abraham, King David,
Israel with his father and sons
and the Rachel he laboured for,   60
and many more, whom he made blessed;
but before this, you should know
human spirits had no salvation.'   63
We hadn't stopped while he spoke
but went on through the forest,
forest, that is, of packed ghosts.   66
And when we'd still not gone far
from the entry, I saw some fire
lighting a circle in the dark,   69
and even though we were distant
I half-realised that that part
was for people of some eminence.   72
'O you who grace science and art,
who are these honoured so much
they're separate from the others?'   75
He says, 'Their mighty reputation
that resounds up in your life,
it means heaven graces them so.'   78
And meanwhile I heard a voice:

52 **I'd recently come:** Virgil, who died in 19 BC, would have been in Limbo just over fifty years on Christ's arrival.
55 **our very first father:** Adam.
60 **he laboured for:** Jacob (Israel) served his future father-in-law Laban for fourteen years in return for his daughter Rachel (Genesis 29: 18–28).

72 **people of some eminence:** Dante's reservation of a special part of Limbo for pagan notables and heroes (including Muslims), which he describes later in this canto, seems to be entirely his own invention.
73 **science and art:** or knowledge and technique, two requisites for the epic poet.

'All honour to the glorious poet,
81   his departed ghost now returns.'
When this voice became silent
    four majestic souls approached us,
84   their faces neither sad nor happy,
and my master starts to speak:
    'See the one with sword in hand,
87   preceding the rest like the chief.
That's Homer, the king of poets;
    then there's the satirist Horace,
90   Ovid's the third and last Lucan.
Because they each share with me
    that title that the voice spoke,
93   their tribute to me is proper.'
And so I watched their assembly,
    that rare school, under a master
96   of highest verse, of eagle-song.
After talking together a little
    they turned round to salute me,
99   and my master smiled at this;
then they honoured me even more,
    yes, taking me into their order,
102   so that the sages now were six.
We walked on towards the light,

84 **neither sad nor happy**: not only because of their 'middling' situation in Limbo, but also because of the traditional idea of the sage as maintaining an emotional mean.

88 **Homer** etc: Homer's work was not known to Dante directly, but only through the testimony of Latin authors like Horace and Cicero; his reputation as the 'greatest' of poets is similarly taken over by Dante from his sources. He carries a sword as the poet of the Trojan war. Horace (here as satirist rather than as author of the *Odes*), Ovid (primarily of importance to Dante through his *Metamorphoses*) and Lucan (whose *Pharsalia* recorded the civil war between the forces of Caesar and Pompey) were all widely read in the Middle Ages.

91 **Because** etc: because in honouring me they honour themselves and poetry generally.

95 **a master** etc: probably Homer again, rather than Virgil; 'eagle-song', i.e., the highest form of poetry, is epic, and Homer has historical precedence here.

saying things silence suits now
as much as our speech did then,   105
and we came to a noble castle
with seven high walls round it,
and a lovely stream as defence.   108
This we crossed like hard earth;
then after entering seven gates
we reach a fresh, green meadow.   111
Here, people have slow, grave eyes
with faces of great authority;
they speak sweetly, discreetly.   114
Now we drew apart to one side,
to a high, luminous open space
where everyone could be seen,   117
and up there on that emerald
magnificent spirits were shown me,
an exhibition I exult in still.   120
I saw Electra with many people
including, I noted, Hector, Aeneas,
armed Caesar with his hawk's eyes.   123
I saw Camilla and Penthesilea,
King Latinus in another part
sitting with his daughter Lavinia.   126
I saw Brutus, who ousted Tarquin,

---

104 **saying things** etc: presumably talking about the art of poetry, which would constitute a digression here.

106 **a noble castle** etc: the allegorical significance of the castle has been much debated; it may represent philosophy or human wisdom, with the seven walls representing the various parts of philosophy (metaphysics, ethics, etc.) or the seven liberal arts, with the stream representing eloquence or some moral qualification the philosopher should possess. The meadow is a version of the Elysian fields (*Aen.*, VI).

121 **Electra** etc: mother of Dardanus, founder of Troy, with her descendents, including Julius Caesar.

124 **Camilla** etc: see note to I, 107. Penthesilea was queen of the Amazons, who helped Troy in the Trojan war and was slain by Achilles (*Aen.*, I, 490-4). Latinus, king of Latium, had betrothed his daughter Lavinia to Turnus, from whom Aeneas won her in single combat (see note to I, 107).

127 **Brutus**: leader of the Roman revolt against Tarquinius Superbus, and subsequent founder of the Roman Republic.

Lucretia, Julia, Marcia, Cornelia,
129   I saw the Saladin alone and apart.
When I looked a little higher
I saw the head of all knowledge
132   sat in the family of philosophers,
and all watching him in veneration;
here I saw Socrates and Plato
135   nearer to him than the others.
Democritus, whose world is chance,
Diogenes, Thales, Anaxagoras,
138   Empedocles, Heraclitus, Zeno;

128 **Lucretia** etc: the four women are respectively the wife of Collatinus, who killed herself through a sense of disgrace after being raped by Tarquinius Superbus's son; the daughter of Caesar and the wife of Pompey; the wife of Cato; and the daughter of Scipio Africanus the Elder and mother of the Gracchi. All four women had the status of moral paragons.

129 **the Saladin:** sultan of Egypt from 1174-93, and reputedly a model prince and warrior in the Middle Ages.

130 **a little higher:** the philosophers proper have a superior status to those celebrated for virtuous deeds.

131 **the head** etc: Aristotle, whose praises are sung throughout Dante's works, especially in the *Convivio*. His numerous treatises on ethics, politics, metaphysics, poetics, etc., were widely read in the Middle Ages and were incorporated into Christian teaching through the writings of Thomas Aquinas in particular. The ethical scheme of *Hell* itself owes a great deal to Aristotle, as canto XI will illustrate.

134 **Socrates and Plato:** Dante knew of them through the testimony of Cicero, and considered them the originators of the moral philosophy which Aristotle then brought to perfection.

136 **Democritus** etc: who believed the universe was a chance grouping of atoms with no purpose behind it; Diogenes the Cynic, whose life of ascetic virtue involved living in a tub; Thales, philosopher, astronomer, mathematician, founder of the Ionian school of philosophy; Anaxagoras, who rejected a materialist theory of the universe for one of an omnipresent mind or *nous*. All were Greek thinkers living between the seventh and fourth centuries BC.

138 **Empedocles** etc: fifth century BC, theorist of the construction of all material bodies from combinations of the four elements; Heraclitus (fl. sixth century BC), taught that fire was the primary form of matter, and that the universe was in a constant state of flux as it attempted to realise this primal element; Zeno (c. 336-264 BC), founder of the Stoic school of philosophy; Dioscorides (first century AD), author of a treatise on the medicinal qualities of plants.

that skilful recorder of qualities,
  Dioscorides I mean; Orpheus I saw,
  Tullius, Linus, the moralist Seneca,   141
Euclid the geometer and Ptolemy,
  Hippocrates, Galen, Avicenna,
  Averroës the great commentator.   144
I can't describe them all fully –
  my great theme hounds me on,
  words will often lag behind truth.   147
The company of six loses two:
  my trusty master brings me away,
  from stillness back to the sighs,   150
and we arrive where nothing shines.

140 **Orpheus** etc: Orpheus and Linus, mythical Greek poets referred to by both Ovid and Virgil. Their being placed with the celebrated Roman writer and orator Cicero (Tullius) and with the moralist Seneca (distinguished here from the tragedian, but in fact the same writer) is puzzling, unless reference to the legendary civilising and ennobling power of Orpheus's song is intended. 142 **Euclid** etc: (323–283 BC), famous for his exposition of the principles of geometry; Ptolemy, mathematician, geographer and astronomer, working at Alexandria in the second century AD. His celebrated exposition of the geocentric model of the universe held sway throughout the Middle Ages, and is the basis of Dante's cosmography in the *Comedy*. Hippocrates and Galen are the most famous medical practitioners and writers of antiquity; Avicenna (d. 1036) was an Arab philosopher and physician who wrote an important commentary on Aristotle, though the commentary on the same writer by Averroës (Arab philosopher, d. 1198) was of more consequence for Dante and for Thomas Aquinas.

CANTO FIVE

So I drop from the first circle
  to the second, its girth smaller
  but its pain and grief much more.   3
There is Minos, horrible, snarling:
  he examines sins at the entrance,
  damns with his tail in a twist.   6
What I mean is, when evil souls
  get to him, everything's confessed;
  and that supervisor of sinfulness   9
sees what part of Hell is needed,
  then twists his tail round his body
  as many levels as they go down.   12
Crowds are before him always:
  they go for their hearings in turn;
  they speak, they listen, they drop.   15
'You, here in the hopeless hotel,'
  Minos says to me when he sees me,
  interrupting his enormous office,   18
'look who you trust to enter with:
  don't be fooled by the wide doors!'

---

2 **its girth smaller**: the structure of
Hell as funnel shaped, with the circles narrowing in diameter as Dante
goes deeper, is indicated here.

4 **Minos**: mythical king of Crete, son
of Jupiter and Europa, used by Virgil
as an infernal judge and magistrate
(*Aen.*, VI, 432–3). Dante retains his
function but converts him into a
medieval grotesque (II. 11–12).

20 **don't be fooled etc**: cf. the famous lines from the *Aeneid*: 'fa-
cilis descensus Averno;/Noctes atque
dies patet atri ianua Ditis;/ Sed revo-
care gradum superasque evadere ad
auras,/Hoc opus, hic labor est' (VI,
126–9), and Matthew 7: 13: 'wide is
the gate, and broad is the way, that
leadeth to destruction'.

21   But master says, 'What's the noise?
        Don't obstruct it, his fated visit:
        it's wished where there's power
24   for any wish, so say no more.'
        And now the sad screaming starts
        in my ears; now I've come there
27   where I'm hit by proper misery.
        It's a place where light is silent,
        but it bawls like a stormy sea
30   when it's hit by opposite winds.
        The gale of Hell, that never stops,
        it sweeps the ghosts in its force
33   and spins and flings them along.
        When they come to the rock-ruin
        then it's screams, howls and tears;
36   here they curse the divine power.
        And I was told about this torture,
        that it was the Hell of carnal sins
39   when reason gives way to desire.
        And just like starlings in winter
        go grouped into big, broad flocks,
42   so this blast herds the bad spirits
        and shoots them here, there, up, down;
        there's never any hope of comfort,
45   never any rest or the rarest lull.
        And as cranes sing their songs
        and cross the sky in a long line,
48   so shrieking I saw them come,

23 **it's wished** etc: see note to III, 95.
32 **it sweeps the ghosts** etc: as often, we have the *contrapasso* here, the symbolic concordance of the punishment to the sin (the headstrong, unrestrained nature of the lust that leads to damnation).
34 **rock-ruin:** Dante's meaning is not clear, though it has been suggested that he refers to one of the falls of rock which form descents from one circle to another elsewhere in Hell. If the lustful came down by such a route after Minos's sentence, they might moan and curse with renewed energy each time they were blown near the place of their descent.

some ghosts spun out by this gale:
so I say, 'Master, who's this lot
the black air thrashes so hard?'   51
'The first one you want news of,'
he says, answering my question,
'she was empress of many lands.   54
She was so addicted to lustfulness
that anything went under her laws
to annul any charge she incurred.   57
She's Semiramis, and books say
she wed Ninus and ruled after him,
holding the land that's the sultan's.   60
The next killed herself for love,
and her pledge to Sichaeus's ashes;
then there's that tart Cleopatra.   63
You see Helen, the cause so long
of such evil; see great Achilles
who battled with love in the end.   66
See Paris, Tristan . . . ' – a thousand
he pointed out to me and identified

58 **Semiramis:** legendary queen of Assyria, wife and successor to Ninus, and builder of Babylon with its hanging gardens. Dante takes his information on her from the *History* of Paulus Orosius, who reports among her other sexual excesses an incestuous relationship with her son. The statement that the sultan of Egypt now holds her lands (l. 60) probably arises from confusing the Babylon in Assyria with the city of the same name in Egypt. Stories and traditions that she and all the figures Dante goes on to mention 'met their death through love' (l. 69) (either by suicide or murder) circulated in the Middle Ages.
61 **The next** etc: Dido, queen of Carthage, whose love for Aeneas (re-counted in *Aen.*, (IV) led to her breaking her pledge of fidelity to her dead husband Sichaeus, and to her suicide on Aeneas's leaving her to sail for Italy.
63 **Cleopatra:** queen of Egypt, died 30 BC. Mistress in turn of Julius Caesar and Mark Antony, whose defeat by Octavian led to her suicide.
64 **Helen** etc: her abduction by Paris (l. 67) sparked off the Trojan war. Achilles died during the same war: according to medieval rewritings of the Trojan story his love for Priam's daughter Polyxena led him into a Trojan ambush where Paris killed him.
67 **Tristan:** hero of numerous Arthurian romances, slain by Mark, king of Cornwall, after the discovery of his affair with Mark's wife Isolt.

69   who met their death through love.
After I listened to my instructor
    naming the ancient women and knights,
72   I felt bewildered, lost in thought.
I said, 'Poet, I'd appreciate it
    if I spoke to those two together,
75   who seem so weightless on the wind.'
He says, 'Just wait till they blow
    closer to us, then you invoke them
78   by their driving love; they'll come.'
When the wind bent them near us
    I spoke up: 'Oh vexed spirits,
81   come and talk to us, if God allows!'
Just like doves summoned by desire
    sweep across the sky on impulse,
84   gliding towards their happy nest,
so these came from the Dido group
    and to us through the brutal air,
87   so strong my compassionate cry.
'Oh gracious, good-natured soul,
    visiting through this black weather
90   those like us who bloodied earth,
if the cosmic king was our friend

---

72 **I felt bewildered** etc: the pilgrim Dante's response throughout this canto is characterised by complexity and uncertainty. He here begins to brood on what the heroes of medieval and classical legend and romance have come to, and on the moral status of the whole medieval 'religion of love', the poetry of which has greatly influenced his own work.

74 **those two together**: the famous pair of lovers Francesca (daughter of Guido da Polenta, lord of Ravenna) and Paolo Malatesta, brother of Gianciotto, lord of Rimini, to whom Francesca was married around 1275. The rest of the canto describes Francesca's and her brother-in-law's mutual passion, and its disastrous outcome. Their togetherness now is part of their torment, though the many references to their continuing susceptibility to passion (ll. 75, 78, 82) led many 'romantic' commentators to see the episode as a vindication of their love, and of its triumph over their damnation. Dante the pilgrim's obvious pity for them does not however preclude the judgemental perspective Dante the poet insists on throughout.

90 **who bloodied earth**: referring back to the cases of murder or suicide listed above.

we'd pray to him for your peace,
since our evil rouses your pity.   93
Whatever you want to hear and say,
we can speak with you and listen
while the wind keeps low as now.   96
The town sits where I was born
on the coast, where Po runs down
with his streams to final peace.   99
Love, swift in seizing noble hearts,
it took this man with the loveliness
taken from me, and still it hurts.   102
Love insists the loved loves back,
and pleased me with him so much
that it's still with me, as you see.   105
Love brought us both to one death:
Caina awaits him, our assassin.'
These were the words they spoke.   108
After I'd heard these hounded souls,
I looked at the ground so long

97 **The town etc:** Ravenna, on the Adriatic coast, where the different tributaries of the river Po converge.

100 **Love etc:** Francesca here outlines some of the cardinal points of the medieval cult of *fin amour*, or 'courtly love', notably the idea that only the noble-hearted can be true adherents of Love (an idea treated throughout medieval literature, from *The Romance of the Rose* to Chaucer's *Troilus and Criseyde*, and asserted by Dante himself in his own lyric poetry). Francesca makes of 'Love' a powerful, sentient, universal force, reducing her own part in the adultery to that of passive victim; her extremely stylised speech, with its repetitions and word-play, mimics poetic convention, and it is entirely appropriate that the passion she speaks of was sparked off by lit-erature, as we learn later (ll. 127ff.). Dante's own involvement in the literary tradition of *fin amour* helps to explain the pilgrim's extreme sensitivity throughout the episode (see note to l. 72), as does the manifest appeal of Francesca's courtly politeness (e.g., ll. 88–93).

102 **taken from me etc:** i.e., bodily beauty taken from her when she died. The 'it' of this line refers back to the Love of l. 100, indicating that she remains oppressed by her passion as part of her punishment.

107 **Caina:** the outermost part of the deepest circle of Hell, described in canto XXXIII and reserved for those who betray members of their own family; the name is taken from the fratricide Cain (Genesis 4: 1–17). Francesca identifies their murderer as Paolo's brother and her husband.

111   the poet asked me 'What's wrong?'
    And I said in reply, 'Oh dear,
     how many sweet thoughts or hopes
114   led these to that awful moment!'
    Then I turned to them and said,
     'Francesca, these torments of yours
117   dismay me to the point of tears.
    But tell me: when sighs were sweet,
     by what means did love arrange it
120   that you knew its dubious desires?'
    She says, 'The worst thing there is
     is to remember the happy times
123   in misery; your master knows that.
    But if you're keen to know them,
     these first rootings of our love,
126   I'll talk even while I'm in tears.
    We were reading one day for fun
     how Lancelot was seized by love:
129   we were alone, but didn't suspect.
    Several times the book made us pale,
     making us look in each other's eyes,
132   but only once it became too much.
    When we read of that adorable smile
     and how the great lover kisses it,
135   this man, who'll always be by me,
    he kissed my mouth all quivering.
     Both book and author were panders:
138   we didn't read any more that day.'

121 **The worst thing** etc: repeats a maxim from a text well-known to Dante, Boethius's *Consolation of Philosophy*, II, iv: 'In all adversity of fortune, the most wretched kind is once to have been happy' (Penguin Classics translation, p. 61). The 'your master' of l. 123 is Virgil himself, who can also remember his earthly glory from his present state in Limbo.

128 **Lancelot:** the French medieval romance of *Lancelot du Lac* recounts its hero's love for Guinevere, the wife of Arthur, she of the 'adorable smile' of l. 133. In the original it is Guinevere who takes the initiative in kissing Lancelot. Dante may have known of some lost version of the story, or may be emphasising Francesca's disingenuousness.

While one of the ghosts told us this
  the other wept – I felt so awful
  I fainted as if I'd actually died,   141
and down I went like a dead body.

CANTO SIX

I came to, after blacking out
   before the two piteous in-laws
   who dazzled me with dismay,   3
and new pains and new victims
   I see near me, wherever I move,
   wherever I turn, wherever I look.   6
It's the third circle, where it rains
   forever, malign, cold and heavy;
   it never eases, it never changes.   9
Heavy hail, dark rain and snow
   sheet down through the black air;
   the earth they soak into stinks.   12
That strange savage beast Cerberus
   bays doglike from three throats
   over the folk who are pelted here,   15
with bloody eyes, black oily beard,
   an enormous belly and huge claws
   to hook, skin and tear the ghosts.   18
The rain has them howling like dogs:
   one side shelters their other one
   as the lost sods toss and turn.   21

---

7 **It's the third circle**: as at the beginning of canto IV, the manner of
Dante's progression is left a mystery
here.
13 **Cerberus**: the three-headed dog
who guards the entrance to the underworld in classical mythology, referred
to by both Ovid (*Metamorphoses*, IV,
448–53) and Virgil (*Aen.*, VI, 417–23).
In his ravenous hunger he stands here
as the embodiment of gluttony, the sin
punished in this circle.

So Cerberus saw us, the great worm,
  his mouths open, fangs on show,
24   with every inch of him bristling.
But my leader reaches his hands
  to grab some mud, and full fistfuls
27   he throws into those greedy gobs.
Like a dog whining to be fed
  who's quiet once he's got meat,
30   turning all his attention to it,
so it was with the filthy mouths
  of the devil Cerberus, who howls so
33   the ghosts would love to be deaf.
We pass over them, souls suffering
  the fierce rain, putting our feet
36   on vanity that seems like substance.
Everyone's lying down in the mire,
  except one who sat up quickly
39   as soon as he sees us pass by.
'O you, escorted through this hell,'
  he says, 'recognise me if you can –
42   you were alive before I wasn't.'
I tell him, 'This torment of yours,
  it maybe destroys recall in me;
45   I can't believe I ever saw you.
Tell me who you are, suffering
  a situation like this so vilely
48   that worse pain is less obscene.'
He says to me, 'Your own city,

22 **the great worm**: a similar expression will later be applied to Lucifer himself (XXXIV, 108).

26 **full fistfuls** etc: Virgil's action imitates that of the Sibyl in *Aeneid*, VI, 417–23, who appeases Cerberus's hunger with cakes of honey. The filthy substitute here emphasises the degradation of gluttony.

36 **vanity that seems** etc: although corporeal in appearance, and of course capable of experiencing physical pain, the souls in Hell won't resume their actual material bodies till the Last Judgement (see ll. 94ff.). Dante is thus able to exploit throughout *Hell* the souls' lack of (moral and physical) 'substance' without impairing the reality of their presentation and suffering.

full to overflowing with envy,
its lovely weather was once mine.   51
Your townsmen called me Ciacco:
gutted by the sin of gluttony
I wallow like this in the rain.   54
And I'm not alone in my misery –
all these souls share the one pain,
the one sin.' And he was silent.   57
I tell him, 'Ciacco, your torment
hurts me so, I could almost cry;
but can you say how they'll end,   60
the people of that divided city;
is anyone there honest, why is it
that so much strife assails them?'   63
He says, 'After a lot of tension
it'll come to blood, the yokels
smashing, evicting the other set;   66
but all changes before three suns
and these get on top, backed

52 **Ciacco:** a Florentine like Dante, but beyond what the text tells us very little is known of him, though various identifications have been suggested. In his *Commentary* on Dante's poem and in the *Decameron*, IX, 8, Boccaccio gives us a not wholly unsympathetic portrait of an aristocratic hanger-on at rich men's tables, and Dante retains some compassion for him here. The word 'ciacco' appropriately means 'pig' or 'hog'.

60 **but can you say** etc: this is the first of the famous passages in the *Comedy* in which Dante uses the poem to discuss and criticise contemporary political events, especially those centring on the vicissitudes of Florence, with which his own life is so bound up. The idea that the damned can see the future (but not the present) is explained in X, 94–

108; Dante is thus able to incorporate through them events subsequent to 1300, the fictional date of the poem. At this point Ciacco refers to the imminent civil commotions in Florence between the 'White' Guelphs (or 'yokels', l. 65) headed by the Cerchi family, and the 'Blacks', headed by the Donati. The uncouth manners of the Cerchi, incomers to the city from the surrounding countryside, were remarked on by contemporary chroniclers. The leaders of both parties were exiled by the city governors (one of whom at this time was Dante himself); a year later, in June 1301, a further mandate against the Blacks was especially severe (l. 66); by 1302 however, within three summers ('suns') of Ciacco's making this prophecy (l. 68), the Blacks had returned to regain control.

69 by one playing crafty just now.
 They'll lord it for a long time,
  keeping their enemies well under,
72 whatever their tears or anger.
 There are two just men, but no one
  listens: greed, envy, arrogance,
75 these sparks ignite every heart.'
 And here his dire words stopped;
  I say, 'Tell me something further,
78 make me a gift of more speech:
 the worthy Farinata and Tegghiaio,
  Jacopo Rusticucci, Arrigo, Mosca
81 and the others who aimed at good,
 tell me where and how they are;
  I'm longing to know, is heaven
84 sweet to them, or hell venomous?'
 And he: 'They're with the worst:
  different sins sink them deep below:
87 you'll see, if you drop that far.
 But when you're back on sweet soil,
  I pray you, recall me to others –
90 I've no more words or answers.'
 And then his open eyes narrowed;
  he gave me a look, sunk his head,
93 and fell back among the blinded.
 Master says, 'He won't be up again

---

69 **one playing crafty** etc: Pope Boni-face VIII, who in 1300 had not yet declared his open support for the Black party.

70 **They'll lord it** etc: the reprisals taken by the Blacks included much plunder and destruction, but the fact that the decree of exile made against the Whites (including Dante himself) in January 1302 isn't mentioned offers strong support to those who believe that the earliest part of the *Comedy* was composed before then.

73 **two just men:** i.e., a tiny number; it is not to be supposed that Dante had anyone in particular in mind.

74 **greed** etc: cf. the similar complaint against Florence in XV, 68.

79 **Farinata** etc: all these with the exception of Arrigo we shall meet further down in Hell, as Ciacco promises: Farinata at X, 22ff. (the heretics), Tegghiaio and Rusticucci at XVI, 28ff. (the sodomites) and Mosca at XXVIII, 103ff. (sowers of discord).

till the angels sound their horns
and the enemy chief comes here: 96
each will revisit his sad tomb,
repossess his flesh and figure,
hear what booms through eternity.'   99
So we go on over this filthy mix
of ghosts and mud, slow-footed,
discussing life eternal a little;   102
I ask, 'Master, all this torture,
what about after the great sentence:
will it be more or less, or as now?'   105
He says, 'Remember your learning:
it states the more perfect a thing
the more it feels good and evil.   108
Now this accursed race of people
haven't come into perfection yet,
they wait it then, rather than now.'   111
We took the road that goes round,
saying more than I repeat here;
when we came to our descent   114
there was Pluto, the great enemy.

96 **enemy chief:** Christ, as judge in
the Last Judgement, when his sentence on the damned will thunder
through Hell (l. 99).
106 **your learning** etc: the scholastic
doctrine that the more perfect a
thing, the more it feels good and evil,
means that the damned will suffer
more after the Last Judgement when
they'll be 'complete' in body and soul
(the state of the blessed will also in-
tensify).
115 **Pluto:** see the note to the opening of the following canto.

CANTO SEVEN

'Satan, King Satan, what the hell . . .!'
  Pluto begins in his furious voice,
  and that noble one, all-knowing,   3
offers comfort: 'Don't let any fear
  disturb you; whatever his power,
  it can't prevent us climbing down.'   6
He turns to that puffed-up face
  and says, 'Quiet, you bloody wolf,
  boil your guts in your own anger.   9
Our visiting the deep is official
  and willed on high, where Michael
  revenged that revolt of the proud.'   12
Just as sails swollen by storm
  can collapse when the mast snaps,
  so this monster crumples to earth.   15
So we descended the fourth slope,
  delving deeper into that dire vault,
  that strongroom of every evil.   18
Justice of God! What power packs
  so many strange pains in its bag?

1 'Satan etc: this first line, which is rather obscure in the original, has often been taken as an expression of furious gibberish on Pluto's part. I follow Sapegno's reliance on the early commentators (particularly the paraphrase given by Pietro di Dante) in translating it as I do. Pluto, the classical king of the underworld, was often identified with Plutus, the god of wealth, son of Iasion and Demeter; Dante probably has this composite figure in mind here, appropriately guarding the circle where the misuse of riches is punished.
11 where Michael etc: see Revelation 12: 7–9.

21 Why do our sins bring them on us?
Like the waves do off Charybdis,
 smashing against their partners,
24 so the people are dancing here,
more in number than any I saw:
 they come shouting from each side,
27 rolling weights with their chests.
They crash into one another, then
 each turns round the other way:
30 'Miser!' they shout, and 'Waster!'
Then both parties trundle round
 to the dark circle's opposite side,
33 continuing to chant their insults:
they meet, crash, turn round again
 for their joust half a circle away.
36 I felt sick at heart at it all:
'Master,' I ask him, 'who are they,
 these people; were they all clerics,
39 these tonsured ones on our left?'
He says, 'Everyone here was blind
 in his first life, mentally blind
42 to any moderation over money.
Their howling declares this openly
 at the two points of the circle
45 where vices come into opposition.
They are clerics, these without hair
 on top, popes and cardinals even,
48 in whom avarice triumphs totally.'
I say, 'Master, among these people
 I think I should recognise some

---

22 **Charybdis**: between this whirl-pool and the rock of Scylla in the Strait of Messina, the waves of the Ionian and Tyrrhenian seas smash against each other.
27 **rolling weights** etc: the form of punishment here, inspired by the punishment of Sisyphus in classical mythology, symbolises the weight or burden of riches; the circular path the avaricious and prodigal pursue relates to the way the wheel of Fortune rotates such earthly goods, as explained later in the canto.
39 **on our left**: i.e., amongst the avaricious.

who were rotten with such crimes.'   51
But he says, 'It's a vain thought:
  lack of cognition in their foul life
  makes them past recognition now.   54
Their eternity is these two clashes,
  two teams who'll leave their tombs
  with closed fists, or shorn heads.   57
Hoarding or squandering ends here,
  this brawl instead of blessedness:
  I don't choose fine words for it.   60
So you see, my son, the poor joke
  of the goods we owe to Fortune,
  that humans make such scrums for;   63
for all the gold under the moon,
  past and present, it couldn't calm
  even one of these weary spirits.'   66
'Master,' I say, 'tell me further:
  this Fortune, with all earth's goods
  in her claws, what is she then?'   69
And he says, 'O idiotic creatures,
  how much ignorance oppresses you!
  Now drink deep my meaning here.   72
That all-encompassing wisdom,
  he made the heavens take light
  from intelligences appointed them,   75
distributing his radiance equally;
  similarly with earthly splendours,
  he set up a minister and guide   78
to rotate such vanities regularly,
  nation to nation, house to house,

---

57 **shorn heads**: symbolising the way the prodigal is shorn of his goods.
75 **from intelligences** etc: God has appointed angels, or 'intelligences' (or 'gods', l. 87) to rotate the heavens and to illuminate them; in the same way he appoints the goddess Fortune to preside over the 'sphere' of earthly goods in the manner described. Dante here makes this pagan goddess an agent of the divine plan, in distinction to many classical and medieval writers who see in her a blind and arbitrary force whose injustices are to be deprecated.

81   beyond any provisions men make;
        so one people rules, another falls
           as she intervenes – unsuspected,
84   just like a snake in the grass.
        You can't do anything about her:
           she arranges, judges and rules
87   like other gods in their orbits.
        Her permutations know no pauses,
           always hurried on by necessity,
90   so that men face constant change.
        This is the one who's so cursed
           even though men should praise her,
93   who's blindly attacked, defamed;
        but she's blessedly deaf to this,
           blessed as other primal creatures,
96   turning her sphere in pure joy.
        Now let's descend to deeper pain:
           stars that rose when I started out
99   are setting, delay is forbidden.'
        Across to the circle's inner edge
           we go: there's a frothing fountain
102   and a channel it pours out into,
        the water rather cloudy than black;
           and here we follow this grey flow,
105   going down an awkward pathway.
        It goes into the mire called Styx,
           this dismal stream, after its fall
108   to the foot of the grim bank.
        Here I was keen to look round,
           and I saw people in that marsh,
111   naked, and filthy, and furious.

---

98 **stars that rose** etc: twelve hours therefore must have elapsed since Virgil left Limbo on his mission to help Dante; the time will be around midnight on Good Friday.

106 **the mire called Styx**: in *Aeneid*, VI, 323 the Styx is also represented as a marsh or mire. We learn from Dante later that all the waters of Hell are the same flow under different names (XIV, 112–20); the Acheron of canto III thus resurfaces here as the fountain of l. 101.

They didn't just punch each other
　　but used heads, bodies, feet too,
　　even their teeth to bite bits off.　　　　114
Master says, 'Here they are, son,
　　souls of the slaves of anger;
　　and don't doubt what I say,　　　　117
there are others below the water
　　whose breath bubbles to the top,
　　as you see wherever you look.　　　　120
Mudbound they say "We were sad
　　in the sweet, sun-livened air,
　　carrying our own fog inside us –　　　　123
now we're sad in this black-out."
　　Their throats gargle this hymn
　　since they can't sing it clearly.'　　　　126
So we rounded this ghastly bog
　　between the mud and the dry bank,
　　watching the sludge-swallowers;　　　　129
and finally we arrived at a tower.

116 **slaves of anger:** two kinds of sinners are punished in the fifth circle: those visible on the surface of the Styx, damned for their anger, and those on the bottom, only visible through the bubbles their breath makes (ll. 118–26). This latter category has been variously interpreted, either as the slothful or as those displaying in life a sullen, internalised anger that finds no outlet (unlike those above them) but remains as a poisonous brooding. A more likely explanation is that here, as in the previous circle, Dante treats of contrasting sins: the angry above and below those incapable of feeling anger, even when justice demands it; victims of a kind of emotional sloth, or desensitised torpor.

CANTO EIGHT

Now returning, I say: well before
  we came under this high tower,
  our eyes were drawn to the top   3
by two beacons we saw put there,
  and another that signalled back
  so far away, I could just see it.   6
I turn to him who knows everything:
  'What does it say? And the other,
  what's its reply? Who's lit them?'   9
He tells me, 'Across the slimy mire
  you'll see already who's expected,
  if the marsh gas doesn't hide him.'   12
You don't get an arrow from a bow
  zipping as quickly through the air
  as the small boat I watched now   15
shooting at us over the water,
  with a lone pilot aboard, crying,
  'Wicked soul, now you've had it!'   18
'Phlegias, Phlegias, ranting's no use

1 **Now returning** etc: here Dante goes back on his narrative a little to pick up the detail of the beacons (l. 4) omitted at the end of the last canto. That this type of backtracking occurs nowhere else in the *Comedy* has led some critics to accept the statement of several of Dante's early commentators: that here Dante is also indicating that the composition of the poem was interrupted by political events in Florence and only resumed after his exile. This would mean that the first seven cantos were composed before 1302 (see note to VI, 70).

19 **Phlegias:** in ancient mythology the son of Mars, who, infuriated by Apollo's seduction of his daughter Coronis, set fire to Apollo's temple and was killed in return and sent to Tartarus by Apollo (see *Aen.*, VI, 618–20). Dante converts him into the ferryman of the Styx and the guardian of the fifth circle, an image of furious anger.

this time,' my master says to him:
21   'we're yours only for the crossing.'
Like someone galled when he hears
of a big cheat played on him,
24   this was Phlegias, in his raving.
Master steps down into the boat
and makes me get in after him;
27   only with me does it seem loaded.
As soon as we're both on board
the ancient prow's cutting water,
30   dipping more than it normally does,
and as we voyage the dead slime
someone swims up covered in mud,
33   saying, 'Who's come before his time?'
I say, 'I'm here, but not to stay;
who are you, wallowing in filth?'
36   He replies, 'Just one who weeps.'
'Then stay weeping, you evil devil,'
I tell him, 'keep groaning away;
39   I know you, despite all the muck.'
Well, his hands go for the boat,
but master's ready to push him off,
42   shouting, 'Back with the other dogs!'
Then he embraces me with a kiss
and says, 'O you haughty one,
45   blessed be the womb that bore you!
This one was a tartar on earth;
nothing virtuous adorns his memory,
48   that's why his ghost raves here.
There, many think themselves kings
who'll be like pigs in shit here,

27 **only with me** etc: Dante, still in the body, is the only passenger who would have any weight; the idea is taken from Aeneas's boarding the boat in *Aeneid*, VI, 412–14.
44 **you haughty one**: Dante's 'just anger' here in the encounter with Ar-genti (see l. 61) contrasts with the state of sinful anger the damned exhibit (see note to VII, 116). Virgil's tribute in the next line, 'blessed be the womb', etc., reproduces the woman's words to Christ in Luke 11: 27.

leaving behind some awful curses!'   51
I say, 'Master, I'd really like it
  if I saw him dunked in this swill
  before we finish our crossing.'   54
And he says, 'You'll be contented
  before the far bank comes in view:
  it's right you enjoy such a wish.'   57
And very soon I saw the pain
  the slimy people put him through,
  for which I'm still thanking God.   60
They all shout, 'Get Filippo Argenti!'
  and that fiery fool from Florence
  goes at himself, with his teeth.   63
We left him, and I say no more:
  for now I heard some lamenting
  making me fix my eyes ahead.   66
My good teacher tells me: 'Son,
  we're nearing the city called Dis,
  its grave citizens, its vast army.'   69
'I can see their mosques already
  master,' I say, 'clear down there,
  and they're fire-red like furnaces.'   72
And he tells me: 'It's eternal fire

---

61 Filippo Argenti: Dante and Argenti were clearly known to each other before this fictional encounter, and some commentators have seen personal and political antagonisms in the extent of Dante's disdain. Early sources supply not much more on Argenti than what we deduce from the passage: we are told of a knight who was arrogant about his status and given to bouts of furious temper and self-display. Boccaccio tells us that the name Argenti derived from his having his horse shod with silver (*argento*).
68 Dis: another name used by the Romans for Pluto, god of the under-world, and applied elsewhere by Dante to Lucifer (e.g., XI, 65). Here, as in the *Aeneid* (VI, 127), the name is applied to the underworld itself. The walls of Dis mark the boundary between lower, or 'nether' (l. 75) Hell, in which the more serious sins of violence and fraud are punished (as will be explained in canto XI), and the sins of incontinence we've already seen in 'upper' Hell.
70 mosques: Dante means the towers of the city, first visible; but the word he chooses indicates the heretical allegiance, or devil-worship, of the citizens.

that makes them red, burning inside
75   in this nether hell, as you see.'
At last we're at the deep ditches
          fortifying this dire land, whose walls
78   seemed to me built out of iron.
Then we've to circle a fair way
          before the boatman bellows at us,
81   'Out you get – here's the entrance.'
On the gates I saw hundreds,
          all slung from heaven, grumbling
84   and asking, 'Who's this living one
crossing the kingdom of the dead?'
          Then my wise master made a sign
87   he'd like words with them, apart.
Now they're mollified a little,
          and say, 'Just with you – he can go,
90   who was fool enough ever to come.
Let him retrace his mad path alone,
          or try to; you're staying here
93   after lighting him the dark lands.'
Well reader, think how bad I felt
          when I heard these hellish words –
96   I thought I'd never get back.
'O dear master, all those occasions
          you've saved me from real danger
99   menacing me, and given me heart,'
I say, 'don't let me die like this;
          if we're not allowed to go on,
102   let's go back together right now.'
But that lord who'd led me there
          says, 'Be easy; no one can remove
105   our passports, given who gave them.
Wait for me here, and be comforted,
          feed your tired spirits with hope,

83 **all slung from heaven**: i.e., the
rebellious angels who fell with
Lucifer.

I won't leave you in the deep.'   108
Then off he went, my dear father,
 leaving me here in uncertainty
 with no, yes, battling in my head.   111
I couldn't hear what he told them,
 but he didn't stay there long
 since they all raced back inside.   114
Then our enemies shut their gates
 in master's face; locked outside,
 he walked slowly back to me,   117
eyes on the ground, no assurance
 in his look, speaking in sighs:
 'They deny me the house of horrors!'   120
Then he says, 'If I get annoyed,
 don't despair, I'll beat them yet
 whoever's busy defending inside.   123
This boldness of theirs isn't new;
 they tried it at an outer gate
 that's still without any locks.   126
You saw the dead script above it:
 but one's already left it, alone,
 descending here through the circles,   129
who'll get this place open for us.'

125 **they tried it** etc: the fallen angels
attempted to bar Christ's Harrowing
of Hell (see IV, 46–61) by closing
Hell-gate itself (III, 1–9), which
Christ smashed open.

128 **but one's** etc: we'll learn more
about the divine rescuer in the following canto.

CANTO NINE

Fear paints its pallor on my face;
   master turns and sees, at once
   curbing his own strange colour.   3
He stops like one listening keenly:
   eyes couldn't take him very far
   in that black air, that dense fog.   6
'It's certain we'll win,' he begins,
   'unless . . . But remember who came;
   the second coming seems slow now!'   9
I saw quickly how he changed,
   how what he began by saying
   was ended with different words,   12
but his speech still gave me fear;
   perhaps I took the cut-off part
   at a worse value than it had.   15
'This far down in the sad crater,
   have any ever come from level one
   where pain is only hopelessness?'   18
I put this to him. 'It's only rare,'
   he says, 'that any of us come down

8 **unless . . . etc:** Virgil's doubt and potential dismay are cancelled by his reaffirmation of who it was that originally came to him (Beatrice), leading him to anticipate, however fretfully, the 'second coming' (l. 9) of divine assistance which he's already mentioned at the conclusion of the last canto.
16 **This far down** etc: Dante seems to be fishing here for Virgil's reassurance that he does 'know the way' (l. 30) by asking him if any from 'level one' (Limbo, see canto IV) have made the descent previously. Virgil's story of an earlier visit induced by Erichtho, the necromancer described in Lucan's *Pharsalia*, VI, 508–827, seems to be entirely an invention of Dante's.

21   along this route I'm taking now.
It's true I've been here before,
    conjured by that pitiless Erichtho
24   who recalled souls to their bodies.
My flesh was just deprived of me
    when she made me enter these walls
27   to spring a ghost from Judecca,
the lowest, darkest place, furthest
    from that sphere that rotates all:
30   I do know the way; so rest easy.
This marsh that smells so awful,
    it goes all round the city of pain
33   which we need force now to enter.'
He said more that I've forgotten:
    my eye dragged all my attention
36   to a tower high on the red walls,
where bolt upright and all bloody
    a trio of furies suddenly came,
39   female in appearance and figure,
ribboned with bright green snakes;
    their hair was a nest of vipers
42   braiding their hideous heads.
Of course, he knew these handmaids
    of the queen of eternal misery:
45   'Regard,' he says, 'the dire Erinyes.
It's Megaera, that one on the left,
    and Alecto wailing on the right;
48   Tisiphone's between.' So he spoke
as they tore themselves with their nails,

27 **Judecca**: the final section of Hell's lowest circle, named after Judas, where those who betray their benefactors are punished (see canto XXXIV); consequently the place furthest from the *primum mobile* (l. 29), or the ninth and outermost heavenly sphere that imparts motion to the other spheres.

45 **Erinyes**: Virgil knows all about the Furies (see l. 43) because he had himself described them at several points in the *Aeneid* (VI, 570–2, VII, 324–9, XII, 845–8), as had other classical writers like Ovid and Statius. The 'queen' whose 'handmaids' they are is Hecate or Proserpine, wife to Pluto.

beating their breasts, howling so
I sheltered near the poet for fear.   51
'Come, Medusa: let's make him stone'
– they say this, looking downwards –
'we were wrong not nailing Theseus.'   54
'Turn right round, close your eyes:
if the Gorgon comes and you see her
there'll be no returning upwards.'   57
That's what master said. And himself
he turns me – not relying on mine,
he masks me with his hands too.   60
O you out there with your faculties,
ponder my message now, hidden
by the mysterious veils of poetry.   63
But now across the sluggish waters
there came a real fracas, terrifying,
making both the banks tremble;   66
just like a wind, all whipped up
by different zones of temperature,
that ransacks the yielding woods,   69
smashing boughs, hurling them out,

52 **Medusa:** one of the three Gorgons of classical mythology. Her head became the trophy and shield of Perseus, turning to stone any who looked on it, as recounted in Books IV and V of Ovid's *Metamorphoses*.
54 **we were wrong** etc: Theseus, king of Athens, attempted unsuccessfully to rescue Proserpine from Hell, and was imprisoned there, an exploit mentioned in the *Aeneid* (VI, 391–7, 617–18). Dante accepts the tradition that he was rescued from Hell by Hercules; the Furies lament the fact that others would have been deterred from entering Hell had he not been rescued.
62 **ponder my message** etc: the allegorical meaning implied here has al-ways been the subject of much debate. There is however a general but by no means unanimous agreement about this most serious obstacle in cantos VIII and IX on Dante's infernal journey: that it represents threats to the understanding of and contrition for sin that that journey signifies. The bad angels on the gates are thus held to represent temptation, the Furies fruitless remorse or bad conscience, and Medusa despair or religious doubt, all conspiring to truncate the allegorical journey. Reason, represented by Virgil, helps in the fight against such forces, but is powerless without the divine Grace which the angel (l. 80), whose intervention is imminent, represents.

imperiously driving the dust on
72   and routing shepherds and flocks.
He uncovered my eyes and tells me,
      'Look over the ancient slime now,
75   there where the fog is bitterest.'
And as before the hostile snake
      frogs fade down through the water
78   and huddle on the pond bottom,
so I saw a thousand lost souls
      scatter from the path of someone,
81   someone crossing Styx on dry feet.
He used his left hand as a fan,
      waving the thick air from his face,
84   and this seemed his only worry.
I was sure that Heaven sent him;
      I turn to master, who signals me
87   to keep quiet, and bow to him.
Lord, how much disdain he showed!
      He reached the gate, opening it
90   with his wand, as easy as that.
'You miserable rejects from heaven,'
      he says across the grim threshold,
93   'what sustains this bravado in you?
Why kick against the pricks, against
      that will whose end can never fail
96   and that only adds to your pain?
What's the good of fighting fate?
      Don't forget your own Cerberus,
99   still chafed all down his throat.'
Now he retraces the filthy path
      without a word to us, seemingly
102   a man consumed by other cares

94 **Why kick** etc: from Acts 9: 5 and
26: 14.
98 **Don't forget** etc: the last of the
twelve labours of Hercules was to
drag Cerberus, who had impeded

him on his mission to rescue Theseus
(above, note to l. 54), up from
Hell, which he did with the help of a
chain round his neck (see *Aen.*, VI,
391–7).

than those right in front of him;
   and we step on towards the city,
   fearless now after his holy words.   105
In we enter without any problem;
   I'm wanting to see what it is
   that's locked in such a fortress,   108
and I'm looking as soon as in;
   I see vast lands all around me
   full of pain, guilt tormented.   111
As at Arles, where the Rhone ends,
   or at Pola, where the Quarnero
   encloses Italy and wets its edges,   114
the tombs make the land uneven –
   so it was here in all directions,
   though there was misery on top: 117
there were fires between the tombs
   making them absolutely scalding,
   like iron needing no more bellows.   120
The covers were all propped open,
   and such harsh laments came out
   you really knew here was anguish.   123
I ask, 'Who is it now, master,
   buried inside these vaults here,
   announcing themselves so bitterly?'   126
He tells me, 'It's the arch-heretics
   and their disciples, of every sect,
   packed in tighter than you'd think.   129
Like is buried with like inside,
   some tombs are hotter than others.'
   Then to the right we head, between   132
these tortures and the high walls.

---

112 **As at Arles** etc: there are still a few remains of this celebrated Roman burial ground in Provence, though not as many as in the Middle Ages. The other Roman necropolis Dante mentions, at Pola, in Istria (former Yugoslavia) has disap-peared.

127 **the arch-heretics:** founders of various heresies, each allocated a separate tomb, or set of tombs, with their followers. The symbolic meaning of the punishment is developed in the next canto.

CANTO TEN

On we go down the narrow way
  between the walls and tortures,
  master first, me following him.   3
'O mighty virtue,' I say, 'winding me
  round these evil circles, as you like,
  speak to me, satisfy my wishes.   6
These people lying in the coffins,
  are they on show? The tomb-lids
  are open, and nobody guards them.'   9
He says, 'They'll all be shut down
  the day they return from Jehoshaphat
  with the bodies they left up there.   12
It's the graveyard all round here
  of Epicurus and his followers,
  who say soul dies with the body.   15
And this question you put to me,
  it'll be answered here, very soon,

---

5 **as you like:** Dante probably refers to the fact that for the first time in their descent the two pilgrims are moving to the right, not the left (see the end of the previous canto). It is possible there may be some kind of symbolic connection here with the sin they are encountering, heresy.

11 **Jehoshaphat:** the valley mentioned in Joel 3: 2 and 12, where the Last Judgement is staged after souls have been reunited with their bodies.

14 **Epicurus:** Greek philosopher (342–270 BC), whose emphasis on the aim of life as earthly happiness (often falsely identified with hedonism) involved the denial of the immortality of the soul. This latter heresy was, according to some contemporary chroniclers, widespread in medieval Florence; the Florentines we're about to encounter retain an addiction to secular concerns and achievements, and their being tortured in a tomb is a graphic illustration of the *contrapasso* (see note to III, 52).

18   as well as the other you're hiding.'
I say, 'Master, I hide my heart
only to be not always talking,
21   as you've urged more than once.'
'O Tuscan, in the city of flames
alive as you go, with such dignity
24   in speech, I pray you halt here.
It's plain from the way you talk
how you come from that noble city
27   that I bruised too much, perhaps.'
These sounds shot out suddenly
from one of the graves: trembling,
30   I move a bit closer to my guide.
But he says, 'What's wrong with you?
It's Farinata, look, on his feet –
33   you can see the top half of him.'
My eyes were already fixed on his
as he lifted his chest and forehead
36   as if he thought Hell was nothing.
And master's hand encourages me,
pushing me to him among the tombs
39   with the warning, 'Watch your words.'

---

18 **the other you're hiding:** Virgil understands that Dante's desire, soon to be satisfied, is to see Farinata, of whom he'd already asked at VI, 79.

21 **as you've urged** etc: e.g., at III, 76–81, IX, 86–7.

32 **Farinata:** or Manente di Jacopo degli Uberti, leader of the Ghibelline party in Florence from 1239. He therefore played an important part in the expulsion of the Guelphs from the city in 1248, though after their return in 1251 and the resumption of civil struggle he and his family were expelled in turn in 1258. A great showdown between the two parties took place at Montaperti, on the banks of the Arbia (see l. 86) near

Siena in 1260, after which the Ghibellines resumed control of Florence. Farinata died in 1264, after which the Guelph fortunes revived, leading to their second return to the city in 1267; Farinata's posthumous condemnation in Florence for heresy (in 1283) smacks of political recrimination.

39 **Watch your words:** Virgil's insistence that Dante speak respectfully to Farinata is heeded by Dante, who shows a courtesy to him throughout (e.g., 'praying' him for information, ll. 95, 116), even though Dante came from the Guelph stock that Farinata assailed (ll. 46–8). The presentation of Farinata

So I reach his vault. Studying me
a while, looking almost scornful,
he asks, 'Who were your people?'   42
And I who was keen to obey him,
I hid nothing, but told him all:
he raises his eyebrows a little   45
and says, 'Furious foes they were
to me, to my fathers, to my party,
so I had to scatter them twice.'   48
'Routed, they returned from all sides
both times,' I reminded him,
'which is more than your set did.'   51
Up through the coverless hole then
a soul rose to his chin, alongside:
I suppose he'd got to his knees.   54
As if wanting to see if someone
was with me, he looks all round;
but when he finds he was wrong   57
he bursts into tears: 'If it's genius
that's won you entry to this dungeon,
where's my son? Isn't he with you?'   60

through the entire canto stresses both
his grandeur and its inherent limitations, its obsession with lineage and
worldly triumph.

49 Routed etc: the two returns of
the defeated Guelphs, in 1251 and
1267, contrast with the final defeat
of the Uberti family, who were condemned to permanent exile and
whose property was razed to the
ground in the later thirteenth century
as revenge for Montaperti, as Dante
explains (ll. 85–7).

53 a soul rose etc: Cavalcante dei
Cavalcanti, previously a political
adversary of Farinata's, a Guelph
whose property was destroyed after
Montaperti; his son Guido (see
below) was betrothed to Farinata's

daughter Beatrice in 1267 to seal the
peace between the two factions.

60 where's my son?: Guido Cavalcanti was the foremost Florentine
philosopher and poet of his day (as
Dante confirms in *Purgatory*, XI, 97–
8), a writer who had greatly influenced Dante's own early poetry
and to whom Dante dedicated his
New Life (where Guido is addressed
as the first among Dante's friends).
His writings tend to confirm the
reputation he had in his own day as a
free-thinker and even atheist. He
played a leading role in the politics
of late thirteenth-century Florence,
siding with the 'White' Guelphs (see
note to VI, 60) and being one of those
banished by the city governors (one

I say, 'I'm not here on my merits:
that one waiting there guides me,
63   I hope, to one your Guido spurned.'
His question and his type of pain
meant I already knew his name,
66   that's how I gave this full reply.
At once he's on his feet, shouting
'What? He spurned? Isn't he alive?
69   Doesn't sweet light touch his eyes?'
And when he realises my delay
in answering him, he falls down
72   and doesn't poke out a second time.
But the one who asked me to stop,
that lordly one, he didn't change
75   or turn his neck, or bend over
but continued our first conversation:
'If they can't learn that,' he says,
78   'it pains me more than this bed.
But that lady who governs here,
her face won't relight fifty times
81   before you learn how hard it is.
And so you return to sweet earth,

of whom was Dante) in June 1300. Confined at Sarzana, where he wrote the famous ballad of exile 'Perch'i'no' spero', he died from an illness in August 1300; he was still alive therefore at the date of the fictional setting of the *Comedy*. His father's belief that the trip to Hell is occasioned solely by Dante's own 'genius' (l. 58) shows the exclusive reliance the Epicureans place on worldly endowments.

63 **to one** etc: the simplest meaning of this much debated line (and translated here accordingly) is that Guido spurned the one Dante is being led to; i.e., Beatrice, in her signification as Theology. Dante is thus indicating Guido's heterodoxy. The alternative reading that Guido spurned Virgil seems only to increase the difficulties of explication.

70 **my delay** etc: the reason for Dante's delay in answering is explained later in the canto.

79 **But that lady** etc: Proserpine or Hecate, queen of Hell, often identified with the moon. Farinata is prophesying that within fifty months (i.e., from Easter 1300) Dante would learn the difficulties of returning from exile (see note to VI, 70). This would take us to the summer of 1304, when the Whites had largely given up on their attempts to return.

tell me: why are they so pitiless
to mine, those people, in every law?'   84
I say, 'All that pain and slaughter
that made the Arbia run scarlet,
that's what speaks in our councils.'   87
And he sighs, shaking his head:
'It wasn't only me,' he says; 'besides,
I didn't join in without reason.   90
And it was I alone, when the rest
agreed to Florence's destruction,
I alone who stood out for her.'   93
'So your seed finds rest some day,'
I pray him, 'untie me a knot
that has my understanding tangled.   96
As I understand it, you can see
what the future is before it comes,
but the present's totally otherwise.'   99
'We see like him with bad vision,'
he says, 'things that are far off;
the Light yet shines to us enough.   102
But our minds dim as they near
or arrive; without news from others
we're ignorant of your human state.   105
So you can see, from that point on
when the future won't be any more,

---

91 **And it was I** etc: at the Council of
Empoli, after Montaperti, Farinata
successfully resisted the plans of the
victorious Ghibellines to destroy
Florence completely. The complexity
of the encounter in this canto results
as much from what Dante shares
with Farinata (love of Florence, political misfortune) as from what divides
them.
100 **We see like him** etc: commentators are divided on whether all the
damned (who can see the future: see
note to VI, 60) are barred from seeing
the present, or merely the Epi-

cureans. Certainly Ciacco in canto VI
seems acquainted with both present
and future, and it would be appropriate to the Epicureans (who believed
only in a present, rather than future
life) if their punishment involved this
ironic reversal.
106 **from that point on** etc: i.e., after
the Last Judgement, when eternity
replaces temporal categories, and the
'future' will no longer be. Virgil has
already told us that the graves will be
closed down then (ll. 10–12), resulting in the Epicureans' utter physical
and mental entombment.

108   our minds will go completely null.'
        And then, like one feeling guilty
            I say, 'Tell him who keeled over
111   his son is still with the living;
        and if I was slow in replying,
            let him know that puzzle did it
114   that you've cleared from my mind.'
        But now master was calling me,
            so I hurry to pray the spirit
117   if he can name his bedfellows.
        'I lie with over a thousand here,'
            he says, 'there's the cardinal,
120   Frederick II, the rest is silence.'
        He went in. I pondered his words
            that seemed to mean trouble for me
123   while I walked back to the poet.
        He moved off, and as we go on
            he asks, 'Why are you so dazed?'
126   so I tell him everything about it.
        'You just remember what you heard
            against you,' the sage commands,
129   'and listen' – he raises his finger:
        'when you reach the bright light
            of her whose eyes see everything,
132   she'll teach you your life's course.'
        Then he went over to the left:
            we go inland, away from the wall,
135   and our path ends in a chasm
        whose stink wafts right to the top.

110 **Tell him** etc: Dante's delay in answering Cavalcante (l. 70) is now explained; he couldn't understand how the father was ignorant of whether the son was alive or not. The imminence of Guido's death (in August 1300) means it's too near in time for the Epicureans to see.

119 **the cardinal** etc: Ottaviano degli Ubaldini, bishop of Bologna 1240–4, then cardinal; died 1273. Like the Emperor Frederick II (1194–1250), of whom we learn more in canto XIII, he had a reputation as a heretic.

132 **she'll teach you** etc: as it happens it is not Beatrice who elucidates the prophecies concerning his future that Dante learns in Hell (e.g., here and from Brunetto Latini in canto XV), but Dante's ancestor Cacciaguida (in *Paradise*, canto XVII).

CANTO ELEVEN

Right on the lip of a deep bank,
   or curve of great broken rocks
   we arrive, with hordes below us   3
in worse pain; and it's so bad,
   the stink the great abyss exhales,
   that we draw back to the cover   6
of a huge tomb, chiselled, I see,
   with: 'I guard Pope Anastasius,
   lured by Photinus from the truth.'   9
'We ought to delay our descent
   till we're used to this dire smell
   a little; then it won't bother us.'   12
So my guide. 'Can we use our time
   so it won't be wasted?' I ask,
   and he: 'I'm thinking that too.   15
My son, you've three lesser circles
   rimmed by these rocks,' he begins,
   'narrowing like those we've left.   18
They've all got evil spirits inside:
   but so the sight's enough for you
   hear why and how they're kept.   21
Every evil that earns heaven's hate
   has injustice as its end, an end
   that uses force or fraud to hurt;   24

---

8 Pope Anastasius: Anastasius II, pope from 496 to 498. Tradition held that he had admitted the heretic Photinus, a deacon of Thessalonica, to the communion, thus indicating his support for Photinus's alleged belief in the non-divinity of Christ.

as fraud is man's particular sin
  God hates it more, so bottommost
27   the fraudulent are, in most pain.
The violent are in the first circle;
  but because force has three targets
30   the circle is built in three rings:
at God, at oneself and at others
  violence can aim, at the person
33   or the possessions, as I'll explain.
You have death or physical harm
  inflicted on others, or their goods
36   can be smashed, stolen, extorted;
so murder and all unlawful assault,
  robbers, ransackers, all are damned
39   in the first ring, in various groups.
Men can be violent to themselves
  or their own goods; so ring two
42   is where this type repents in vain,
the self-remover from your world,
  the fritterer who wastes his means,
45   crying where he should be happy.
Then there's violence to the deity,
  the heart's denial or open curses
48   or abusing nature and its gifts;
so the badge of the smallest ring
  marks Sodom and Cahors, also those
51   who insult and disparage God.
Fraud, gnawer of every conscience,
  this works in two different cases,

25 **as fraud is** etc: the distinction between employing force and fraud to others' harm is taken from Cicero, *De officiis*, I, 13, as is the assertion that the use of fraud is the more culpable (because man's 'particular' faculty, reason, is thus perverted). The fraudulent are thus 'bottommost', in the two lowest circles, the last of all being reserved for the traitors, users of fraud against those who trusted them.

50 **Sodom and Cahors:** abusers of nature, named from the cities of Sodom (sexual malpractice, see Genesis 18–19) and Cahors in southern France (famous for its great number of usurers in the Middle Ages). Virgil will explain later in the canto how usury is a sin against nature.

where trust is, and where it's not.   54
This latter case means the murder
  of the natural bond of love only;
  so the second circle's the lair   57
of hypocrisy, flattery, enchantment,
  counterfeiting, thieving, simonists,
  pimps, swindlers, crap like this.   60
The other means the disregarding
  of natural love, but added to this,
  the further love that creates trust;   63
so the smallest circle, that point
  of all the universe where Dis sits,
  traitors are there, tortured always.'   66
I say, 'Master, your explanation
  is totally clear, and your division
  of this abyss and all its residents.   69
But tell me: those in that marsh,
  those thrashed by the wind or rain,
  those cursing, meeting head on,   72
why aren't they in this fiery city
  and hurt here, if they annoy God?
  Why their situation if they don't?'   75
He says, 'Why do your wits wander
  out of their normal way so much?
  Or what's your mind got hold of?   78
Don't you remember those words
  in your Ethics, treating thoroughly

65 **Dis:** see note to VIII, 68.
70 **those in that marsh** etc: in ques-
tioning Virgil Dante recapitulates the
sinners he's already visited: the wrath-
ful in the Styx, the lustful and the
gluttons (hounded by wind and rain
respectively) and the misers and
wasters, clashing 'head on'.
78 **Or what's your mind** etc: Virgil
suggests here that Dante may be confused by those thirteenth-century
theologians (against whom Thomas

Aquinas had written) who proposed
that all sins are equally offensive to
God.
80 **in your Ethics** etc: Aristotle's *Ni-
chomachean Ethics* divides sins into
three types, those of incontinence,
bestiality and malice (VII, 1). The
first is less blameworthy, as it consists in the immoderate pursuit of
things not evil in themselves and does
not aim directly at injury to others;
the circles of 'upper' Hell, outside the

81 the three dispositions heaven rejects,
incontinence, behaving like beasts
and malice? And how the first
84 offends God less, is less to blame?
If you digest this judgement well,
and recall who those are above
87 undergoing the torments outside,
you'll see why they're kept apart
from this evil bunch, also why
90 the divine hammer is less cruel.'
'O sun that clears up every mist,
your clarifying delights me so much
93 I enjoy doubt as much as knowing.
But go back a little,' I tell him,
'to where you say usury is a sin
96 against God's gifts: untie that knot.'
'Philosophy notes more than once,'
he replies, 'if you understand it,
99 how nature's realm takes its course
from the divine mind, and its art:
if you examine your Physics well,
102 you'll find early on in the book
that your arts as far as possible
follow her, as students to teacher:
105 so they're like God's grandchildren.
Recall Genesis from the beginning,
where she and they are the means

city of Dis, are allocated to sins of
this type. The sins of malice are punished in lower Hell, as has been explained; there is, however, no precise
division in Dante's scheme corres-
ponding to the category of bestiality.
The heretics of the previous canto,
who don't fit into the Aristotelian
framework, are appropriately on
the border between Hell's two main
divisions: within the city of Dis, but
above the abyss.

97 **Philosophy notes** etc: Virgil
draws particularly on a passage in
the *Physics*, II, 2 (l. 101) in bringing
Aristotelian philosophy forward to
explain how the human arts and industry can be called God's 'grandchildren' (l. 105)
106 **Recall Genesis** etc: man was
originally put in the Garden of Eden
'to dress it and keep it' (Genesis 2:
15); he was later ordered to labour
'in the sweat of [his] face' (3: 19).

that humanity is to live and grow;   108
but the usurer takes another way,
   slighting nature and her follower
   and putting his hopes elsewhere.   111
But come now, it's time to leave;
   the Fish glitter on the horizon,
   the Bear is right over Caurus   114
and over there we can climb down.'

Usury tries to avoid the divine imperative whereby existence is sustained through the partnership of nature and human industry.

113 **the Fish** etc: Pisces immediately precedes Aries (where the sun at present is, see I, 38) in the zodiac; the twelve zodiacal signs each rise over the eastern horizon at two-hourly intervals, so the dawn of Easter Saturday is not far away. The Great Bear lies in the north-west, above the Caurus, or north-west wind.

CANTO TWELVE

So we reach a place to descend
 this rocky drop, an awful scene
 especially with what was coming.   3
That landslide down from Trent
 that crashed into the river Adige
 because of earthquake or erosion,   6
that's all fractured from its start
 on the peak, to the plain below,
 so there's a kind of pathway down –   9
well, the stairs here were similar,
 and right on the shattered brink
 the shame of Crete was stretched,   12
the one conceived in the fake cow;
 he gnawed himself on seeing us,
 like someone consumed by anger.   15
Master shouts: 'Are you worrying
 the duke of Athens is here again,
 your butcher in the world above?   18

---

4 That landslide etc: Dante almost certainly alludes to the landslide south of Rovereto, known as the Slavini di Marco, which he may have seen in person or read about in Albertus Magnus's *De meteoris* (III, ii, 18).

12 the shame of Crete: the Minotaur, part man, part bull, conceived by Pasiphaë (wife of Minos, king of Crete) who encased herself in a wooden cow in order to satisfy her lust for a bull (see Ovid, *Metamor-* *phoses*, VIII, 131–7). Critics disagree on whether the Minotaur has the function of guardian of the seventh circle (the violent), or as seems more likely, solely of the landslide that leads to the circle.

17 the duke of Athens: Theseus, who killed the Minotaur with the help of Minos's and Pasiphaë's daughter (hence the Minotaur's half-sister) Ariadne.

Keep away, animal; this man
hasn't your sister as his guide,
21   he's here to see your tortures.'
Like a bull that they unharness
the moment the death blow falls,
24   who flings himself here and there,
so the Minotaur was hopping mad;
ever ready, master shouts, 'Run,
27   descend the path while he raves.'
Thus we went down the rock fall
that often shifted under my feet
30   at the strange load of my weight.
He spoke my thoughts: 'You're musing
at these ruins, perhaps, patrolled
33   by that brutal anger I've annulled.
Note that on that other occasion
I climbed down here to deep Hell,
36   this rock hadn't collapsed then;
but if I remember, shortly before
that One came for all the booty
39   he lifted out of Dis's top circle,
all around this deep dire abyss
shook so, I thought the universe
42   felt love, which in one theory
means the world's return to chaos;
and just then this ancient rock
45   here and elsewhere broke like this.
But look below now, coming up

---

30 **at the strange load** etc: cf. VIII, 27.

34 **that other occasion** etc: for Virgil's previous descent, which took place shortly after his death, see IX, 22–7; he explains now how the present landslide occurred shortly before the Harrowing of Hell (ll. 37–9, see IV, 46–63), in other words at the time of the Crucifixion.

42 **which in one theory** etc: Empedocles maintained that the universe was constituted out of a discord between the elements, and that any resolution of this discord ('love') would mean the collapse of matter and its return to original chaos.

45 **elsewhere**: in the *bolgia* of the hypocrites (see XXI, 106–8) and in the 'rock-ruin' of V, 34.

is the river of blood, that stews
those who were violent to others.'   48
O blind greed and mad anger,
    you hound us in our short lives
    then boil us like this eternally!   51
I could see a broad, bowed river,
    like one totally ringing a plain,
    the ring master had mentioned;   54
and between it and the landslide
    Centaurs chased, armed with arrows
    like they used to raid on earth.   57
Seeing us climb down, they stop,
    and three came from their troop
    with bows and arrows all ready,   60
and from a distance one shouted:
    'What torture are you dropping to?
    Tell us from yonder, if you don't   63
I'll shoot.' And master: 'We'll tell,
    but when we get to Chiron –
    your malice hasn't rusted much.'   66
Nudging me, he says, 'It's Nessus,
    he died for the lovely Dejanira
    and made himself his own revenge.   69
The middle one with head bowed
    is big Chiron, Achilles's tutor:

---

47 **the river of blood**: Phlegethon,
the river of fire in the *Aeneid* (VI,
550–1). We learn its name later, at
XIV, 130–5.
54 **master had mentioned**: i.e., at XI,
34–9.
56 **Centaurs**: famous for their raping
and pillaging exploits, and thus appropriate guardians of those punished in
the Phlegethon; they echo the Minotaur in their man-beast composition.
65 **Chiron**: son of Saturn and Phil-
yra, celebrated for his wisdom and
learning, and tutor of Achilles (l. 71)
and other ancient heroes. Tradition-

ally the leader of the centaurs, he has,
in Dorothy Sayers's words, 'the most
amiable character of all the inhabitants of Hell'.
67 **Nessus**: whose attempted rape of
Dejanira, Hercules's wife, led to Hercules slaying him with a poisoned
arrow. Nessus gave his robe, soaked
in the poisoned blood, to Dejanira,
telling her it had the power to win for
her the love of anyone who wore it,
but Hercules went mad and died as
soon as she persuaded him to put it
on. See *Metamorphoses*, IX, 127–33,
152–62, 166–9.

72   furious Pholus is the third one.
Thousands of them patrol the river,
           shooting souls out of the blood
75   more than their sins allow for.'
So we approach these swift beasts;
           Chiron takes an arrow, with it
78   parting the curtain of his beard,
so revealing his enormous mouth;
           he says to the others, 'You see
81   him behind, moving what bears him?
That's not normal for dead feet.'
           And my master, right by his chest
84   where the two natures join, says
'He lives indeed, and to him alone
           I have to show this black hole:
87   need brings him, not pleasure.
One left off her alleluia singing
           to assign me this astounding role:
90   he's no felon, I'm no past one.
But by the power that so permits
           that I can travel this grim path,
93   give us a scout from your ranks,
one to show us where we can ford
           the river, and to carry him over
96   since he's no airborne spirit.'
Then Chiron turned to his right,
           to Nessus: 'Guide them like this,
99   keep away any others you meet.'
So on we move with our expert
           by the bank where the blood boils,
102   and those boiling scream out.
They were under to their eyebrows;
           the huge Centaur says, 'Tyrants,

---

72 **Pholus:** who attempted to rape the bride and other Lapithaean women at the nuptials of Pirothous and Hippodamia, *Metamorphoses*, XII, 219ff.

88 **One left off** etc: Beatrice, see II, 52ff.

creatures of blood and pillage,   105
lamenting here their heartless acts;
here's Alexander, hard Dionysius too
who gave Sicily its brutal years.   108
That head of really black hair
is Ezzelino; that other blond one
is Obizzo d'Este, truly killed   111
by his so-called son up above.'
Then I turn to the poet, who says,
'He's leader now, I'm in reserve.'   114
A little further the Centaur stops
above people who from chin up
poke out of these scalding baths.   117
He shows us one all by himself:
'In God's lap he spilt the heart
still praised beside the Thames.'   120
Next in this river came people
with head and chest stuck out,
and I knew a number of these.   123
So on it flows lower and lower
till only feet get blood-stained,

107 **Alexander** etc: either Alexander the Great (356-23 BC), whose cruelties were recorded by several writers, or Alexander the tyrant of Pherae (4th century BC); 'hard Dionysius' is likely to be Dionysius the Elder, tyrant of Syracuse (405-367 BC), rather than his son who succeeded him.

110 **Ezzelino** etc: Ezzelino III da Romano (1194-1259), Ghibelline leader and tyrant of Marca Trivigiana. Guelph chroniclers, referring to him as the 'son of Satan', told plentiful tales of atrocities committed by him in Lombardy, Padua and elsewhere. Obizzo d'Este (l. 111), Marquis of Ferrara (1264-93), was a Guelph leader with a similarly bloody reputation; here Dante affirms the truth of the rumour that he was killed by his (possibly bastard) son, Azzo.

119 **he spilt** etc: Guy de Montfort, whose father had been killed at the hands of Edward I of England, took revenge by stabbing Edward's cousin, Prince Henry, during Mass in the church at Viterbo ('in God's lap') in 1272. Henry's heart was subsequently set up as an object of veneration on a column beside the Thames.

121 **Next in this river** etc: we pass from the tyrants to the more everyday men of violence, many of whom are known to Dante but are too numerous to dwell on.

126 and this was where we crossed.
'Just as you see this hot bath
draining itself on this side,'
129 the Centaur says, 'on the other
you should know it gets deeper,
the river bed, until it rejoins
132 the place where tyranny weeps.
There the divine justice pierces
that scourge on earth Attila,
135 and Phyrrhus and Sextus; eternally
this steaming distils the tears
of Rinier da Corneto, Rinier Pazzo,
138 turners of streets into battlefields.'
He turned then, back over the ford.

134 **Attila** etc: king of the Huns in the 5th century AD, the famous 'scourge of God' (*flagellum Dei*). Phyrrhus is either the king of Epirus (318–272 BC), a notorious adversary of the Romans, or the son of Achilles mentioned in *Aeneid*, II, 526–8. Sex- tus is probably the son of Pompey the Great, whose acts of piracy are de- scribed by Lucan (*Pharsalia*, VI, 113– 15). Rinier da Corneto and Rinier Pazzo were well-known brigands and murderers who plagued northern Italy in Dante's day.

CANTO THIRTEEN

Nessus hadn't finished crossing
  when we reached a kind of wood,
  one without any paths marked.   3
Its leaves were all brown, not green,
  its branches knotted, not straight,
  with no fruit, just poisoned thorns: 6
beasts between Cecina and Corneto
  that shun any cultivated places,
  they've no cover as rough as this.   9
Here the wild Harpies nest, chasers
  of the Trojans off the Strophades
  with their sad news of future pain;   12
huge wings they have, human faces,
  clawed feet, big feathered bellies;
  their moans fill the weird wood.   15
Master says: 'Before we go further,
  you should know we've crossed now
  to the second ring of this circle   18
that lasts till the horrid sandbath;
  so keep your eyes open – you'll see
  things I'd never dare describe.'   21

7 **beasts between** etc: the two towns mentioned mark the northern and southern limits of the Tuscan Maremma, a notorious tract of swampland and forest.

10 **wild Harpies** etc: daughters of Thaumas and Electra, with women's faces and the bodies of predatory birds. Virgil tells how they chased Aeneas and his men from the Strophades islands and prophesied the sufferings they would have to face (*Aen.*, III, 209ff.).

19 **the horrid sandbath**: as described in the following canto.

I could hear groans everywhere
   but no one who was making them,
24   so I stopped, completely lost.
I think he thought that I thought
   these groans came from the foliage
27   from people who were hid there,
so master tells me, 'Take a twig
   and snap it off from the branch –
30   your illusion will snap as well.'
There was a big thorn tree there,
   but when I reach to pluck it
33   the trunk howls, 'Why pick on me?'
And now that it starts to bleed
   it screams again, 'Why pick me?
36   Haven't you a heart inside you?
Before we were wood, we were men,
   but even if we were snakes' souls
39   your hand should have more pity.'
It's like you light a green stick
   at one end: the other whistles
42   as the sap sputters out of it,
so from where this was splintered
   words and blood came; terrified,
45   I drop the twig, and just stand.
The sage speaks: 'O wounded soul,
   if he could have already believed
48   what he's found only in my poem,
he'd never put his hand on you;
   but disbelief made me make him
51   do that which saddens me too.
But speak your name; he'll amend
   by reviving your fame on earth,
54   where he's allowed to go back.'

34 **it starts to bleed** etc: in the encounter with the tree Dante is inspired by the episode in *Aeneid*, III, 22–48, where Aeneas visits the tomb of his dead companion Polydorus, out of which grow trees that bleed when plucked.

And the tree: 'Such a sweet lure
  can't be resisted – don't object
  if it draws me on to speak fully.   57
I'm the one who held both keys
  to the heart of Frederick; so soft
  I turned them, to open or lock,   60
I was sole in his secrets, almost;
  I was wed to this glorious post
  enough to lose sleep, then life.   63
But that bitch is always awake
  and snooping in Caesar's palace,
  deadly to all, especially at court;   66
and she fired everyone against me,
  and their flames fired Augustus,
  so happy honour became sad woe.   69
Then it was to my soul's bitter taste
  to try to fly bitterness by dying,
  and to sin against my sinless self.   72
But I swear by my recent roots
  that I never once broke fidelity
  to my lord, so worthy of honour.   75
And if either of you do return,
  comfort my memory, laid low,
  yet, from the blows envy gave it.'   78
After waiting a little, the poet says,
  'He's silent; now's your chance
  to ask anything more you'd like.'   81
But I tell him, 'You ask again

---

58 **I'm the one** etc: Pier della Vigna, chief adviser to the Emperor Frederick II (see X, 120), whose two 'keys' governed his master's approval and disapproval, and who was imprisoned on a charge of treachery in 1248. Poet and legislator as well as statesman, he shows a fondness in his speech for word-play, repetition and antithesis (e.g., in ll. 68–72) that shows not only linguistic sophistica-

tion but the paradox of the act of suicide itself (l. 72), emblematised by the elaborately knotted form of the trees. Pier died in prison in 1249, according to some commentators by dashing his head against the prison wall.

64 **But that bitch** etc: Pier's periphrasis for envy, which circulated the charges of treachery towards the Emperor ('Caesar', l. 65).

what you think I'd like to know –

84   I just can't, it's too upsetting!'

And he went on: 'So this man does
      willingly what you plead of him,

87   poor prisoned soul, do inform us

how the spirit comes to be held
      in these gnarled knots; if you can,

90   tell us if anyone ever gets free.'

At this the trunk gives a big sigh,
      then his sigh becomes this answer:

93   'I'll reply as quickly as I can.

When the desperate soul gets free
      from the body it rips itself from,

96   Minos sends it through gate seven.

It drops at random into this wood,
      so wherever chance catapults it

99   it germinates here like any seed.

It becomes a sapling, then a tree:
      then the Harpies browse its leaves,

102   giving agony, and vents for agony.

We'll return for our human remains
      like the rest, but won't wear them:

105   it's only just, we cast them away.

No, we'll trail them here, our bodies,
      and hang them in this awful wood,

108   each one on his own soul's thorns.'

While we attended to the trunk,
      thinking he wanted to say more,

111   we were startled by some noise;

just like one hearing the hurry
      of the boar, and the hunt after it,

114   with foliage rustled by the chase.

And then, two shot from our left,

---

96 Minos etc: see V, 4–15.
103 **We'll return** etc: in answer to Virgil's second question (l. 90), Pier explains the peculiar nature (in ac-cordance with the *contrapasso*, see note to III, 52) of the suicides' re-union with their bodies at the Last Judgement (see VI, 94–9, X, 11–12).

scratched and naked, racing so fast
  they broke any branch in their way.   117
'O Death, hurry to me now, hurry!'
  the first shouts, the too-slow second
  crying, 'Lano, you weren't this quick   120
to escape at the battle of Toppo!'
  And maybe his breath failed then,
  since he clings closely to a bush.   123
Behind them the wood is seething
  with hunting dogs, fierce and black,
  and raring as if just unchained,   126
and they sink their teeth into him,
  the one hiding, ripping him apart,
  then go off with his poor limbs.   129
Now master takes me by the hand,
  leading me to the bush, that weeps,
  in vain, at its bloody breakages.   132
'O Giacomo da Santo Andrea,' it says,
  'what help was it hiding by me?
  Why's your guilty life my fault?'   135
When master reaches it, he asks it,
  'Who were you, with all these wounds
  that your sad words bleed out of?'   138
And he replies, 'O souls that arrive
  in time to see this unjust havoc

---

120 **Lano etc:** this figure has been identified with Ercolano Maconi of Siena, a notorious spendthrift who after ruining his fortunes wilfully sought death at the battle of Pieve del Toppo (near Arezzo) in 1287, in which the Sienese were defeated by the Aretines. We have moved from the suicides to those who were 'violent' to their own goods, the two types explained in XI, 40–5.

125 **hunting dogs etc:** allegorically, these may represent the perils attendant on profligacy: poverty, shame, remorse, even creditors who assail the profligate in life. Musa is right to point out how the present figures are to be distinguished from the 'wasters' of canto VII by the sheer intensity and violence of their spending and self-ruin.

133 **Giacomo da Santo Andrea:** Paduan, died 1239, reputedly murdered on the orders of Ezzelino III (see XII, 110). Famous tales exist of his throwing his money into the river Brenta to while away the time, and of burning one of his villas to the ground for the fun of it.

141   that sunders me from my leaves,
   rake them up round my poor stem.
    I'm of the city that changed patrons,
144   having the Baptist instead of him
   whose revenge will always sadden her;
    and if it wasn't that by the Arno
147   some sight of him still remains,
   those citizens that refounded her
    on the embers Attila left behind,
150   they'd have done it all for nothing.
   I gibbeted myself on the premises.'

143 **I'm of the city** etc: the original patron of Florence was Mars, god of war, supplanted by John the Baptist. The civil war that afflicts the city is here thus explained as Mars's 'revenge', mitigated by the fact (ll. 146–7) that the remains of a statue of him still existed on the Ponte Vecchio, over the Arno. The identity of the speaker here remains something of a mystery; even the early commentators cannot agree on who he is, nor on whether Dante deliberately chose not to name him.

149 **Attila** etc: Dante follows tradition in confusing Attila (see XII, 134) with Totila, king of the Goths, who laid siege to Florence in 542.

CANTO FOURTEEN

Then the love of my native city
    made me gather the shed leaves
    to return to him, silent now.   3
Next between rings two and three
    we reach the frontier, and see
    justice in all its horrible art.   6
I stress these unheard-of things:
    I say we saw a level plain,
    only not a plant grew there.   9
The wood of misery garlands it,
    as the sad river does the wood;
    here we stop, right at the edge.   12
The country was thick, arid sand,
    no way different from that land
    trodden by the soles of Cato.   15
How much, O vengeance of God,
    how much you ought to terrify
    every reader of what I saw now!   18
Different herds of naked spirits
    were all weeping wretchedly,
    apparently under different laws: 21
some were lying along the ground;
    some sat, their legs drawn up;
    others paced about all the time.   24

15 **Cato:** Dante is referring to the crossing of the Libyan desert by the army of Cato of Utica in 47 BC (Lucan, *Pharsalia*, IX, 371–410).
22 **some were lying** etc: those lying, sitting and in motion are the blasphemers against God, the usurers and the sodomites respectively. See XI, 46–51 and notes.

These last were the most numerous,
and those least who were lying,
27   though pain was on their lips more.
Over all the desert, slowly falling,
it rained broad flakes of fire
30   like snow in the windless Alps.
Just as in the hotlands of India
flames fell on Alexander's army
33   and dotted the ground, entire,
so that he had all his soldiers
trampling the soil, snuffing them
36   before they could join together;
so the eternal ardour fell here;
and it lit the sand, like tinder
39   lit by flints, doubling the pain.
There was no declining the dance
of their poor hands, here, there,
42   fending away the fresh firefalls.
So I say: 'Master and conqueror
of everything, save the dour demons
45   who confronted us in the gateway,
who's that he-man seeming to scorn
the fire, and writhing in disdain
48   as if the rain couldn't ripen him?'
But the same one realised himself
I was asking master about him,

29 **it rained** etc: the punishment here is inspired by the brimstone and fire poured down on Sodom and Gomorrah in Genesis 19: 24.

31 **Just as in the hotlands** etc: the story involving Alexander's army here is taken from Albertus Magnus, *De meteoris*, I, iv, 8.

44 **save the dour demons** etc: see VIII, 82ff.

46 **who's that he-man** etc: the blasphemer is identified later (l. 63) as Capaneus, one of the seven Greek kings taking part in the famous siege against Thebes, described in Statius's *Thebaid*. His physical grandeur, as well as his defiance of the gods, is described by Statius; Jupiter finally killed him with a thunderbolt (ll. 53–4) as he vaunted himself on the walls of Thebes (*Thebaid*, x, 897ff.). Dante thus chooses a classical, rather than Christian, exemplum here of humanity in its pride setting itself up against God.

and cries, 'As my life, so my death.   51
If Jupiter tired out the blacksmith
    who armed his fury with the bolt
    that shot me on my final day;   54
or if those others sweated shifts
    for him, in Mongibello's black forge,
    as he shouts, "Good Vulcan, help!"   57
just as at the battle of Phlegra;
    if he shot all his strength at me
    he'd never be happy in revenge.'   60
At this my leader cried out so
    I'd never heard him so loud:
    'In that your pride won't lie down,   63
O Capaneus, you're punished more:
    no pain could match your madness,
    your fury is its own fulfilment.'   66
Then he turns more softly to me:
    'This was one of the seven kings
    besieging Thebes, a scorner of God   69
as now, it seems, and of prayer;
    but as I told him, his own oaths
    are the right medals for his chest.   72
Move behind now, guard your feet
    from the scalding sand, as before,
    keep your path well to the wood.'   75
In silence we reached a brook
    spurting from the wood, and today
    its bloody colour still unnerves me.   78
Like the stream out of Bulicame

52 **the blacksmith** etc: Vulcan, who
aided by 'those others' (l. 55) – the
Cyclops – manufactured Jupiter's
thunderbolts in the furnace of
Mount Etna in Sicily ('Mongibello',
l. 56).
58 **the battle of Phlegra:** Phlegra, in
Thessaly, was where Jupiter defeated
the giants who were attempting to
climb Mount Olympus – another
example of blasphemous presumption. See Virgil, *Georgics*, I, 278–83;
Ovid, *Metamorphoses*, I, 151–62.
79 **Bulicame** etc: the lake of boiling
sulphur near Viterbo, which apparently had a reddish cast. I follow
those critics who in l. 80 read *petta-
trici* (i.e., combers [of hemp or flax],
who used the waters to steep the
fibre) rather than *peccatrici* (pros-
titutes, who supposedly used the
water for washing).

the hemp-workers share, so this

81   as it flowed down over the sand.
The bottom and both the slopes
were of stone, the bankside too,

84   so I realised this was the path.
'Among all that I've shown you
since we came through that gate

87   whose welcome no one is denied,
your eyes haven't seen anything
as worth noting as this beck

90   that all the flames die out on.'
These words came from my leader;
so I prayed him to feed me,

93   now he'd whetted my appetite.
'There's a ruined spot in mid-sea,'
he begins, 'that's known as Crete:

96   its king once ruled a pure world.
There's a mountain there called Ida,
once an idyll of watery glades,

99   now hoary in its total desertion.
Rhea trusted to it as the cradle
of her son, and when he cried

102   she orchestrated noises to hide it.
In the mountain stands an ancient,

---

86 **that gate**: the main entrance to Hell, in III, 1–12.

90 **the flames die out on**: as explained in XV, 1–3.

94 **There's a ruined spot** etc: the Mediterranean island of Crete, already described by Virgil (*Aen.*, III, 104–6, VIII, 324–5) as the setting of the Golden Age under 'its king' (l. 96) Saturn.

100 **Rhea** etc: Rhea was Saturn's wife and mother of Jupiter. To thwart the prophecy that he would be deposed by one of his sons, Saturn devoured them when they were born; Rhea however hid Jupiter in Mount Ida, and had her followers, the Curetes, drown his cries out with their noise (see *Aen.*, III, 111–13; *Georgics*, IV, 150–2; Ovid, *Fasti*, IV, 197–214).

103 **an ancient** etc: this colossal statue is inspired by that described in the dream of Nebuchadnezzar (Daniel 2: 31–3). The progressive degradation (from the head down) of its material symbolises, following Ovid (*Metamorphoses*, I, 89–131), the decline of the world and of human nature from the Golden Age through subsequent historical periods. The statue's position in Crete is mid-

vast in size, his face facing Rome,
  his back turned towards Damietta.   105
His head is formed from fine gold,
  his arms and chest pure silver,
  then he's brass down to his crotch;   108
from there he's of unalloyed iron,
  except his right foot's terracotta
  and it bears most of his weight.   111
Everything, the gold apart, is split
  by a fissure that drips tears
  that collect and bore the rock;   114
they drop here from level to level,
  making Acheron, Styx, Phlegethon,
  then down along this tight canal   117
until there's no further to fall:
  thus Cocytus; and this still lake
  you'll see yourself, so I'll stop.'   120
I ask him, 'If this brook here
  comes as you say from our world,
  how is it we only see it now?'   123
'The place is round as you know,'
  he says, 'and turning leftwards
  you've circled much going down,   126
but not yet the entire circuit:
  and so, if anything new appears
  you shouldn't be amazed at it.'   129
'What about Lethe and Phlegethon?'
  I ask; 'you ignore one, master,

way between the cradle of civilisation in the east (represented by Damietta in Egypt) and Rome, centre of the west. Its fissure and the tears running down it (which form the rivers of the underworld) represent the corruption and sorrow that have overtaken humanity since the Golden Age.
110 **except his right foot** etc: the terracotta right foot probably represents the Church in its corruption,

which yet exercises more authority (is leant on more) than the other, iron, foot, the Empire.
116 **Acheron, Styx, Phlegethon**: see cantos III, VII and XII respectively. Cocytus (l. 119), envisaged as a lake of ice, is at the lowest point of Hell; see canto XXXII.
130 **What about Lethe** etc: Virgil hasn't mentioned another famous river of the classical underworld,

132   you say his tears make the other.'
     'I like you asking such questions,'
     he says, 'but that boiling blood
135   ought to answer one of them.
    Lethe you'll see, not in this pit,
     but where souls wash themselves
138   when repented sin is removed.'
    And then: 'Now it's time to leave
     this wood, so follow behind me:
141   the path is this unscorched bank
    where every flame is extinguished.'

Lethe, the river of forgetfulness (see *Aen.*, VI, 705, 749), and goes on to inform Dante (ll. 137–8) that it is situated in Purgatory (see *Purgatory*, XXVIII). Dante hasn't realised that Phlegethon was the river of blood in canto XII. The fact that it was 'boiling' (l. 134) should have alerted him to its identity; its heat is referred to in the *Aeneid* (VI, 548–51) and glosses on Virgil's poem had explained how Phlegethon means 'burning' in Greek.

CANTO FIFTEEN

Now we're up on the stone bank;
  the beck's vapour makes a screen
  saving bank and water from the fire.   3
In Flanders, from Bruges to Wissant,
  they fear the flood crashing in
  and build dykes to repel the sea;   6
in the same way, along the Brenta
  Paduans shield towns and villages
  before Chiarentana feels the thaw –   9
well, this was like those in form
  though not as high or as broad,
  whichever master actually made it.   12
We'd already gone from the wood
  so far, that I couldn't have seen it
  if I'd turned back round to look,   15
when we met a group of ghosts
  coming by the bank, and each one
  peered at us, as in the darkness   18
you eye each other at new moon;
  and they really scrutinised us,
  like an old tailor threads a needle.   21
And as this school made their study,
  one recognised me, and takes me
  by the hem, and cries: 'Amazing!'   24

9 **Chiarentana:** an Alpine region including part of modern Austria and the upper valley of the river Brenta (l. 7), which rises in the Tyrol.

12 **whichever master** etc: Dante leaves indeterminate the identity of the master: either God or some divine agent.

Now when he reached out his arm,
　I gazed hard at his cooked face,
27　　so though the features were burnt
my mind recognised who it was;
　and I bend my face down to his
30　　and say, 'Are you here, Dr Brunetto?'
He replies, 'My boy, don't object
　if Brunetto Latini turns with you,
33　　while his group goes on a little.'
I tell him: 'It's my dearest wish;
　we can sit together, if you like,
36　　as long as my guide doesn't mind.'
'Son,' he says, 'any of us who stops
　at all, he has to lie a century
39　　without fanning the fire off him.
So keep on: I'll stay at your heels,
　then I'll get back to my party
42　　who weep at never-ending pain.'
I don't dare climb from the bank
　down to his level: with head low
45　　as in respect, I keep on going.
So he begins: 'What fate or fortune
　brings you before your final day?
48　　Who's this showing you the path?'
'Up there above, in the air serene,'
　I say, 'I foundered in a vale

30 **Dr Brunetto**: Brunetto Latini, born in Florence c.1220, died 1294. Guelph politician and writer, he went into exile in France between 1260 and 1266 after the Guelph defeat at Montaperti (see note to X, 32), but afterwards held many public offices in Florence including that of city notary and scribe. During his exile he wrote, in French, the *Tresor* (Ital. *Tesoro*, l. 119), an encyclopaedic prose work incorporating history, science, politics, rhetoric, etc., as well as the *Tesoretto*, a long didactic poem in Italian. He also translated Cicero's writings on rhetoric. He is credited with introducing political and rhetorical theory into Florentine intellectual life. I have translated the title Dante gives him ('ser') as 'Dr', to indicate Brunetto's standing; as with Farinata and Cavalcante in canto X, Dante addresses him in the second-person plural form ('voi') throughout.
50 **I foundered** etc.: i.e., in the 'dark wood' of canto I.

before my middle age was full.   51
Only yesterday morning I got out,
    but as I fell back, he appeared
    to lead me home by this route.'   54
He replies, 'If you follow your star
    you can't fail to dock in glory,
    if I saw right in life's lucency;   57
and if I wasn't dead too early,
    seeing heaven smile on you so
    I'd have aided you in your work.   60
But that thankless, malignant race
    who dropped from Fiesole ages back
    and still smack of mountain flint,   63
they'll do you for doing a good job;
    and it's right – among crab apples
    you'll never get the fig to fruit.   66
They've always been known as fools,
    greedy, spiteful, arrogant people:
    you sever yourself from their ways.   69
You're destined to such great honour
    that both sides will hunger for you,

54 **to lead me home** etc: i.e., to God, the eventual destination of humanity's pilgrimage on earth.

55 **your star**: the constellation of Gemini, which the sun was situated in at Dante's birth, and whose influence predisposed man to a life of study and letters. The common medieval belief in astrological influence (n.b. not determinism) is reiterated by Dante in *Paradise*, XXII, 110–20.

62 **who dropped from Fiesole** etc: tradition had it that the hill town of Fiesole, on the outskirts of Florence, became a refuge for Catiline and his troops in the struggle against Julius Caesar; when Caesar destroyed the town he established the new city of Florence, stocking it with the Fieso-lans themselves under the jurisdiction of a small number of Roman families and colonists (l. 77). Florence's original 'mixed stock' was thus seen as the reason why the city was torn by civil discord.

65 **among crab apples** etc: cf. Luke 6: 44: 'For every tree is known by his own fruit. For of thorns men do not gather figs, nor of a bramble bush gather they grapes.'

68 **greedy, spiteful** etc: cf. Ciacco's words on the Florentines in VI, 74–5.

71 **that both sides** etc: Brunetto seems to be prophesying the antagonism towards Dante shown by both the Black and the White Guelphs; the former in the decree of exile against the Whites (see VI,

72   but goats won't get near the grass.
        So let the bloody beasts of Fiesole
        eat each other, and leave the crop
75   – if any still grows in their dung –
        in which the holy seed is reborn
        of those Romans, who stayed there
78   when it became the nest of evil.'
        'If my wish was granted completely,'
        I tell him, 'from humankind
81   you wouldn't yet be under ban:
        what's indelible in me hurts me now,
        that image of the good, dear father
84   you were, always reminding me
        how a man immortalises his name;
        and as long as I move my lips
87   they'll declare how thankful I am.
        I note your words on my future:
        I save them and others for glossing
90   by an able lady, if I reach her.
        So I want you to have no doubts,
        as long as my conscience is clear,
93   however Fortune acts, I'm ready.
        I've already heard similar warnings –
        Fortune can get turning her wheel,
96   the yokel his hoe, when they like.'
        At this, master turns to his right
        then faces round to look at me,
99   saying, 'Well heard is well noted.'

67–72, and notes) and in the particular condemnation against Dante; the latter in their recriminations against Dante after his break with them in the early years of exile (more on this is given in *Paradise*, XVII, 61–9).

76 **holy seed** etc: on Dante's belief in the divinely ordained significance of the Roman Empire and its people, see Introduction.

84 **always reminding me** etc: it is uncertain whether Brunetto was ever Dante's teacher in any formal sense, though it is clear that his achievements and ambitions were an important stimulus to Dante's own.

89 **and others** etc: i.e., Farinata's words in X, 79–81, which will also be kept for 'glossing' by Beatrice (l. 90); cf. X, 130–2, and note.

99 **Well heard** etc: Virgil's epigrammatic utterance has been variously interpreted, though critics largely agree that he seems to be approving

And I'm still continuing to speak
  with Dr Brunetto, wanting to know
  any in his group famous or great.   102
He says, 'It's worth knowing some;
  others are better left to silence
  since there's no time for so many.   105
In short, know they were all clerics
  and writers, of authority and renown,
  their lives fouled by the same sin.   108
Priscian is in that wretched crowd
  and Francesco d'Accorso; you also see
  – if you've a taste for such dirt –   111
the one who the servant of servants
  moved from Arno to Bacchiglione,
  where he left the body he abused.   114
I'd say more, but our walk and talk
  can't go any further – I see there
  some new smoke rising off the sand.   117
People are coming I can't mix with:
  remember my *Tesoro*, where I live
  still; I ask for nothing further.'   120
Then he turned, appearing like one
  who races for green cloth at Verona
  through the country; and like him   123
who wins, he seemed, not a loser.

of Dante's speech and of his determina-
tion to take the prophecies to heart
and not be caught off guard by
Fortune.
106 **clerics**: i.e., men of the Church.
The sinners include Priscian, l. 109,
the sixth-century grammarian born
in Mauretania whose *Institutiones
grammaticae* were an important text-
book in the Middle Ages (the fact that
there is no other record of his supposed sodomy has led some commentators to suggest that Dante intended
someone else here); and Francesco
d'Accorso (1225–94), l. 110, cel-

ebrated professor of law at the
universities of Bologna and Oxford.
112 **the one who** etc: Andrea de'
Mozzi, bishop of Florence (on the
river Arno) until 1295, then trans-
ferred by Boniface VIII (referred to
by the traditional papal title of 'servant of servants') to the bishopric of
Vicenza (on the Bacchiglione), where
he died in 1296. Tales of his sexual
misdemeanours were widespread.
122 **who races** etc: the Veronese
palio, a foot race (run naked) for a
prize of green cloth, held on the first
Sunday in Lent.

CANTO SIXTEEN

We hear the water echoing now
    as it drops into the next circle
    with a drone like a beehive,   3
and three ghosts hurry up together,
    leaving a gang that was going by
    under the grim flogging of the rain.   6
They approach us, and each shouts:
    'You, stop – from the way you dress
    you seem from our own evil city.'   9
Ah, what scars I saw them bear,
    some new, some old, from the fire!
    It hurts me whenever I recall it.   12
Their cry had made master pause;
    he turns to me, and, 'Wait now,'
    he says, 'we owe these courtesy.   15
But if it wasn't the weather here
    to rain arrows of fire, I'd advise
    you to hurry, rather than them.'   18
After we stopped they began again
    the old refrain; then they reach us
    and arrange themselves in a ring,   21
just like greased, naked wrestlers
    testing out their grip and balance

---

5 **a gang:** the previous canto had focused on a group of clerics and writers, whereas the sodomites here are men from political and military life, as we'll see.
20 **the old refrain:** i.e., of tears and laments.
21 **a ring:** the device whereby the sinners manage to stop and talk to Dante whilst keeping in motion, to avoid the penalty described in xv, 37–9.

24   before they aim a punch or throw.
        Then they wheel, each spirit's face
        fixed on me, so their necks went
27   in a motion contrary to their feet.
        'If the woes of this crumbling land
        make us and our pleas despicable,'
30   one says, 'and our peeling tans,
        may our reputations move your soul
        to tell us your name, you going
33   so safe through Hell on live feet.
        This one whose tracks I tread in,
        though he hasn't much skin left now
36   he was grander than you'd think:
        he was good Gualdrada's grandson,
        Guido Guerra – during his lifetime
39   his brains and his sword did much.
        This other treading sand after me
        is Tegghiaio Aldobrandi – his voice
42   should have been welcome up there.
        And me, tortured with them, I was
        Jacopo Rusticucci; and it's a fact
45   my bitch of a wife hurt me most.'
        You know, if it wasn't for the fire

26 so their necks etc: i.e., at some
point in their circling the sinners
would have to twist their necks in
this 'contrary motion' in order to
keep their eyes on Dante.
38 Guido Guerra: descended from
the illustrious Lombard family the
Conti Guidi, Guerra (born c.1220)
was a grandson of Gualdrada di Bel-
lincione Berti de' Ravignani, a celebrated female paragon of beauty,
morality and domestic virtue. As
Guelph leader he led the Florentines
against the Arezzo Ghibellines in
1255, but was exiled after Montaperti (see note to X, 32), a battle he tried
to dissuade his party from fighting.

He further distinguished himself at
the battle of Benevento (1266) and
died in 1272.
41 Tegghiaio Aldobrandi: another
Florentine Guelph commander (died
before 1266), and another who advised against Montaperti (ll. 41–2).
44 Jacopo Rusticucci: little is known
of him, beyond his being mentioned
in Florentine records between 1235
and 1266; l. 45 is usually interpreted
as meaning that the unsympathetic
nature of his wife drove him to homo-
sexuality. Both Rusticucci and Tegghiaio were among those Florentines
who 'aimed at good' whom Dante
asked Ciacco about in VI, 79–80.

I'd have cast myself down to them,
  and I think with master's assent;   48
but since I'd have been barbecued
  terror overcame my real desires,
  and my craving to embrace them.   51
And I replied, 'Grief, not loathing,
  so much as is shed only slowly,
  that's what your state fixed in me   54
when master here spoke some words
  that made me ready to believe
  people like you were approaching.   57
I am from your city, and always
  your deeds and your great names
  I'd repeat and hear with feeling.   60
I'm leaving rotten fruits for ripe
  that my trusty guide promised me;
  but first I've to sink to the core.'   63
'So your spirit conducts your limbs
  for a long time yet,' he replies,
  'and your fame sparkles after you,   66
tell us whether merit and manners
  still dwell in our city as they did,
  or whether they're exiled totally;   69
since Guiglielmo Borsiere over there
  who's just joined our tortured set,
  he pains us enough with his news.'   72
'Newcomers mixed with quick money

---

55 **some words:** i.e., l. 15, which indicated that people worthy of respect
were approaching.
63 **the core:** i.e., the centre of the
earth and bottommost part of Hell.
70 **Guiglielmo Borsiere:** little is
known of this court figure, who according to Boccaccio had a reputation as a peacemaker and man of
refined etiquette.
73 **Newcomers** etc: Dante's stric-
tures on the decay of Florence recur

throughout the *Comedy*; here he as-
sumes an oratorical and prophetic
stance (l. 76) and specifically blames
the 'new people' coming into Florence
from the surrounding country during
the thirteenth century for the city's
demise. Quick money was to be made
from Florence's commercial expansion and from its usury business. The
present inhabitants of the city are thus
contrasted with the great figures of the
past whom Dante meets in this canto.

97

that puffs people up beyond measure,
75 Florence, you weep for this already.'
I raised my face and shouted this;
and the three took it as my reply,
78 swapping looks that saw the truth.
'If it's always so little inconvenience,'
they all say, 'to satisfy enquiries,
81 lucky you with such gifts of speech!
Therefore, so you leave this dark pit
and return to see the bright stars,
84 when you rejoice to say "I was",
make sure you tell folk about us.'
Then the wheel broke, they shot off
87 with legs seeming quick as wings.
Yes, you'd never get out an Amen
as rapidly as these disappeared;
90 so master said we should go on,
and I followed him a short while
till the water sounded so close
93 we'd hardly have heard ourselves.
That river running right to the sea,
the first to do so after Monviso
96 on the left slope of the Apennines,
the one at first called Acquaqueta,
though it sinks along several valleys
99 and changes its name at Forlì –
well, it roars above San Benedetto
dell'Alpe, going over in one jump
102 instead of a thousand small stages,
and just so, down this craggy bank
we found the dark water crashing,
105 so ears couldn't bear it for long.
I had a cord around my waist:

95 **the first** etc: going eastwards
from Monviso, all the rivers running
off the Apennines flow into the Po,
until the Acquaqueta (today called
the Montone) which was then the
first to go straight to the sea.
106 **a cord** etc: there is obviously an
allegorical meaning in the episode of

at times I'd thought to use it
to trap the bright-skinned cat,   108
and after I'd taken it right off
just as my guide instructed me,
I gave it him, rolled in a knot.   111
Then he turned towards his right
and threw it out from the summit,
down into that enormous ravine.   114
'Something unusual is likely here,'
I thought; 'it's a strange signal
my master follows with his eyes.'   117
Ah, how carefully we have to go
when those who see your actions
can see your thoughts as well!   120
He tells me, 'He'll soon come up,
him I expect and you guess at;
he'll have to show himself soon.'   123
Whenever the truth seems a lie,
silence is best, as far as possible,
else there's blame without fault,   126
but I must speak here: reader,
I swear by the lines of my comedy,
so they'll long be in good grace,   129
that I saw in that murky darkness
something swim up towards us,
wondrous even to the stout-hearted,   132
like one surfacing who dives down
perhaps to get the anchor loose
if it's snagged in rocks or weed,   135
who pulls upwards, kicking his feet.

the cord, though what it is remains one of the most uncertain parts of the entire poem. Few commentators now accept that Dante was a member of the Franciscan order in his boyhood, and that the cord of the order's habit represents the novice's battle with lust ('the bright-skinned cat', cf. I, 31ff). That it represents the virtue that would tame lust, or virtues such as truth and justice opposed to the Fraud we're about to meet (personified by the monster Geryon) is however widely accepted. On the other hand some critics see the cord as representing weaknesses that Dante has to *lose* before overcoming such vices.

CANTO SEVENTEEN

'Here's the thing with needle tail
  that leaps mountains, busts walls
  and defences, infects the world!'   3
So master begins to address me
  as he beckoned it to the brink
  near where the stone walk ended.   6
And that filthy image of Fraud
  arrives, shows his head and chest,
  but keeps his tail below the bank.   9
The face you felt you could trust
  as that of a just-looking person,
  but the rest of him was reptile;   12
he had two hairy claws for arms
  and back, chest and both sides
  had designs of knots and circles: 15
there's no sewing with such colours
  on stuff from Turkey or Tartary,

---

1 **the thing etc**: we only hear 'the thing' 's name, Geryon, at l. 97; in classical mythology he was a tyrant killed by Hercules in the course of his labours, and is described by Virgil, Ovid and other poets as a monstrous combination of three human bodies. Dante retains the triform nature, but recasts him as a combination of human, animal and reptile (ll. 10–13), possibly inspired by Revelation 9: 7–10. Dante may have been inspired more generally by any number of zoological fantasies in the writing and art of the Middle Ages; such a figure in any case makes an obvious personification of Fraud.

15 **designs of knots etc**: signifying the snares of Fraud, with the 'circles' indicating the devious paths of the fraudulent.

18   Arachne never wove such patterns.
   So exactly like boats by the shore,
    half in water, half on the bank,
21   or like the beaver sits to fish
  in Germany, that land of guzzlers,
   so this horrible beast sticks out
24   on the curb that halts the sand.
  He darted his tail about in the air,
   twisting up the poisonous fork
27   that arms its tip, like a scorpion's.
  'We've to twist a little ourselves,'
   master says, 'to get over there
30   to where that beast's stationed';
  so down we climbed on the right,
   and ten steps across the stone rim
33   made us safe from sand and fire.
  When we'd reached this creature
   I saw spirits a little further on
36   sat on the sand, near the abyss,
  and master says, 'So it's complete,
   your experience of this last ring,
39   go and see how that lot manage.
  But keep your conversation short:
   I'll talk to him while you're gone
42   so he'll lend us his strong back.'
  Well, on I went, all by myself

---

18 **Arachne**: the maiden of Lydia who challenged the goddess Minerva to a weaving contest; her beautiful handiwork so enraged Minerva that she changed her into a spider (*Metamorphoses*, VI, 5–145).

21 **or like the beaver** etc: the beaver was supposed to catch fish by dangling his tail in the water; Geryon's half-concealed position is of course a further indication of Fraud.

22 **in Germany** etc: proverbial.

28 **We've to twist** etc: the travellers have to go out of their usual direction (which is always leftwards) and move to the right to get to Geryon (see l. 31), a reversal that only happens in one other place in Hell (see IX, 132, and note to X, 5). Here the 'twisting' obviously underlines the crooked nature of Fraud.

36 **sat on the sand**: those sitting, the usurers, had already been introduced at XIV, 23. Dante makes sure he meets a group who are almost entirely Florentine (l. 70).

at the seventh circle's very edge,
to where these tortured folk sat.   45
Their agony burst from their eyes;
their hands went flapping all over
at the flames, or the hot sand –   48
dogs in summer are just like this,
going crazy with feet or snouts
when fleas get them, or horseflies.   51
I looked at some of their faces
browning under that terrible heat
but didn't know any; then I notice   54
each has a pouch round his neck
of different colours and stamps
that their eyes seem greedy for.   57
And as my gaze goes among them
I see azure on a yellow purse,
shaped in the figure of a lion.   60
I look further, and see another,
the purse red as blood, the stamp
a goose, whiter than any butter.   63
And one that had a white purse
with the fat blue sign of a sow
shouts: 'Why are you in this pit?   66
You shove off; since you're living,
I tell you my neighbour Vitaliano

60 **the figure of a lion** etc: all the usurers we are about to meet are of noble family, which increases that sense of degradation communicated throughout Dante's encounter with them by the extensive use of animal imagery: these are all aristocrats debased by the passion for filthy lucre, and seemingly unrecognisable as individuals. An azure lion on a yellow ground was the arms of the Gianfigliazzi, a Florentine Guelph family; Dante may have had particularly in mind Catello di Rosso Gianfigliazzi,

who practised usury in France (died after 1283).
63 **a goose** etc: arms of another Florentine (Ghibelline) family, the Obriachi.
65 **a sow** etc: arms of the Scrovegni family of Padua, whose money built the famous chapel painted by Giotto in the early fourteenth century.
68 **Vitaliano:** usually taken to be Vitaliano del Dente, who was in fact *podestà* of Padua in 1307. As we go deeper into Hell, many shades not only do not wish to be reported in

69 will come here, to sit on my left.
I'm Paduan, among these Florentines;
 they're always bawling in my ears,
72 "Wait till that perfect knight comes
who'll have three goats on his bag!"'
 Then he made faces with his tongue,
75 like an ox when it licks its nose.
Now, afraid that staying too long
 would annoy him who said not to,
78 I left those shattered spirits.
I found he was already mounted
 on that horrible animal's back;
81 he said: 'Now courage, now daring:
in future our stairs are like this –
 get up in front, I'll go between
84 so that tail can't do any damage.'
A man that feels fever coming on
 with his fingernails already white,
87 shivering when he sees the shade,
this was me when I heard him;
 but shame threatened everything
90 that makes us copy brave leaders.
I perched on those vast shoulders:
 I wanted to say, 'Hold me tight,'
93 but found my voice wouldn't come.

the world above, but start to condemn those living with malicious predictions of future damnation.

72 **that perfect knight** etc: the arms given in the next line identify the awaited Florentine as Gianni Buiamonte of the Becchi family (died 1310). That a usurer held high public office in Florence and was knighted is the point of Dante's sarcasm against the city here.

74 **Then he made faces** etc: i.e., as an insult to Dante.

82 **in future** etc: Dante will in fact be lifted down from the eighth to the ninth circle by the giant Antaeus (XXXI, 130–45), and at the centre of Hell will have to climb along Lucifer's body to begin his journey up to Purgatory (XXXIV, 70ff).

84 **so that tail** etc: i.e., reason, personified by Virgil, is a defence against the snares of Fraud. Dante's actual physical contact with Geryon implies that the overcoming of sin in these lower parts of Hell involves much more a recognition of and active struggle with it, rather than bypassing it as a mere spectator.

But he who had helped me before
  in other dangers, after I was up
  he held me steady with his arms;   96
then he says, 'Geryon, move now:
  glide down in wide, easy circles:
  remember your unusual cargo.'   99
Like a ship backs out of dock
  slowly, slowly, so he moved away;
  and when he felt himself free   102
he manoeuvred his body right round,
  then shot out his tail like an eel
  and raked in air with his arms.   105
Ah, no one was ever so frightened,
  I think, Phaeton chucking the reins
  so Heaven still seems scorched today,   108
or poor Icarus, after he realised
  feathers were melting off his back,
  his father crying, 'Watch your path!' –   111
neither could feel worse than I did
  when I saw only air all round me,
  and nothing else but this brute.   114
He sailed onwards, ever so slowly:
  I only knew he circled downwards
  from the wind on my face and legs.   117
Now I hear the water on my right
  in a horrible tumult beneath us,
  and I stick my head out to look.   120
And then I fear going down more,
  I see fires and I hear screams
  so I shiver and sit more tightly.   123
I see now what I couldn't before,
  how we circle down: on all sides

107 **Phaeton:** who was unable to control his father Apollo's chariot, so that the sun went astray from its course and left the scorchmark of the Milky Way across the sky; see *Metamorphoses*, II, 1-324.

109 **Icarus:** son of Daedalus; the two tried to escape from Crete using wings fastened to them with wax, but when Icarus flew too near the sun the wax melted and he was drowned; *Metamorphoses* VIII, 203-33.

126   awful evils are coming up closer.
   As a falcon airborne a long time
    returns tired to where he shot off,
129   having seen no prey or signal,
   so his owner sighs: 'He's dropping!'
    and as he lands in wide spirals
132   far from his master, disdainful;
   so Geryon takes us precisely down
    to the bottom of the sheer rock,
135   and with his burden unloaded
   he vanished as quick as an arrow.

CANTO EIGHTEEN

Hell has a part called Malebolge,
  a place of iron-coloured rock,
  as is the cliff that encircles it.   3
Exactly in this evil plain's centre
  is a huge hole, deep and wide,
  as I'll describe in due course.   6
From here the land forms a ring
  back to the base of the high cliff,
  its floor cut into ten valleys.   9
Like the earth's lay-out appears
  when you've got ditch after ditch
  guarding the walls of a castle,   12
so these valleys appeared here;
  and as from the fortress gates
  bridges run to the outer circle,   15
so crags go from the cliff's base
  across the valleys, bank to bank,
  meeting their terminus at the hole.   18
So here, off-loaded from the back
  of Geryon, we now were, the poet
  heading left, and me behind him.   21
On my right I see fresh anguish,
  new pain, new hands on the whip,
  all packed into this first ditch.   24

---

1 **Malebolge:** the meaning of the Italian word, coined by Dante to describe the eighth circle, is 'Evilbags', or 'Evilsacks', a set of circular valleys, as Dante will explain, where the fraudulent sinners described at XI, 52–60 are 'bagged'.

At the bottom were naked sinners
in a faster, two-way traffic,
27   against us this side, with us that,
just like Rome handled the ranks
this jubilee year, over the bridge,
30   organising the flow of people
so on one side they all headed
to the castle, going to St Peter's,
33   the other moving to the mount.
On both banks of the dark rock
horned devils with huge whips
36   flayed folk fiercely, on their backs.
Hell, how they made them skip
at the first course! No one wants
39   a second or third helping here.
While I walked, my eyes hit on
one of them; immediately I said,
42   'I've already had a taste of him,'
and I stop to make him out better;
my kind guide stops too, agreeing
45   that I can turn back a little.
Him with the weals tries to hide,
lowering his face; but it's no use
48   since I say: 'You looking down,
if your face hasn't been falsified
you're Venedico Caccianemico:

27 **against us this side** etc: the first
bolgia is that of the pimps and sedu-
cers of women, divided into a 'two-
way traffic' on either side of the
ditch's midpoint. Dante compares
the arrangement with the traffic control instituted in Rome in the jubilee
year of 1300, when over 200,000 pilgrims visited the city: on the ponte
Sant' Angelo, those going to St
Peter's (and facing the Castel Sant'
Angelo, l. 32) had to keep to one
side, and those leaving the basilica
(facing Monte Giordano – 'the
mount', l. 33) to the other.
50 **Venedico Caccianemico**: born
c.1228 into a leading Bolognese
Guelph family, and prominent in the
civil intrigues and political struggles
in Bologna throughout the thirteenth
century; he also held high office in
Milan, Pistoia and elsewhere. Dante's
early commentators report that he
procured his sister Ghisolabella
for the Marchese of Ferrara (either
Obizzo II or Azzo VIII d'Este) for

why is your sauce here so spicy?'   51
And he says, 'I grudge telling you;
   but your meaning forces me to,
   it brings back the ancient world.   54
I was him who made Ghisolabella
   do the wishes of the Marchese,
   whatever the smutty story says.   57
I'm not the only Bolognese here,
   rather this place is full of them,
   more than all the tongues today   60
saying "sipa" from Savena to Reno;
   if you want assurance of this,
   remember the greed in our hearts.'   63
As he speaks, a devil hits him
   with his lash, saying, 'Get going,
   pimp! Women aren't for sale here.'   66
And now I go back to my guide;
   and only a few strides later
   there's the crag, rising off the bank.   69
We can climb it easily enough,
   and so heading right up the rock
   we leave the circling outer wall.   72
We reach where the bridge yawns
   below, letting the lashed go under;
   master says, 'Stop, absorb the sight   75

monetary and political gain. He died in 1302, though Dante must have thought he was dead by 1300; where and when Dante had previously encountered him (l. 42) isn't known.

51 why is your sauce etc: Dante is punning on the word *salse* (sauces) which is a metaphor for the pungent pains undergone by Caccianemico and also the name of a mass burial-pit outside Bologna where the bodies of criminals and suicides were thrown. Caccianemico recognises the local reference (ll. 53–4).

57 whatever etc: other versions of the story, less damning to Caccianemico, are here rejected in his own confession of guilt.

61 saying "sipa" etc: Bolognese dialect word for the third person present subjunctive of the verb *essere* (to be) = *sia*, often used for *sì* ('yes'). Caccianemico claims that there are more Bolognese in this first *bolgia* than in the territory of Bologna itself, between its eastern and western confines marked by the rivers Savena and Reno. The Bolognese obviously had a reputation for covetousness (l. 63).

of these other evil-born ones now,
these whose faces you haven't seen
78 since they went in our direction.'
From the old bridge we watch them,
this other crowd coming towards us,
81 flayed just as much as the first.
I needn't question my kind master:
he says, 'See that grand one come,
84 seeming to scorn any tears at pain;
how regal his appearance is still!
He's Jason, whose skill and courage
87 won the ram from the Colchians.
He went to the island of Lemnos
after its cruel, fanatical females
90 had murdered all their menfolk:
here his ploys and gilded speech
tricked Hypsipyle, the young girl
93 who before tricked the other women,
and he left her, all alone, pregnant;
such torture fits such a crime,
96 and Medea's avenged here too.
With him go all tricksters like that;
and that'll do for this first ditch
99 and all those stuck in its jaws.'
We'd come where our narrow path
crosses over the second bank
102 that shoulders the following arch.
We heard people's stifled moans
in the next pit, snuffling, wheezing,
105 the sound of self-inflicted blows.

86 **Jason**: who led the Argonauts to the successful capture of the golden fleece from King Aeëtes of Colchis (*Metamorphoses*, VII, 1–158). On the way he stopped at the island of Lemnos, and seduced and abandoned Hypsipyle; later he tricked Aeëtes's daughter, Medea, in the same way (l. 96).

93 **who before tricked etc**: outraged by the behaviour of their menfolk, the 'cruel' (l. 89) women of Lemnos decided to kill all the males on the island. Hypsipyle hid her father, King Thoas, and pretended that she'd murdered him.

The sides were crusted with plaque,
 deposits of vapour that floated up
 to trouble their eyes and noses.   108
The bottom's so deep, that to see
 the only place was right on top
 of the rock, where it arches most.   111
Here we came; and down in the pit
 I see the people plunged in shit
 that seemed on tap from the sewer.   114
And while I'm poring over them,
 I see a head so crapped over
 you couldn't say if lay or cleric.   117
He yells, 'Why's your greedy gaze
 on me, more than the other shites?'
 I say, 'Because, if I remember,   120
I've seen you before, with dry hair:
 you're Alessio Interminei of Lucca –
 that's why I'm watching you most.'   123
Then he smacks his bonce, saying
 'What sunk me here was flattery,
 that my tongue never got tired of.'   126
Master steps in now: 'Look further,'
 he tells me, 'over there a little;
 look closely at that woman's face,   129
that filthy and tousled prostitute
 clawing herself with shitty nails,
 now squatting, now on her feet.   132
It's Thaïs the whore: to her man's
 "Am I much in your good books?"
 her reply was, "Oh, marvellously!"   135
And that's enough looking at them.'

---

122 **Alessio Interminei:** next to
nothing is known of him, nor why he
is to be found in this second *bolgia* of
the flatterers (or more appropriately,
given their punishment, arse-lickers).
He was still alive in 1295.
133 **Thaïs:** a prostitute in Terence's
play *Eunuchus*, known to Dante
through its being quoted by Cicero
(*De amicitia*, 26) as recording an in-
stance of excessive flattery, with
Thaïs responding thus fulsomely to
her lover's gift of a slave.

CANTO NINETEEN

O Simon Magus, O paltry crew
crazy for gold and for silver,
prostituting the things of God   3
that should be wed to goodness;
now the trumpet sounds for you
since you're in the third ditch.   6
Already on this next death row
we'd climbed up along the bridge
to right over the ditch's middle: 9
O mighty wisdom, how much art
you show, in Heaven, earth, Hell,
how justly you dispense power!   12
I saw on the bottom and sides
the livid rock all full of holes,
all round, all of the same width.   15
They seemed no bigger or smaller
than those they have for baptism
in my beautiful San Giovanni,   18

1 **Simon Magus**: see Acts 8: 9–24,
where Simon the sorcerer attempts to
buy from the apostles the power to
communicate the Holy Ghost through
the laying on of hands. From him the
term simony derives, referring to the
buying and selling of ecclesiastical
offices and the trafficking in sacraments.

3 **prostituting** etc: i.e., selling office
to those who can pay for it, rather
than those who merit it.

5 **the trumpet sounds**: the towncrier
would announce himself in this
way, before declaring the judgements
of the magistrates.

18 **San Giovanni** etc: the Baptistery
at Florence, where Dante himself was
baptised. It seems that the priests
baptising there stood in circular vessels
arranged round the font, to protect
themselves from the crush of the crowd
(verification of this is difficult because of destruction to the Baptistery

one of which, a few years back,
    I broke as someone choked there –
21   this be the truth, to any doubters.
From each hole came thrusting out
    the calves and feet of a sinner,
24   just visible down to the knees;
and their soles were all on fire,
    so they danced away so frenziedly
27   no stocks would ever hold them.
And just like flame on a pudding
    goes licking its outermost surface
30   so here from their toes to heels.
'Who's that tormented one, master,
    jiving more than his companions,'
33   I ask, 'kissed by a redder fire?'
He says, 'If you let me carry you
    down there, down the lower bank,
36   he'll name himself and his sins.'
I say, 'I like whatever you like:
    you know your wish is law, master,
39   you know what my silences hide.'
So we went on to the fourth bank,
    turning and descending leftwards
42   into those narrow beds of holes.
My good master didn't unload me
    until we came to the manhole
45   of him who wept with his legs.
'Whoever it is upside-down here,
    poor soul like a stuck stake,'
48   I began, 'speak if you're able.'

since Dante's time). Little else is known of Dante's account here of breaking one of these, but he obviously wishes to refute the charge of sacrilege that presumably circulated (l. 21). The parody of baptism in this *bolgia* emblematises the *contrapasso*.

35 **the lower bank:** i.e., the inner bank of the third *bolgia*. Dante explains in XXIV, 34–40 how the inner bank of each *bolgia* is lower and less steep than the outer because the entire region of *Malebolge* slopes down towards the central well.

I stood like a priest confessing
  the evil murderer already fixed,
  called back by him to delay death.   51
He cries, 'You stand there already,
  you're already up there, Boniface?
  The script's tricked me by years.   54
You've retired from the lucre early,
  after conning our lady fearlessly
  into marriage, then defiling her?'   57
Well, I stood there dithering then,
  like those baffled by some reply
  they don't know how to answer.   60
Virgil intercedes: 'Tell him quickly,
  "I'm not him, not him you think,"
  and I replied as he told me to.   63
Then the shade's feet had a spasm;
  he sighs, and in a bitter voice
  says, 'So why go pestering me?   66
If you're so wanting to know me
  that you've run down the bank,
  know I wore the great mantle;   69

49 **like a priest** etc: Dante compares the sinner's situation to that of a murderer, executed as was common at the time by being put upside-down in a hole which was then filled in with earth; here as elsewhere in *Hell* the fiction seems less brutal than the everyday reality. Dante images himself as the priest, stooping over to hear the last confession, and 'called back' by the murderer to gain him a few more minutes (l. 51).

52 **He shouts** etc: the sinner is Giovanni Gaetano Orsini, who was Pope Nicholas III from 1277 to 1280 and who grew wealthy through the sale of ecclesiastical positions to relatives. He mistakes Dante (l. 53) for the pope in office in 1300, Boniface VIII

(1294–1303); see note to III, 59. He therefore feels 'tricked' by Boniface's arrival in Hell three years before his death (l. 54). Boniface will take up Nicholas's position in this hole of the popes, as explained later (ll. 73–8), when Nicholas will join his predecessors.

56 **after conning** etc: 'our lady' is the Church, which the pope is seen as 'marrying'. That Boniface tricked Celestine V into abdicating in 1294, then bought his way into office, was widely believed. As pope, his simony was notorious.

69 **the great mantle:** i.e., of popehood. Nicholas's talk of being the 'bear's offspring' (l. 70) puns on his family name of Orsini (*orsa* = bear).

I truly was the bear's offspring
and greedy to advance the cubs,
72   slotting coin there and myself here.
Others are sunk below my head,
simonists in the job before me,
75   laid now in the rock's clefts;
I drop down too when he comes,
the one I believed that you were
78   when I shot at you my question.
But I've been stuck upside-down
and my feet are already scorched
81   for longer than he'll be like this:
because after him, a filthier comes,
that lawless priest from the west
84   who'll hang here over both of us.
Another Jason he'll be, that one
thick with his king in Maccabees;
87   so him with the French throne.'
Well, I may have gone too far now,
but I actually replied like this:
90   'Tell me how much he asked for,
I mean Our Lord from St Peter
before he handed him the keys?
93   No, all he asked was, "Follow me."
And did they take Matthias's cash,
Peter and company, in their ballot
96   to fill the guilty soul's place?
You stay put, you're well punished,

82 **a filthier comes** etc: Clement V, pope from 1305 to 1314 (thus replacing Boniface in this *bolgia* after eleven years, as opposed to Nicholas's longer wait for Boniface, l. 81). A native of Gascony ('from the west', l. 83), he was notoriously corrupt.
85 **Another Jason** etc: Jason became the Jewish High Priest by bribing King Antiochus Epiphanes of Syria (2 Maccabees 4: 7–27), just as it's here claimed that Clement bought his office from the French king, Philip the Fair, becoming his puppet.
92 **before he handed him** etc: Matthew 16: 19.
93 **Follow me**: Matthew 4: 19; John 21: 19.
94 **Matthias's cash** etc: Matthias was elected by the apostles to take the place of Judas (Acts 1: 21–6).

and look after those evil gains
that made you hostile to Charles.   99
And if I wasn't still restrained
by my respect for the great keys
you held in the happier life,   102
I'd use even stronger language;
for greed like yours sours the earth,
trampling goodness, raising the bad.   105
The Evangelist intended you pastors
in her who sits upon the waters
and fornicates with the kings,   108
the woman born with seven heads
and sustained by the ten horns
as long as her spouse was virtuous.   111
God is just gold and silver to you:
how are you other than idolators,
only their one is your hundred?   114
Constantine, how much bad you bred,
not your conversion, but that grant
the first rich pope had off you!'   117

99 **that made you hostile** etc: the rumour ran that Nicholas had received money to support the Sicilians against their French king, Charles of Anjou.

106 **The Evangelist** etc: see the famous passage describing the whore of Babylon in Revelation 17, here interpreted (as was common in the Middle Ages) as representing the corrupt Church in its political intrigues. The seven heads and ten horns are symbols of the Seven Sacraments and Ten Commandments, sources of strength to the Church given an honest pope (or 'spouse', l. 111).

112 **God is gold** etc: see Hosea 8: 4. The Jews worshipped one gold idol, the golden calf (Exodus 32), whereas Nicholas and his like worship a 'hun-dred' (individual pieces of money, l. 114).

115 **Constantine** etc: after Pope Sylvester I had healed him of leprosy, the Roman emperor Constantine was converted to Christianity in 312. He moved the capital of the Empire to Constantinople in 330, leaving the dominion of Rome and the western Empire as a gift to the Church (the famous 'donation of Constantine'). The donation was later shown to have no historical basis, but Dante accepts it here as the origin of the Church's corruption through its intervention in temporal matters. In his political treatise *Monarchia* he returns to attack Constantine's action, and its disastrous effect on the Church (II, xii, 8, III, x, xiii).

And while I chanted on like this
   anger or conscience was eating him,
120   his feet kicked away like crazy.
I'd say my master was delighted,
   he looked so pleased to hear
123   these words of truth spoken out.
So he took me in both his arms:
   after lifting me up to his chest
126   he retraced our downward path,
and didn't weary of cradling me
   till he made the top of the arch
129   that bridges banks four and five.
Here he unloads me, gently, gently,
   because of that rough, steep rock
132   that even goats would find tough.
Then another valley comes in view.

CANTO TWENTY

Now, new torture is my topic,
  in this twentieth canto of part one
  dealing with those below earth,   3
and I was ready straight away
  to study the deep new opening
  that runs with unhappy tears;   6
and I saw in this round moat
  people go along weeping quietly,
  pacing slowly like a procession.   9
As they arrived underneath me,
  I saw them twisted amazingly
  between their chins and chests,   12
so their faces faced backwards
  and they walked by in reverse
  since they couldn't see before.   15
It may be that people paralysed
  have been screwed round like this,
  but I never saw or heard of it.   18
May God help you derive fruit
  from your read, reader – think
  if I could keep my sight dry,   21
seeing our image under my nose
  so deformed, tears from their eyes
  ran down the cleft in their arse.   24

---

11 **twisted amazingly** etc: the punishment of the astrologers, soothsayers and those dealing in magic in this *bolgia* is to have the power of seeing 'before' (which supposedly extended to the future on earth) taken away from them. Virgil explains this succinctly in ll. 38–9.

Indeed I wept, leant on a crag
of the hard rock; my guide says,
27   'Are you still as silly as this?
Pity thrives here when it's dead:
is there anyone worse than him
30   who'd usurp divine foresight?
Come on now, look up, and see
one that the earth gulped down
33   as the Thebans cried, "Anfiaraus,
what's the hurry to go on leave?"
and his plummeting only stopped
36   with Minos, who bags them all.
Note his shoulders are his chest:
since he ached to see in front
39   he looks and moves in reverse.
See Tiresias, whose looks changed
in a man–woman mutation
42   when his entire body altered;
he had to take his stick twice
to the two entwined snakes
45   before he got his manhood back.
Backing on to his belly is Aruns;
in the mountains by Luni, cleared
48   by the Carrarese who live below,
he had among the white marble
a cave dwelling, so that the sea

---

33 **Anfiaraus** etc: one of the seven kings who besieged Thebes, his story is told in Statius's *Thebaid*, VII–VIII. Having foreseen that he would die during the siege, he tried to avoid going but was betrayed by his wife Eriphyle; during battle the ground opened up and swallowed him.

36 **Minos** etc: see V, 4–15.

40 **Tiresias** etc: Theban soothsayer, whose encounter with the snakes described here is told in Ovid, *Metamorphoses*, III, 324–31. Having experience of being either sex, he judged that women got more pleasure from lovemaking, whereupon Juno in anger struck him blind. Jupiter gave him the gift of prophecy as compensation.

46 **Aruns**: Etruscan diviner who foretold the civil war between Caesar and Pompey (Lucan, *Pharsalia*, I, 584ff.). Luni (l. 47) was an ancient Etruscan city destroyed by Dante's day.

and stars opened to his view. 51
And the woman whose pubic parts
and whose hair-buried breasts
are all hidden round the back, 54
she was Manto, who tried many lands
before she chose my native place,
on which I'd like your attention. 57
Following the death of her father
and the slavery of Bacchus's city,
she wandered the world at length. 60
There's a lake up in lovely Italy
in the Alps that shut off Germany
above Tiralli, called lake Benaco, 63
and from Garda to Val Camonica
I'd think over a thousand streams
water their way down into it. 66
Trent's, Verona's, Brescia's bishops,
they might all bless at one point
in the middle, if they visited, 69
and Peschiera's strong, splendid fort
fronts Bergamese and Brescians too
where the lake bank is lowest. 72
Here everything comes to cascade
that the lap of Benaco can't hold,
forming a river through the green 75

55 **Manto**: Tiresias's daughter, who
fled Thebes ('Bacchus's city', l. 59)
and the tyranny of Creon after her
father's death. Reference to the
founding of Mantua (which Virgil is
about to describe) is in *Aeneid*, x,
198–200; see also *Metamorphoses*,
vi, 157–62 and *Thebaid*, iv, 463–6,
vii, 758ff.
63 **lake Benaco**: today known as
lake Garda. Tiralli is a castle north of
the lake.
64 **Garda** etc: the city of Garda is
on the eastern side of the lake, the

Camonica valley on the west.
67 **Trent's** etc: the confines of the
three bishoprics actually met at a
point on the lake, where all three
bishops might therefore officiate;
critics have recognised in 'if they
visited' (l. 69) a sarcastic reference to
their negligence.
70 **Peschiera's** etc: the fort of Peschiera had been built on the south-
east side of the lake by the lords of
Verona to repulse attacks from the
Bergamese and Brescians.

meadows; once the water moves,
  Benaco is renamed the Mincio,
78   till it joins the Po at Governol.
Now, before long it finds a level
  where it spreads to make a marsh
81   that can be rank in the summer,
and here the cruel virgin passed
  and saw some untenanted land
84   in the middle of the marshes.
To get away from any society
  she settled there with servants,
87   practising her arts till she died.
Then the men around those parts
  drew to that spot, fortified
90   by surrounding marsh as it was,
and raised a city on her bones,
  named because of her settlement
93   Mantua, with no need of sorcery.
Its citizens used to be numerous,
  before da Casalodi's stupidity
96   was exposed by Pinamonte's ruse.
So I warn you, if ever you hear
  of any other origin for my city,
99   don't let tales oust the truth.'
I say, 'Master, your explanation

---

82 **cruel virgin**: Virgil 'corrects' the *Aeneid* here, where Manto is a wife and mother (and whose son, Ocnus, actually founded Mantua). Statius in the *Thebaid* however refers to Manto as a virgin, and describes her cruel participation in the magical rites of her father.

93 **with no need of sorcery**: the reason for Virgil's account of the founding of Mantua, which seems to be a digression, might now be explained. According to legend, ancient peoples would decide the names of their cities using sorcery or augury, whereas Vir-

gil suggests that the derivation of 'Mantua' is perfectly rational. Virgil could be attempting to cleanse his native city of any 'stain' of magic, and himself from his own reputation in the Middle Ages as a magician.

95 **da Casalodi** etc: in 1272 Alberto da Casalodi, lord of Mantua, was persuaded by Pinamonte dei Bonaccolsi to exile his nobles, who were widely hated by the populace. Pinamonte was then able to depose the defenceless Alberto, which he did with much slaughter.

convinces me so completely
any other would be mere dross.   102
But these people walking round,
tell me if any are noteworthy –
they absorb all my attention.'   105
So he says, 'That one whose beard
stretches down over his back,
he used augury, when in Greece   108
the only males were in cradles;
he and Calchas chose the time
to cut the moorings in Aulis.   111
He's Eurypylus – this deed of his
is sung of in my high tragedy
as you know – you know it all.   114
The other one with the thin body
was Michael Scott, who really knew
every trick of bogus magic.   117
Guido Bonatti's there, and Asdente
who'd regret now it's too late
not keeping to twine and leather.   120
See the wretched witch-women
who left spinning and stitching
for herbal charms and evil images.   123
But come now; Cain and his thorns

---

112 **Eurypylus:** at the time of the Trojan War (taking all the men from Greece, ll. 108–9) Eurypylus and Calchas were the augurs who divined the most favourable time for the Greek fleet to set sail (from Aulis). In fact the *Aeneid* ('my high tragedy', l. 113) doesn't refer to Eurypylus's part in this operation, though in II, 113–18 he is referred to as an emissary to Apollo's oracle to find the best time for the Greeks' return journey.
113 **my high tragedy:** see note to I, 86.
116 **Michael Scott:** Scottish philosopher in the court of Frederick II

(see X, 120), reputedly an augur and astrologer.
118 **Guido Bonatti** etc: from Forlì, a magician in the service of many lords in Italy during the thirteenth century; Asdente was an ex-shoemaker from Parma.
124 **Cain and his thorns** etc: the equivalent of our man in the moon. The moon is setting in the west, near Seville (on the boundary between the northern and southern hemispheres); the time is about six a.m. There is no reference in canto I to the moon helping Dante there in the 'deep wood'.

already touch the sea at Seville
126   and the hemispheres' boundary,
and last night was the full moon:
you'll remember, it did no harm
129   to you, crossing the deep wood.'
Thus he spoke, and on we moved.

CANTO TWENTY-ONE

From one bridge to another we go,
   talking of things that don't concern
   my comedy; when we reach the top   3
we stop to witness the next ditch
   of Malebolge, more fruitless tears;
   and we see it's incredibly dark.   6
If you know the arsenal at Venice,
   the gluey pitch they boil in winter
   to smear on their leaking boats   9
since they can't put to sea; instead
   some get on with new boats, others

2 **talking of things** etc: it has been argued that the 'things' omitted here may refer to the charge of barratry made against Dante in the decree of exile of 1302. The new *bolgia* is indeed that of the barrators (swindlers in civic and public office, the secular counterparts of the simonists of canto XIX), and its peculiarly vituperative energy may be motivated by Dante's scorn of the charge against him.

7 **If you know** etc: the comparison between the arsenal at Venice and the present *bolgia* centres on the quantities of black pitch present in both places; what might seem like a digression in the extent of Dante's description of the arsenal is generally justified on the grounds that it sets the tone for the busy activity of this and the following canto. The narrative that follows, the so-called 'comedy within the *Comedy*', owes much to medieval popular theatre: 'a mixture of savage satire and tearing high spirits', in Dorothy Sayers's words, that can be 'a little disconcerting to the more solemn-minded of Dante's admirers'. Certainly, Dante's reference to his 'comedy' at l. 3, coming so soon after Virgil's mention of his 'high tragedy' (XX, 113), indicates succinctly the contrast between the *bolgia* of the magicians, with its personages from classical literature and its discourse on the founding of Mantua, and this thoroughly unclassical narrative of 'low' language and crude actions that now follows, culminating in the famous last line.

12 plug holes from all the voyages,
some work on the poop or the prow;
 some carve oars, some twist ropes
15 and others darn rips in the sails –
so with no fire, but with holy art
 a thick pitch bubbled down there
18 and coated every bit of the bank.
Watching it, all I could see in it
 were the bubbles the heat lifted,
21 and the way it swelled and sagged.
While I was having a good look
 master cries, 'Careful, watch out!'
24 drawing me from where I was,
so I turn like a man dithering
 who looks when he ought to run,
27 and in a second is terrified,
and still looks, but now sets off:
 behind us was a black demon
30 coming racing over the bridge.
Hell, he sure was evil looking!
 How grim his whole body seemed,
33 flitting along with his wings out!
His high, sharp shoulder bore up
 an evil-doer, in a fireman's lift,
36 gripped tight by both the heels.
From the rock he says: 'Hey, Malebranche,
 here's one of Saint Zita's elders!
39 Shove him under, I'm off for more,
off back there where there's lots:
 they're all swindlers except Bonturo,

---

37 **Malebranche:** name coined by Dante ('Evilclaws') for the devils guarding the fifth *bolgia*.
38 **Saint Zita's elders:** i.e., a governor or magistrate of Lucca, whose patron saint, Zita, died in the thirteenth century. One of Dante's early commentators identifies the elder as Martin Bottaio, who died during the night between Good Friday and Easter Saturday, 1300.
41 **except Bonturo:** Bonturo Dati, leader of the popular party in Lucca in the early fourteenth century; his reputation for corruption means that Dante is being ironic here.

they change no to yes for money.'   42
He threw him over, turning back
   along the bridge, and a loosed dog
   wouldn't be after a thief as fast.   45
The soul sank, and twisted back up;
   but the devils beneath the bridge
   shouted: 'There's no Holy Face here: 48
it's another swim from the Serchio!
   If you don't like our backscratchers,
   don't poke from the pitch.' Then   51
they prong him with all their hooks
   and shout, 'Keep a low profile –
   swindle on the quiet, if you can.'   54
A chef has his lads do likewise,
   pushing the joint down in the pot
   with their forks, to make it cook.   57
'So it doesn't seem you're here,'
   my good master says, 'set down
   behind a rock that can hide you;   60
and whatever threats they offer me
   don't you worry, I'll handle them,
   I've known brawls like this before.'   63
He went to the end of the bridge;
   and when he made the sixth bank
   he needed to keep himself steady.   66
Just like house-dogs go berserk,
   jumping all over the poor tramp
   who turns up at the door to beg,   69
so they come from under the bridge
   and go for him with their hooks,
   but he shouts, 'Don't you try it!   72

---

48 **no Holy Face** etc: the line has several possible meanings, relating to an ancient Byzantine crucifix of black wood in the church of San Martino in Lucca. The sinner's face, blackened by the pitch, may be being compared sarcastically with the crucifix, or his posture of supplication might be drawing from the devils a reminder that there's nothing to pray to in Hell.
49 **Serchio**: a river near Lucca.
63 **brawls like this before**: see IX, 22ff. and cf. l. 81 of this canto.

Before you get those spikes going
   one of you come out to hear me,
75   then see if it's wise to grapple.'
They all shout: 'You go, Malacoda!'
   so one comes – the others stay –
78   saying, 'What good can it do him?'
'Do you really think I've come,
   Malacoda,' master addresses him,
81   'safe before from all your traps,
without God's will and fate's favour?
   Let us pass; Heaven requires me
84   to show someone these wild paths.'
That took him down a peg or two;
   he dropped his fork at his feet
87   telling the others, 'No game here.'
Now master calls to me, 'You there,
   crouched low in the rock's clefts,
90   it's safe to come out to me now.'
I was at his side in a second;
   and all the devils came forward
93   so I worried they wouldn't obey –
just like the scared troops I saw
   who left Caprona after the truce
96   seeing all their enemies round them.
I got as much of me as possible
   behind master, not taking my eyes
99   off them, who hardly seemed nice,
waving their pitchforks and saying
   to themselves, 'Give him a tickle!'
102   or, 'Shall I scrub his back for him?'
But that devil who was conversing
   with master, he turns round fast

76 **Malacoda**: 'Eviltail'.
95 **Caprona**: a castle belonging to
Pisa, taken by the Guelphs from
Lucca and Florence, with Dante
among them, after a siege in 1289.
The defeated soldiers were offered
their lives in return for the surrender.

and says, 'Lay off, Scarmiglione!'   105
Then he tells us, 'You won't get far
    along this avenue, the sixth arch
    lies all smashed on the pit floor.   108
If you're still wanting to go on
    then keep to the top of this bank;
    nearby's another bridge to cross.   111
Yesterday, five hours after this,
    twelve hundred and sixty-six years
    passed, since the road was closed.   114
I'll send some of my band along
    to see if anyone's airing himself:
    you go with them, they won't bite.   117
Come here Alichino, and Calcabrina,'
    he starts to say, 'and you, Cagnazzo;
    and Barbariccia, you be in charge.   120
Take Libbicocco and Draghignazzo,
    Graffiacane, Ciriatto and his tusks
    and Farfarello and mad Rubicante.   123
Patrol all round the bubble-bath:

105 **Scarmiglione:** from the verb *scarmigliare*, to dishevel, or ruffle (someone's hair); an obvious euphemism.

111 **nearby's another bridge etc:** in fact, as the pilgrims will find out, *all* the bridges over the sixth *bolgia* have been smashed for the reason Malacoda goes on to explain. The way that Virgil is thus deceived, as with the barring from the city of Dis in cantos VIII–IX, again allegorises the limited powers of reason unaided by divine Grace.

112 **Yesterday etc:** the road was broken by the earthquake, already described in XII, 31–45, that shook the earth on Christ's death, the 1266th anniversary of which was yesterday, Good Friday (the Crucifixion having taken place in AD 34).

Debate continues as to whether the time of day on Easter Saturday is now five hours before noon or 3 p.m., according to whether Dante accepted the hour of Christ's death as the former (as he interpreted the account in St Luke) or the latter (as in the other gospels).

118 **Alichino etc:** as with the devils mentioned earlier in the canto, the names that follow have various meanings. *Alichino* comes from the French *Harlequin*, *Cagnazzo* is a vicious *cane* (dog), *Barbariccia* means 'Curlybeard' and so on. Whether or not their derivation is always clear, Dante's use of hard and grating consonants in the names speaks for itself. Some of the names are similar or identical to those of Dante's actual contemporaries.

protect these until the next rock
126   that crosses the pits in one piece.'
'Hey, master, what's happening?'
        I say – 'Let's go alone, unguided,
129   since you know how; I don't like this.
If you're as observant as usual
        don't you see them gnashing teeth,
132   looking as if they mean trouble?'
He tells me: 'Don't start worrying:
        they can gnash just as they want,
135   they do it at those simmering souls.'
They turned to take the left bank;
        but first, each blew a raspberry
138   at their leader, for a salute,
and he trumpets back with his arse.

CANTO TWENTY-TWO

I've seen troops get under way,
   whether to attack or to parade
   or sometimes to make a retreat;   3
I've seen horsemen on your land,
   you Aretines, I've seen raiders,
   clashes at tournament and jousts;   6
I've witnessed clarions and bells,
   drum-rolls, signs from battlements
   or other signals, native or foreign;   9
but I never heard a bugle like this
   get horses or infantry into action,
   or ships steering by land or stars.   12
So we depart with the ten devils,
   grisly company! – but then in church
   with saints, with scum in the pubs.   15
My eyes were fixed on the pitch
   to study everything in this valley
   and the people being stewed here.   18
Like dolphins arch out their backs
   and give a warning to sailors
   that they should save their boats,   21
so occasionally, to ease the pain,
   a sinner's back would curve out
   then in again, quick as lightning.   24

5 **you Aretines:** Dante was a combatant at the battle of Campaldino (1289), in which the Guelphs from Lucca and Florence defeated the Ghibellines, headed by Arezzo.

19 **Like dolphins** etc: that dolphins announced the approach of storm in the manner described was commonly believed at the time.

Or like at the edge of a ditch
the frogs poke their noses out,
27   keeping the rest of them hidden,
so here the damned, everywhere;
but when Barbariccia approached
30   they go back under on the boil.
I saw – and I still shudder at it –
one stay put, as it can happen
33   every frog slips away but one;
and Graffiacane, who was nearest,
he hooks him by the tarred hair
36   and out he comes, like an otter.
I knew the names of the devils,
I'd listened when they were picked,
39   and when they called each other.
'O Rubicante, get your claws going,
shred his skin for him a bit!'
42   so the others all start shouting.
'Master,' I ask, 'can you find out
who he is, this poor devil here
45   who's plumb in his enemies' hands?'
So my master went over to him
to ask who he was. He replies:
48   'I'm from the kingdom of Navarre.
My mother put me to the service
of a lord, my dad being a lout
51   who ruined himself and his goods.
Then I served good King Thibault:
here I began my shady dealing
54   that I sweat to pay back now.'
But Ciriatto, his mouth sporting
tusks like a boar's on both sides,
57   he lets him have a feel of one.
Yes, cats have got the mouse now:

48 'I'm from . . .' etc: early commentators name the sinner as Ciampolo or
Giampolo (= *Jean Paul*), but tell us
little more about him and his service
under Thibault II of Navarre (1253–
70) than the text does.

so Barbariccia forks his arms
round him, with 'Off, he's mine,'   60
and then he turns to my master:
'If you want any more,' he says,
'ask, before he gets ripped apart.'   63
So master asks: 'These other damned,
do you know any who are Italian
in the pitch?' And he answers,   66
'I've just left one from that way,
I wish we were both still under,
balls to claws and hooks then!'   69
Libbicocco says, 'We've had enough,'
and he gets his fork into his arm
and tears away nerves and sinew,   72
while Draghignazzo wants a shot
at his legs; but their commander
whips round with an angry look.   75
When they'd all quietened a bit
master questions him quickly
as he's mooning at his wound: 78
'This one you said it was bad
to be fished from, who was he?'
He says, 'It was brother Gomita   81
of Gallura, that old box of tricks
who managed his master's foes
so they all sang his praises.   84
He took cash "behind closed doors",
to use his formula – a swindler
in every office, and a big one.   87
He's with the Hon. Michel Zanche

67 that way: i.e., Sardinia (see below).

81 brother Gomita etc: deputy of Nino Visconti, governor of Gallura, one of the then four districts of Sardinia. Nino had him hanged when it was discovered that he accepted bribes to release prisoners in his care.

85 "behind closed doors": i.e., dismissing cases *di piano*, in a summary hearing with no formal trial.

88 the Hon. Michel Zanche: the details of his career are unclear, though he was said to be governor of Logodoro (another district of Sardinia) under King Enzo, and later took over

of Logodoro; their two tongues
90   never weary talking of Sardinia.
But Hell, watch him gnashing now:
I'd say more, if I didn't worry
93   it wasn't to scale my ringworm.'
Their prefect turns to Farfarello
whose eyes goggled with menace
96   and says, 'Back, you great brute.'
The worried one starts off again:
'You want Tuscans or Lombards,
99   and I can get some to appear:
but let the Malebranche keep off
so no one's frightened by them,
102 and I'll stay just where I am
and for one of me, I'll get seven
when I whistle; that's our sign
105 whenever anyone can come out.'
Cagnazzo twitches his snout at this
and shakes his head: 'Evil sod,
108 he's invented this to dive under!'
The other one, never short of tricks,
replies: 'More evil than that,
111 getting my own into more trouble.'
Unlike the rest, Alichino accepts:
he tells him, 'If you jump down
114 I can't go galloping after you
but I'll hover above on my wings –
we'll go up and behind the bank,
117 then see if you can beat us all.'
Well, reader, this is an odd sport;
they make for the bank's far side,
120 him first who liked it all least.
The Navarrese chose his time well;
in a flash his feet touch earth,

the rule of the island. He was murdered by his son-in-law Branca
d'Oria (see XXXIII, 134–47).

120 **him first** etc: i.e., Cagnazzo,
ll. 106–8.

he jumps, he slips their leader.   123
Now they're all sobered by this,
    and him most whose fault it was;
    he's up and cursing, 'I'll get you!'   126
but it's no use: wings are slower
    than fear is, one's already under,
    the other pulls out of his dive –   129
just like a duck would go down
    in a shot, if a falcon swooped,
    who then soars up, beaten, mad.   132
Calcabrina's furious at the cheat:
    flying behind, he really wants
    to make trouble over the escape,   135
and since the sinner's disappeared
    his talons are into his fellow
    and they're clawing over the pit.   138
But the other could hawk it too:
    he fights back, till they plunge,
    together, into the seething ditch.   141
The heat quickly unsticks them;
    but there's no way to fly out,
    their wings have got so smeared.   144
Barbariccia's mad with the others,
    he has four fly with their hooks
    to the other bank, and quickly   147
they're in position on each side:
    their forks rake for these pigeons,
    already cooked in the casserole,   150
and we leave them to the problem.

---

125 **and him most** etc: Alichino, whose acceptance of the sinner's 'challenge' (l. 112) led to his escape. 134 **he really wants** etc: the devils have no scruples in this narrative of trickery and fraud about attacking and betraying each other, just as Ciampolo was ready to do with his companions. Of course, whether Ciampolo invented the whole story of whistling an 'all clear' (ll. 104–5) is an uncertainty that deepens the atmosphere of trickery in this canto.

CANTO TWENTY-THREE

Then on we went all by ourselves
  in silence, one behind the other,
  like Franciscans walk in the street.   3
The brawl had brought to my mind
  one of those stories of Aesop's,
  the one about the frog and mouse;   6
it's very like what had happened,
  if you think about it, the end
  and beginning are just the same.   9
But as when you've begun thinking
  one thought leads you to another,
  so I grew twice as frightened   12
when I thought, 'It was our fault
  that that lot made such a show
  of themselves – they'll be really mad.   15

3 **like Franciscans** etc: original Franciscan statutes do suggest that the friars go about their missions in pairs, one behind the other as portrayed here.

5 **one of those stories** etc: all animal fables were attributed to Aesop in the Middle Ages, though there is much debate over the precise application of the frog and mouse fable to the episode in the previous canto. A frog offers to ferry a mouse across a river by tying their legs together, intending to drown the mouse by then pulling him under; a hawk then swoops down and carries both off, tied together as they are, and eats them (the mouse is freed in some versions). The frog may be understood as Calcabrina, supposedly intending to help Alichino (the mouse) in the chase after Ciampolo, but really wanting to harm him; the two devils end in the pitch like the two animals in the hawk's beak. Other interpretations see Ciampolo as either frog or mouse, or Dante and Virgil as more generally representing the mouse (in their escape).

If they're furious as well as evil
   they'll be after us more fiercely
18   than dogs, when they get hares.'
I could feel all my skin tingling
   with fright; I looked behind me
21   and said, 'Master, can you think
where to hide us – I'm terrified
   these Malebranche will catch up:
24   I can feel them on to us already.'
And he says, 'If I was a mirror
   your outside wouldn't show in me
27   quicker than your inside has –
I saw how you thought just now
   when I thought the same things,
30   so I've a plan for both of us:
if this right bank slopes conveniently
   we can slip into the next ditch
33   and avoid any chance of capture.'
And he'd hardly suggested this
   when I saw them swooping along
36   after us, and not very far away.
So master grabbed me immediately,
   like a woman woken by shouting
39   who sees that fire's broken out,
who picks up her baby and runs
   without even a vest on her back,
42   more worried for it than herself;
and down that rough, rocky face
   that walls in the next circuit
45   he slid all the way on his back.
Water running through a conduit,
   even when it gets to the blades
48   of a water-wheel, it's more slow
than master was down that bank,
   with me in his lap all the time,
51   more like a son than companion.
His feet just touched the bottom

when they arrived at the brink
  above us, but we needn't worry: 54
high Providence made them warders
  of the fifth ditch, but took away
  any power of theirs to leave it.   57
Down here were people all painted,
  going immensely slowly, their faces
  weeping with effort and fatigue;   60
they all wore cloaks with low cowls
  down over the eyes, in that style
  the monks are fitted with in Cluny.   63
These have a surface of dazzling gold,
  but are actually made from lead:
  Frederick's would be straw beside them. 66
What costumes to play eternity in!
  We turned as usual to our left,
  going their way, hearing their cries;   69
but they were so tired of walking
  with that weight, that every step
  we had new neighbours beside us.   72
So I ask master: 'Can't we find
  if there's anyone celebrated here
  while we're going along like this?'   75
And someone heard my Tuscan speech
  and shouted behind us, 'Stop,
  don't run away into the darkness!   78

63 **Cluny:** the famous Benedictine monastery of Cluny, in Burgundy, was noted for the copious robes of its inhabitants. Some editors read 'Cologne' instead of Cluny.

66 **Frederick's would be straw etc:** i.e., Frederick's cloaks would weigh nothing beside these. Unconfirmed reports told of the Emperor Frederick II (see X, 120) using thick lead cloaks on those guilty of the crime of lese-majesty. The cloaks were supposedly heated and melted while on the criminals' bodies. In this present *bolgia* Dante encounters the hypocrites, and their form of punishment may have been suggested by the etymology given in the *Magnae derivationes* of Uguccione da Pisa, where 'hypocrite' is derived from the Greek *yper* (*above*) and *crisis* (*gold*); i.e., something golden only on the outside. A famous parallel expression is in Matthew 23: 27: 'Woe unto you ... hypocrites! for ye are like unto whited sepulchres ...'

I might have what you're seeking.'
My guide turns and says, 'Wait,
81   and then carry along at his pace.'
So I stand watching two of them
strain with hurry in their faces,
84   checked by their coats and the crowd.
Finally, they make it, and eye me
sideways, not offering to speak;
87   then they consult each other:
'He's breathing as if he's alive;
and if they're dead, why the honour
90   of escaping the ponderous hood?'
And then, 'Tuscan, you join here
the order of the poor hypocrites;
93   don't object to saying who you are.'
I tell them, 'I was born and raised
in the grandest spot on the Arno,
96   and this is my body, as always.
But who are you, in such misery
that your eyes are like waterfalls?
99   What's this glittering penalty?'
And one replies, 'These golden robes
are of lead so thick, the weights
102   make the scales groan, like this.
We belonged to the Jovial Brothers,
both from Bologna; he's Loderingo,

---

86 **sideways:** not only as an indication of the 'shifty' nature of hypocrisy, but also because of the immense weight of the hoods, impeding their movements. Cf. the detail of the 'low cowls/down over the eyes', ll. 61–2.

95 **the Arno:** the river running through Florence.

103 **Jovial Brothers:** the order of the Cavalieri di Maria Vergine Gloriosa, founded at Bologna in 1261 as arbiters in cases of civil and factional discord, and to protect the poor and weak against oppression. The comfortable and relaxed rule of the order seems to have earned its members this name.

104 **Loderingo etc:** Loderingo degli Andalò (c.1210–93) and Catalano de' Malavolti (c.1210–85), both from Bologna, took leading parts in founding the 'Jovial Brothers'. From Ghibelline and Guelph families respectively, they were appointed governors of Florence in 1266. Rather than keeping

I'm Catalano – your city chose us   105
  (though it's one man's job normally)
    to keep the peace; how we fared
    is still visible around Gardingo.'   108
'O brothers, your evil . . .' I began,
  but then I stopped: I saw a figure
    crucified by means of three stakes   111
along the ground; on seeing me
  he moans into his beard, writhing.
Brother Catalan was watching this   114
and says, 'You're wondering at him:
  he it was advised the Pharisees
    "one man should die for the people."   117
He's laid naked across the way
  as you can see, and has to bear
    the weight of everyone who passes.   120
His father-in-law suffers likewise
  in this pit, and all that council
    the Jews owe their misfortunes to.'   123
I could see Virgil was stupefied
  by this, a soul spread on a cross
    in the dirt, exiled for eternity.   126
And then he asked the friar this:
  'Do please tell us, if you're able,
    is there any opening on the right   129
we can get through out of here,
  without making those black angels
    help us escape, by coming down?'   132

---

the peace, however, they covertly aided the Guelphs in their attacks on their opponents and their property, such as the houses of the Uberti family in the Gardingo area of Florence (l. 108); see notes to X, 32, 49.

117 'one man should die . . .' etc: the quotation is from John 11: 50. The crucified figure is Caiaphas, the high priest of the Pharisees, who in council urged the death of Jesus with these words, pretending to have the interests of the Jews at heart. Cf. his punishment with Isaiah 51: 23.

121 His father-in-law etc: Annas (see John 18: 13–14). The council of Pharisees are seen here as responsible for the subsequent misfortunes of the Jews, the destruction of Jerusalem and the dispersal of the race.

He replies, 'Nearer than you hope
      is a rock running from the rim
135   that bridges all these awful pits,
except this one, where it's smashed:
      you can climb up along its ruins
138   that slope down into a big heap.'
Master was thoughtful for a while;
      then he said, 'He was a real help,
141   that one raking sinners over there.'
And the friar: 'I heard at Bologna
      all about the devil and his vices –
144   a liar he is, and father of lies.'
Well, master strode away at this,
      looking a little clouded by anger;
147   so I left them to their burdens,
following those darling footsteps.

139 **Master was thoughtful** etc: because he now realises the deceit of Malacoda ('He was a real help,' l. 140); see note to XXI, 111.

142 **I heard at Bologna** etc: i.e., in the famous theological schools of the city. The sinner's sly 'topping' of Virgil with his superior knowledge of the devil ('A liar he is . . .' etc., cf. John 8: 44), added to the deceit of the devils themselves, accounts for Virgil's anger.

CANTO TWENTY-FOUR

In that part of the tender year
   when the sun warms in Aquarius
   and night lessens to half the day,   3
when frost copies over the ground
   the image of her white sister,
   though her brushstrokes don't stay: 6
the peasant without any fodder
   gets up, looks out, sees the land
   all white; so he smacks his side   9
and paces the house, muttering,
   wretched, not sure what to do;
   goes out again, and now in hope,   12
for things have all changed face
   in a short time, and with his stick
   he chases his flock out to feed.   15
Like this master made me worry
   when I saw him troubled so much,
   but the remedy came as quickly: 18
when we reached the broken bridge
   he turned with the sweet look
   I saw before, at the hill's base.   21
He opens his arms, after considering
   and looking at the ruin carefully,
   and then catches me up in them.   24

---

2 **when the sun** etc: the sun is in Aquarius from 21 January to 21 February; the season is approaching the spring equinox, when the night occupies exactly half the solar day of twenty-four hours.
5 **her white sister:** the snow.
21 **at the hill's base:** i.e., in canto I.

143

Like someone who works things out,
  who always seems to see ahead,
27   so he helps me up on to the top
of an overhang, and eyes another
  and tells me, 'Grab that one next,
30   but make sure it bears you first.'
It wasn't a route for heavy coats:
  we only just did it, rock to rock,
33   him weightless, me being pushed,
and if it wasn't that on this side
  the climb was less than the other,
36   however he did, I'd have been beat.
But since all Malebolge slopes down
  to that hole, that deepest well,
39   it means that for every valley
one bank's high, the other's lower;
  and finally we reach that point
42   where the last rock sticks out.
Now I was up, I couldn't go on,
  air was so milked from my lungs
45   I sat down in the earliest place.
'You have to exercise yourself so,'
  master tells me; 'fame isn't won
48   by loafing about on feather-beds,
and without it one's life is spent
  with no more trace on the earth
51   than smoke in air, foam in water.
And so, up: overcome the agony
  with the will that always wins,
54   unless the heavy body sinks it.
There's a longer ladder to climb;
  it's not enough to escape these:
57   if you understand me, take heart.'
And then I rose, as if I possessed

---

51 **than smoke in air:** cf. Psalms 102: 3.
55 **a longer ladder** etc: the climb
along the body of Lucifer and subsequent ascent from Hell which is
described in the final canto.

more breath than I'd really got,
　and said, 'On, I'm fit and eager.'　　　　60
So up the crag we take our way,
　an awkward, narrow, rocky path,
　much steeper than the one before.　　　　63
I spoke, to avoid seeming tired;
　and this next ditch replies to me
　in a voice struggling to be clear.　　　　66
I couldn't make it out, even though
　I was now on top of the bridge,
　but the speaker seemed in motion.　　　　69
I look down, but even sharp eyes
　couldn't enter those dark depths,
　so I say, 'Master, let's move on　　　　72
and climb down to the other bank:
　I listen and can't understand
　here, I look down and can't see.'　　　　75
'The only reply I make,' he says,
　'is doing it; every fair request
　needs no answer other than action.'　　　　78
We climb down at the bridge-end
　where it joins with the eighth bank,
　and now the whole pit's on show:　　　　81
and I see inside hideous hordes
　of snakes, so monstrous in form
　the memory still drains my blood.　　　　84
Sandy Libya can stop boasting now,
　with all its chelydri, its iaculi,
　its pareae, cenchres, amphisbaenae,　　　　87
for this number of poisonous pests
　it wouldn't have with all Ethiopia,

85 **Sandy Libya** etc: the Libyan desert was renowned for the number and variety of its snakes (according to myth, sprung from the drops of blood of Medusa – see note to IX, 52). Dante's list is based on Lucan (*Pharsalia*, IX, 708–21), who describes chelydri as leaving a smoking track behind them; iaculi as flying snakes; pareae as ploughing a track with their tails; cenchres as moving in a straight line; and amphisbaenae as having a head at both ends of their bodies.

90   plus all those above the Red Sea.
Within this awful, savage spaghetti
people ran about, naked, terrified,
93   without any refuge or heliotrope,
hands fettered by snakes behind
whose tails and heads coiled round
96   their backs, and were tied in front.
And there's one near us, by our bank –
a snake suddenly transfixes him
99   where his neck meets the shoulder.
You couldn't write 'o' or 'i' as quick
as he catches fire and burns; ash,
102   he can't help but crumble away
and when he's spread on the floor
all the dust gathers itself again
105   and he's straight back to himself:
in the same way the sages write
of the phoenix, dead and reborn
108   as five hundred years approach,
who never eats any grass or grain
but only droplets of incense, balm,
111   and dies cradled in nard and myrrh.
Like one who faints, unaware how,
whether a devil hauls him down
114   or some obstruction seizes him,
who's up again and looking round

93 **heliotrope**: a stone reputed to cure snake bites and to make its bearer invisible.

94 **hands fettered** etc: punished in this *bolgia* are the thieves, their 'light fingers' now restrained in this manner. The snakes symbolise the sly, furtive practice of the thief; the metamorphoses we see in this and the following canto show the thieves undergoing the appropriate punishment of having their human form 'stolen' from them.

107 **the phoenix** etc: Dante's description here derives from *Metamorphoses*, XV, 392–400, where the special nest of nard and myrrh that the phoenix builds as her death bed (l. 111), and whence she's reborn, is described.

113 **whether a devil** etc: Dante gives two contemporary explanations for fainting, one supernatural, one 'medical', based on the idea of some blockage in the body's veins or channels.

all bewildered by the great shock
he's had, panting as he gazes;   117
so this sinner, on his feet again.
O power of God, what a tempest,
what a heavy rain of revenge!   120
Master asks him now who he was;
he replies, 'I fell from Tuscany,
only recently, into this wild gulch.   123
I preferred being animal to human,
a proper bastard: I'm Vanni Fucci,
the beast; Pistoia was my fit lair.'   126
I tell master, 'Make sure he stays,
ask him what crime sunk him here:
I knew him, a fellow of brawls   129
and blood.' But he heard – at once
he turns facing me, all attention,
blushing in the agony of shame;   132
he says, 'It's more pain to me now
that you witness me in this misery
than it was having my life taken.   135
I can't deny what you're asking:
I'm down so low because I stole
that treasure, out of the sacristy,   138
and another was falsely accused.
But so it's no joy to have seen me,
if you ever escape this darkness   141
lend an ear to this news, listen:
soon Pistoia will shed its Blacks,

125 **Vanni Fucci** etc: a celebrated thug and troublemaker from Pistoia, where he fought on the side of the Black Guelphs; he was condemned as a murderer and robber by the city in 1295. Dante knew him, and here seeks information as to why he's in this circle and not in that of the violent (canto XII).

137 **because I stole** etc: Fucci's crime was apparently committed in 1293,

when he stole the treasure of the chapel of St James in Pistoia cathedral. As he tells us, another was falsely accused (one Rampino Foresi) and almost hanged. Fucci died shortly before March 1300 (l. 123), his guilt only being discovered after his death.

143 **soon Pistoia** etc: although the Whites in Pistoia, aided by those from Florence, scored a victory over the Blacks in May 1301, the Blacks

144   then Florence will change favours.
Mars takes fire from Val di Magra,
     folded within clouds of tempest,
147   and with harsh and furious storm
will charge over Campo Piceno,
     routing the clouds in its raging,
150   and every White will be wounded.
I tell you this: be hurt by it!'

had gained control of Florence with the help of Charles of Valois and Pope Boniface VIII by 1302 (see VI, 67–72). The 'fire' (or thunderbolt) of l. 145 represents Moroello Malaspina, lord of Lunigiana ('Val di Magra'), who led the Florentine Blacks against the Pistoian Whites and eventually captured Pistoia, the last White stronghold in Tuscany, in 1305–6. Campo Piceno (l. 148), the *Ager Picenus* referred to in Sallust, *Bellum Catilinae*, 57, 1–3, was incorrectly identified with Pistoia.

CANTO TWENTY-FIVE

With this, the thief stops speaking,
   raising his hands in two V-signs
   and shouting out, 'Up yours, God!'   3
Well, the snakes became my friends
   as one clamped round his throat
   as if saying, 'No more of that!'   6
and then another rebound his arms,
   tightening itself into such a knot
   he couldn't move them at all.   9
Ah, Pistoia, Pistoia, why your delay
   in razing yourself off the globe?
   Even your founders weren't as bad.   12
In all the murky circles of Hell
   I saw no one as insolent to God,
   not even him shot down at Thebes.   15
He said no more and hurried away,
   then I saw a Centaur come along,
   crying madly, 'Where's the dog gone?'   18
I bet even Maremma has fewer snakes
   than those over his horse's part,
   right up to where he was human;   21
and there on top of his shoulders
   was a dragon spreading its wings,
   breathing fire on anyone present.   24

12 **Even your founders** etc: Pistoia was supposedly founded by the bloody war veterans who were the remnants of Catiline's army.
15 **him shot down** etc: Capaneus (see XIV, 46–72).
19 **Maremma:** see note to XIII, 7. The region was noted for its abundance of snakes.

Master tells me, 'This is Cacus –
he usually had a moat of blood
27   round his cave, in Mount Aventino.
He's not placed with his brothers
because of that sly theft of his
30   nearby, the great herd robbery;
but his crimes were put an end to
by Hercules's club – a hundred hits
33   he gave him, ten were enough.'
While he spoke Cacus passed on,
and three souls arrive below us
36   that master and I don't notice
till they shout, 'Who are you two?'
so then we stop our conversation
39   and concentrate solely on them.
I didn't know them; as it happens
though, sometimes, just by chance,
42   one of them named someone else,
saying, 'Where's Cianfa got to?'
so I put my finger to my lips
45   as a sign to my master to listen.
I'm not surprised if any readers
can't believe what comes next:
48   neither can I, and I watched it.
While they were there beneath us,

25 **Cacus** etc: the son of Vulcan, his story is told in the *Aeneid*, VIII, 193–305, where he is described as half-human, half-animal. On this hint, Dante converts him into a Centaur, placed here rather than 'with his brothers' (l. 28; i.e., the guardians of Phlegethon, see canto XII) because of the theft described in the following lines.

29 **that sly theft** etc: Cacus stole a neighbouring herd of cattle in the possession of Hercules by leading them backwards to his cave, so that their hoof-prints pointed away from it. On discovering this, Hercules slew him with his club; Virgil seems derisive about the number of blows needed to kill him ('ten were enough', l. 33).

43 **Cianfa**: a knight of the Florentine Donati family, who died between 1283 and 1289. Little further is known of him; he re-enters the action immediately as the 'lizardy thing' of l. 50. On recognising his name, Dante is immediately attentive, ll. 44–5.

this lizardy thing with six legs
shot out, and seized one of them.   51
Its middle legs hugged his waist,
its front legs gripped his two arms
and its mouth bit into his cheeks;   54
its back legs clung to his thighs
and it threaded its tail between,
snaking it upwards along his back.   57
You've seen ivy strangling a tree,
but nothing that twined so tight
as that monster around his body.   60
Then they fused together totally,
mixing colours like melting wax
so no one saw which was which;   63
or as when you set fire to paper
and brown runs before the flame,
not yet black, no longer white.   66
Well, the other two are watching it
and shout, 'Agnolo, what a change!
You're neither nowt nor summat!'   69
The two heads were lumped in one,
and two former faces were mixed
to make one new, with four arms   72
mixed likewise into two front legs;
torsos and back legs were spliced
to make limbs never seen before.   75
The original shape had all gone:
it was something, it was nothing,
horrible; it lurched off, awkward.   78
In the great oven of August days,
when a lizard changing hedgerows

68 **Agnolo**: again, little is known of him, beyond his reputation as a thief (which in the early commentators may simply stem from this passage) and his full name, Agnolo Brunelleschi.

69 **You're neither nowt etc**: the suc-

ceeding passage describing the transformation can be compared with Ovid's description of the merging into one of Salmacis and Hermaphroditus (*Metamorphoses*, IV, 373–9).

81   zips over the way like lightning,
so now comes a small, fiery snake
livid and black as a peppercorn,
84   going for the other two's bellies;
and where we first get nourished
it hits one of them a bull's eye,
87   then trails down in front of him.
He just wonders at it, speechless,
just standing there and gawping
90   as if he felt unwell, or sleepy,
with the snake staring him back;
then smoke pours from his wound
93   and out of the snake's mouth too
and it mixes. Lucan can be silent
about poor Sabellus and Nassidius
96   and listen to what's coming now,
Ovid can keep Arethusa, Cadmus:
his poem changes one to a fountain,
99   one to a snake, but I've no envy –
he never tried having two beings
swapping their nature face to face,
102   taking on one another's bodies.
They time their duet just right,
the snake's tail forking into two
105   as the man's legs grow together:
all the way up to his thighs
the glue sets, so after a minute
108   you couldn't see any join at all.
The split tail takes on the shape
the man surrenders, its covering
111   starts going soft, the man's scaly;
I see his arms shooting upwards

85 **and where we first** etc: the navel.
94 **Lucan can be silent** etc: Lucan tells of two of Cato's soldiers bitten by snakes in the Libyan desert: Sabellus, who was reduced to a pool of liquid, and Nassidius, who swelled up until he died (*Pharsalia*, IX, 763–97). For the transformations of Arethusa and Cadmus (l. 97), see *Metamorphoses*, V, 572ff. and IV, 563ff.

into his armpits, the snake's arms
getting longer as his grow short,   114
while its back feet twist together
to become a man's cock – the man
sees his make two feet, poor sod.   117
So as the smoke makes them swap
each other's colour, putting skin
on one, peeling the other's off,   120
the first rises, the second collapses,
the evil eye still clamping them
as they begin to exchange faces.   123
The standing one has his snout
sucked into his forehead, the flesh
fashioned there to two new ears,   126
and all that didn't run upwards
remains to make a proper nose
and thicken lips, as necessary.   129
The fallen one grows a long face,
his ears smoothed into his head
like a snail draws in its horns;   132
his tongue, that before was single
and could speak, splits into two,
the other's joins; the smoke stops.   135
Then the one who was now snake
hisses himself off down the valley,
the other spits speech after him.   138
He turns his new self to the third,
saying, 'Let Buoso go like I did,
grovelling along through the pit.'   141
So I watched ditch seven's dregs
chop and change; if it's confused,
what I write, let the weirdness   144
excuse me. My sight was reeling

140 **Let Buoso go** etc: the figure transfixed in the navel by the snake (ll. 85–6) and who has changed natures with it, is now named, though commentators disagree whether he is Buoso degli Abati or the Buoso Donati referred to in XXX, 44, or Buoso di Forese Donati, who died c.1285.

by now, and my head felt dizzy;
147   but I recognised Puccio Sciancato
before these last two could escape,
the only one of the original three
150   not changed into anything else;
the other was your curse, Gaville.

148 **Puccio Sciancato** etc: Puccio Galigai, nicknamed Sciancato ('lame'), a Ghibelline exiled from Florence in 1268, though he later made peace with the Guelphs. Although not recognised by Dante at first (l. 40), Dante presumably identifies him from his disability as he moves off.

151 **your curse, Gaville**: the figure who metamorphosed with Buoso is identified now as Francesco dei Cavalcanti, known as Guercio. He was killed by men of Gaville, a village near Florence, whereupon his family took a bloody revenge on the village.

CANTO TWENTY-SIX

Rejoice, Florence, you're so great
   your fame wings over the earth,
   your name sounds all over Hell!   3
I found five citizens like these
   among the thieves, shaming mē
   and not doing you much credit.   6
But if dreams at dawn are true,
   you'll feel that fate before long
   that Prato and other places crave.   9
It can't arrive too quickly now:
   would it had, since it has to!
   For me, waiting only worsens it.   12
So we went, back up the steps
   the rocks made for our descent,
   master drawing me behind him,   15
continuing that solitary journey;
   and on those shattered crags
   feet were no use without hands.   18
I grieved then, as I grieve now
   when I remember the next scene,

4 **like these:** all the Florentines
Dante has encountered as thieves in
the previous canto were of noble
family, which accounts for his opening invective against the city here.

7 **if dreams at dawn** etc: dreams that
occurred near the end of the night
were regarded in both antiquity and
the Middle Ages as particularly prophetic; see for example Ovid,

Heroides, XIX, 195–6.

9 **that Prato** etc: other Tuscan towns
were under Florence's rule, like
Prato, or else feared her supremacy.
Dante may be referring to the mal-
ediction placed on the city by the
Cardinal Niccolò da Prato in 1304,
after the failure of his initiative as
peacemaker there, or to the rebellion
of Prato in 1309.

21   tightening the rein on my talent
      so that virtue keeps it close,
        so that if a good star or better
24   favoured me, I don't foul it up.
    That season when the world's light
      conceals his face from us less,
27   the countryman rests on the hill
    as midges give way to mosquitoes,
      and sees all along the valley
30   fireflies, perhaps where he farms:
    so ditch eight was all illuminated
      with this many flames, as I see
33   as soon as the bottom appears.
    That one revenged by the bears,
      when he saw Elijah's car lift
36   and the horses reaching the sky,
    his eyes couldn't distinguish them
      into other than a single flame
39   rising upwards like a little cloud;
    so each flame threads the throat
      of the ditch, and none reveals
42   the sinner stolen and wrapped.
    Straining to see from the bridge,
      I wouldn't have needed a push
45   to be over, if I hadn't held tight,
    and master, seeing me so intent,
      says, 'Souls inhabit the flames,
48   each burned in his own binding.'

21 **tightening the rein** etc: Dante's insistence that moral constraints need to be kept on his intellectual and imaginative abilities, given to him by a 'good star' or divine Grace (the something 'better' of l. 23), is prompted by his experience in this *bolgia* of those who abused such abilities. Punished here are the fraudulent who used their intelligence for political advantage through craft and deceit; the presentation of the sinners is conspicuously more elevated than elsewhere in *Malebolge*.

28 **as midges** etc: i.e., at dusk in summer.

34 **That one revenged** etc: Elisha, who saw Elijah's ascent into heaven in the chariot of fire – see 2 Kings 2 : 11–12, where the story of the bears' 'revenge' is also given (23–4).

'Master, you confirm the thought
   I'd already had,' I tell him,
     'and I was wanting to ask you: 51
who's in the flame that's forked
   at the top, as if on the pyre
     that Eteocles and his brother had?'   54
He replies, 'In there are tortured
   Ulysses and Diomedes, teamed
     in punishment, as in performance;   57
that flame is lamenting within
   the horse-play that carved open
     an exit for Rome's noble seed;   60
it weeps for deceiving Deidamia
   who still mourns Achilles in death,
     and Palladium is pain to it now.'   63
'If it's possible from that furnace
   to speak,' I say, 'I'd ask you
     and I'd ask you a thousandfold   66
that you don't stop me waiting
   till that horned flame gets here:
     see it's like a magnet to me!'   69
He replies, 'This is an entreaty
   that does you credit, so I agree;
     but keep a rein on your tongue –   72

---

54 **Eteocles** etc: the hatred of the brothers Eteocles and Polynices survived after they'd killed each other in combat, so that the flames from their two bodies remained separate on their pyre. See Statius, *Thebaid*, XII, 429-32; Lucan, *Pharsalia*, I, 551-2.

56 **Ulysses** etc: Ulysses and Diomedes were partners in several nefarious exploits during the Trojan war, detailed in the following lines. The 'horse-play' of l. 59 refers to the trick of the wooden horse, brought inside the walls of the city by the Trojans and, unknown to them, containing Greek soldiers (see *Aen.*, II, 13-297). The resulting downfall of Troy led to Aeneas's escape and the subsequent founding of Rome.

61 **Deidamia** etc: the lover of Achilles, who had been disguised as a woman in order to avoid going to the Trojan war. Ulysses found Achilles out, rewoke his warlike spirit, and took him away from her (see Statius, *Achilleid*, I, 536ff.).

63 **Palladium**: the statue of Pallas Athena, regarded as guaranteeing the impregnability of Troy, until stolen by the two Greeks (*Aen.*, II, 162ff.).

let me speak, since I understand
what you want; these were Greeks,
75   they might disdain your language.'
Now when the flame had arrived
and it seemed to my leader right,
78   I heard him address them thus:
'O you, twinned inside one fire,
if I deserved well of you alive
81   when I penned those epic verses,
however much or little my desert,
don't move on; one of you tell
84   where he disappeared into death.'
The antique flame's greater fork
began labouring and murmuring
87   as if flapped about by a wind,
flickering its tip here and there
like a tongue trying to speak,
90   until a voice was thrown out:
'After I left Circe, who held me
near to Gaeta for over a year,
93   before Aeneas gave it its name,
neither joy in a son, nor my duty

73 **since I understand** etc: Dante's wish is to discover the circumstances of Ulysses's final voyage and his death, which we are about to hear of. This final voyage seems in fact to be an invention of Dante's own, not provided in any previous text; it is 'perhaps the most beautiful thing in the whole *Inferno*' (Sayers).

74 **these were Greeks** etc: these epic figures from antiquity are to be addressed by Virgil, author of the 'high tragedy' (XX, 113) that commemorates them, and Dante's principal link of communication with the classical past. Indeed, Virgil's address to the Greeks deliberately echoes the *Aeneid*: 'if I deserved well of you' (l. 80) repeats Dido's 'si bene quid de te merui' (IV, 37).

91 **Circe** etc: the sorceress who detained Ulysses and his men on their return journey from Troy, turning some of them into swine (*Odyssey*, X). Dante didn't know Homer's poetry (see note to IV, 88) and is dependent here on Ovid's *Metamorphoses* XIV, 154ff. where Ulysses's desire to pursue his homeward voyage, albeit with an aged and tired crew (cf. below, l. 106) is described.

92 **Gaeta:** the promontory near Naples named by Aeneas in honour of his nurse, Caieta, who died and was buried there (*Aen.*, VII, 1-4).

to an aged father, nor the love
I owed to Penelope's happiness,   96
none could beat the thirst in me
to be wise in the ways of men,
to know their strengths and sins;   99
so I put out on the great ocean
with just one boat and its crew,
those few who hadn't deserted me.   102
I traced both shores until Spain
and Morocco, saw Sardinia too
and the other isles that sea bathes.   105
My mates and I creaked with age
when we arrived at that strait
where Hercules had set markers   108
so that men should go no further:
on my right I passed Seville,
Ceuta was past us, on my left.   111
"O brothers, after so many dangers,"
I said, "you've won the west:
and now in this so little vigil   114
that our five senses have left,
don't deny knowing that world
without people, behind the sun.   117
Think on why you were created:
not to exist like animals indeed,
but to seek virtue and knowledge."   120
I made my fellows so fired up
to go on, with this little sermon,
they could hardly be restrained,   123
and with our poop pointed at dawn
we winged on our absurd flight

96 **Penelope** etc: the wife of Ulysses.
From passages in Cicero (*De finibus*,
v, 18, 48–9), Horace (*Epistles*, 1, 2,
17–26) and Seneca (*Epistulae mo-
rales*, LXXXVIII, 7), Dante derived the
idea of Ulysses as an exemplar of the
thirst for knowledge that triumphed
over all earthly ties and obstructions.
107 **that strait** etc: the Strait of Gib-
raltar, where the Pillars of Hercules
signalled the boundary of the habit-
able world. Ulysses now tells of his
momentous voyage beyond them.

126   with oars, always veering to port.
Already, stars of the other pole
all shone, with ours sunk so low
129   they never rose above the sea.
Lit five times and spent in turn
the moon's light appeared to us
132   since we'd entered those deeps,
when we saw a mountain, obscure
in the distance, and one so high
135   I'd never seen its equal before.
We rejoiced, but only to despair:
a storm rose on this new land
138   and hit the prow of the ship.
After three turns with the waters
the poop lifted on the fourth
141   and the bow sunk, as was desired,
until the ocean closed above us.'

126 **to port**: i.e., heading in a south-westerly direction.

133 **a mountain**: Mount Purgatory. Ulysses's shipwreck before reaching the mountain sets the seal on his 'absurd flight' (l. 125), now emphasised as an illustration of the limitations attaching to human endeavour without divine Grace, and to paganism devoid of Revelation.

141 **as was desired**: i.e., by God.

CANTO TWENTY-SEVEN

The flame was upright now, still,
  saying no more, already on its way
  with the licence of the sweet poet,   3
when another that moved behind it
  made our eyes look up to its tip
  with confused sounds that came out.   6
Like the Sicilian bull first bellowed
  – and it was right – with the moans
  of him whose file had finished it,   9
moaning away in the victim's voice
  so that, though it was all brass
  it seemed to be pierced by pain;   12
so, having no passage to begin with
  through the fire, into fire-speak
  the muffled words were changed.   15
But after they'd found their way
  up to the tip, given that vibration
  the tongue had sent them out with,   18
we heard this: 'O you I address,
  you who spoke Lombard just lately,

---

7 **the Sicilian bull** etc: the instrument of torture made by Perillus for Phalaris, tyrant of Agrigentum. The victim was shut in the brass bull, which was then heated, the victim's screams being converted into a noise like a bull bellowing. Phalaris made Perillus himself the first to be tortured in it. Among the many accounts, see Ovid, *Tristia*, III, xi, 39–54.

20 **who spoke Lombard** etc: the speaker addresses Virgil, having heard the actual words of his dismissal to Ulysses (l. 21). 'Lombard' may refer to Virgil's accent as well as to his use of *istra* ('now') in the Italian.

21 saying, "Go now; I ask no more,"
even if I've been slow to arrive
may it not irk you talking to me:
24 it won't irk me, and I'm on fire!
If you've sunk to this blind world
just now, out of that lovely land
27 of Italy, source of all my sins,
say, is Romagna at peace or war?
I'm from its hills, between Urbino
30 and the ridge the Tiber rises in.'
I was already bent over, attentive,
and master nudges me in the side
33 and says, 'You speak; he's Italian.'
In fact, I had my reply prepared,
so without any hesitation I began:
36 'O soul who suffocates down there,
your Romagna never was, it isn't now
without war in its tyrants' hearts;
39 but none was overt when I left it.
Ravenna's as it has been for years:
the eagle of Polenta nests on it
42 and covers Cervia with its wings.
The city that bore the long trial

29 I'm from its hills etc: the speaker identifies his place of origin as Montefeltro in the Romagna, the part of Italy running south of Bologna between the Apennines and the Adriatic coast. He is Guido da Montefeltro, and gives an account of his career later in the canto.

37 your Romagna never was etc: the region was noteworthy in Dante's time for its 'tyrants', i.e., those able to seize power and even establish family dynasties over cities and communes because of the weakness of popular resistance. Dante became well acquainted with the courts of Romagna in his years of exile.

41 the eagle of Polenta etc: the Polenta family (whose crest was an eagle) had ruled Ravenna since 1270. Guido il Vecchio, father of Francesca da Rimini (see canto v) was in power in 1300; his rule extended to the small town of Cervia, on the Adriatic.

43 The city etc: Forlì, the Ghibelline city laid siege to by Guelph forces (including many French soldiers), from 1281–3. Guido da Montefeltro led the successful sortie against the besieging forces which resulted in their massacre. In 1300 Forlì was ruled by Scarpetta degli Ordelaffi (arms a green lion).

and made bloody heaps of French,
   it's caught under the green claws.   45
And Verrucchio's old and new mastiffs
   who took evil care of Montagna,
   their razor-teeth bite where they did.   48
The little lion in the white lair
   has the cities by Lamone, Santerno,
   swapping sides summer and winter,   51
while that city flanked by the Savio,
   it lives between tyranny and freedom
   as it lies between plain and hill.   54
Now who you are, I pray tell us:
   don't be more resistant than others,
   so your name might carry on earth.'   57
After the flame roared a little
   in its way, the sharp end moves
   here, there, then throws out this: 60
'If I thought I spoke to someone
   who could ever return to the world,
   my fire wouldn't flicker any more;   63
but since no one ever exits alive
   from this depth, if I hear truth,
   I'll reply without fear of infamy.   66

46 **And Verrucchio's** etc: Verrucchio
was the castle-seat of Malatesta, lord
of Rimini, 1295–1312, when his son
Malatestino succeeded him (the 'old
and new mastiffs'); his other sons
were the Paolo and Gianciotto of
canto V. Among their many acts
of brutality Dante cites the murder of
their opponent Montagna de' Parci-
tati.

49 **The little lion** etc: a blue lion on
a white field was the arms of Maghi-
nardo Pagani da Susinana, ruler of
Faenza (on the river Lamone) and
Imola (near the Santerno). His 'swapping sides' (l. 51) refers to his keeping in with both Guelphs and

Ghibellines.

52 **that city** etc: Cesena, at the foot
of the Apennines on the river Savio.
In the hands of its own mayor,
Galasso da Montefeltro, in 1300.
Though he seems to have been an
enlightened governor he showed
signs of usurping office permanently
until his death in 1300.

61 **If I thought** etc: Guido was renowned as one of the most astute
soldiers and politicians of his day;
here we see him pondering the wisdom of telling Dante his story, mis-
taken in the belief that Dante is one
of the damned and cannot report him
on earth.

I was a soldier, then took the cord,
  thinking the cord would be amends,
69   and certainly I'd have been right
if the head priest – curses on him! –
  hadn't returned me to my old sins;
72   how and why, I want you to know.
While I was of the bone and flesh
  my mother gave me, all my works
75   weren't of the lion, but the wolf:
every contrivance and covered way
  I knew, managing them so aptly
78   my fame went to the world's end.
When I saw I'd reached that part
  of my life, when it suits all men
81   to slacken sail, gather their ropes,
these former pleasures worried me
  so I repented, confessed, took vows;
84   poor devil! – it would have worked.
The leader of the new Pharisees
  was making war beside the Lateran,
87   and not with Saracens or Jews –
no, all his enemies were Christians,

67 **I was a soldier** etc: born c.1220, Guido had a glittering military career as a Ghibelline leader in Romagna fighting Guelph and papal forces between 1274 and 1282, as in the siege of Forlì (above, ll. 43–4). Excommunicated and confined by the church, he escaped in 1289 to lead the Pisan Ghibellines against the Tuscan Guelphs. Later he became ruler of Urbino, but in 1296 was reconciled with the Church and became a Franciscan ('took the cord', i.e., the rope that girdled the Franciscan habit). He died in 1298. Dante suggests that his late repentance was motivated by a spirit of calculation and self-interest (l. 68) rather than contrition.

70 **the head priest:** Pope Boniface VIII (see note to III, 59). Guido's anger against Boniface is his main stimulus in speaking to Dante.

75 **the wolf:** a symbol of cunning. Guido's account illustrates amply why he has been condemned to this *bolgia* (see note to XXVI, 21).

85 **The leader** etc: Guido returns to his attack on Boniface, seen as leader of a corrupt Church, and in open hostility in Rome itself ('beside the Lateran', l. 86, the papal residence) against the Colonna family. These latter did not recognise the abdication of Celestine V nor Boniface's right to office (see note to III, 59).

none had helped to conquer Acre
or traded in the sultan's country;   90
and he didn't respect his high office
or sacred orders, my cord neither
that used to make waists shrivel.   93
But like Constantine sent to Sylvester
for a leprosy cure, inside Soracte,
so he sends to me as his doctor   96
to make his fevered pride get well:
he wants advice, and I'm silent
since his words seem raving mad.   99
He's at me again: "Don't you worry,
I absolve you in advance: tell me,
how can Palestrina be overthrown?   102
I'm able to lock and unlock heaven,
as you know; I hold the two keys
that my predecessor didn't love."   105
And serious arguments pushed me
to where I thought silence worse:
so I said, "Father, you'll wash me   108
of the sin that I'm falling into:

89 to conquer Acre etc: Acre was the last Christian stronghold in Palestine, conquered by the Saracens in 1291. The Church had banned Christian trade with Muslim countries (l. 91).

93 that used to make etc: i.e., in the days when the Franciscan order was genuinely committed to abstinence and poverty.

94 like Constantine etc: see note to XIX, 115. Soracte is a mountain outside Rome, where Sylvester had taken refuge in a cave from Constantine's persecution of Christians.

102 Palestrina: one of the castle-refuges of the Colonna family, where they held out against Boniface's forces for eighteen months, until tricked into surrendering by his empty promises (instigated by Guido, l. 110) of pardon and reinstatement.

104 the two keys: see Matthew 16: 19. Boniface was rumoured to have tricked Celestine V into abdicating.

106 serious arguments etc: such as the Franciscan rule of obedience, which Guido would break in resisting the pope's request. Guido's weighing up of the pros and cons of helping the pope leads him into accepting a compromise – sinning and being absolved simultaneously – which may be politically expedient but has no justification morally, as he discovers with a shock (l. 121) at the point of death.

promise much and deliver little;
111 here's your high throne's triumph."
Francis came then, when I was dead,
 to take me; but a black cherubim
114 told him: "Hands off – no cheating,
he has to come down to serve me
 for dealing in treacherous advice,
117 since when I've queued to grab him;
absolution minus repentance can't be,
 nor repenting and wanting a thing
120 at once, a complete contradiction."
O misery! I woke with a shock
 when he said, seizing me, "Perhaps
123 you didn't realise, I know logic!"
He took me to Minos; eight times
 his tail went round his grim back;
126 then he gnawed himself in his fury,
saying, "One for the thieving flames;"
 so here I walk, lost as you see,
129 fretting myself inside my costume.'
And so having finished his speech
 the flame moved away in its misery,
132 its sharp end twisting, writhing.
We press onwards, master and I,
 up to the start of the next rock,
135 over the pit where they pay up,
those sinners who sowed division.

124 **eight times** etc: for Minos's
manner of judgement see v, 4–12.

CANTO TWENTY-EIGHT

Who'd be capable, even in prose,
  of showing fully all the carnage
  I saw now? However many goes   3
I had, it could never be achieved;
  language can't cope, human minds
  haven't the faculty to take it in.   6
If all the crowds could assemble
  that in poor-rich Puglia's history
  have wept because of their wounds,   9
whether from Trojans, or the long war
  that made such a mound of rings
  in Livy's account, which is true;   12
these, with those bearing the brunt
  of Robert Guiscard's attack, others
  whose bones can still be found   15
at Ceprano, where all the Puglians

---

8 **poor-rich Puglia** etc: the south-eastern part of Italy, 'poor' because of its being contested in so many wars and battles (which Dante goes on to enumerate), 'rich' because of its beauty.

10 **from Trojans** etc: the first war referred to is that between the Romans ('Trojans,' i.e., descendents of Aeneas) and the Samnites (343–290 BC); see Livy's *History* of Rome, X. The other 'long war' is the Second Punic War, between Rome and the forces of Hannibal (218–201 BC).

Livy (Book XXIII) records that after the battle of Cannae in 216 three bushels of rings were gathered from the hands of dead Romans.

14 **Robert Guiscard** etc: the Norman warrior who conquered much of southern Italy in the eleventh century (died 1085).

16 **Ceprano** etc: a strategic site in the war (1266–8) between Charles of Anjou and Manfred, king of Sicily. The pass at Ceprano was abandoned without a fight by the Puglians, allowing Charles to advance to

betrayed them; and at Tagliacozzo,
18   where old Alard won, holding off:
get every man to show his slashes
and stumps of limbs, it'd be nothing
21   beside the squalor of bolgia nine.
Take a barrel, with a stave lost:
it wouldn't be holed like one I saw,
24   gutted from chin down to crotch:
the bowels hung out between his legs;
you saw his heart and the foul bag
27   that makes shit from all we swallow.
I was stuck, fascinated by him –
he gazed back, opening his chest,
30   saying, 'Have a look at my cardigan!
See how ragged it is on Mohammed!
Ali goes screaming in front of me,
33   sliced from his chin to his brow.
And all these you see down here
were sowers of splits and schisms
36   in life; so they're cut open now.
Back there, a devil dresses us up
so cruelly, with snips of his sword;
39   he fits us all with a new suit
at every lap of this awful track,
because the first is healed again
42   before we get back round to him.
But who are you, up on that rock

Benevento, where Manfred and much of his army were killed. Dante conflates the two incidents in locating the slaughter at Ceprano itself.

17 **Tagliacozzo** etc: here Charles of Anjou went on to defeat Manfred's nephew Conradin, by holding back a reserve troop who made a late and decisive intervention; the ploy was suggested by Charles's adviser Érard de Valéry (Alard).

31 **Mohammed**: founder of the Mus-

lim religion, born at Mecca c.570, died in 632. By tradition he was an apostate Christian cardinal, disappointed in his hopes of promotion to the papacy. Ali (l. 32) was Mohammed's son-in-law and follower, who himself founded a schismatic sect within Islam. The 'sowers of splits and schisms' (l. 35) in this *bolgia* include both religious and secular figures.

musing, perhaps postponing pain
  that your confession has merited?'   45
Master steps in: 'He's not dead yet,
  nor does sin haul him to torture;
  to complete his education, to me   48
– the dead one – it's given to lead him
  down through these circles of Hell:
  this is truth, just as I speak it.'   51
On hearing this, a great crowd
  stood still in the ditch to see me,
  stupefied, forgetting the bloodbath.   54
'Therefore, as you might soon see
  the sunshine, tell brother Dolcino
  if he's not keen to follow me fast   57
down here, to stock up on food;
  or snow will let the Novaran win,
  which otherwise wouldn't be easy.'   60
Mohammed had halted mid-stride
  to pass me this news, and now
  resumed his walk. The next one   63
had a hole right through the neck,
  a nose pruned back to the bridge
  and only one ear; he stood there   66
watching in wonder with the others,
  opening his windpipe to speak
  before them, as it bled everywhere: 69
'O you not condemned by crime
  and who I saw up above in Italy,
  either you or your double, that is,   72
have in mind Pier da Medicina,

---

45 **your confession:** i.e., to Minos
(see V, 8).
56 **brother Dolcino etc:** leader of a
sect known as the Apostolic Brothers, who preached a return to the
ideals of primitive Christianity. Condemned as heretics, they sought refuge in the hills near Novara, where

bad weather eventually led to their
surrender to the local bishop ('the
Novaran', l. 59). Dolcino was burned
at the stake in 1307.
73 **Pier da Medicina:** very little is
known of him, apart from his place
of origin (Medicina is a town in the
Po valley) and his reputation as an

so you see again the lush plain
75   sloping from Vercelli to Marcabò.
And tell the two most eminent men
in Fano, Guido and Angiolello,
78   that if foresight here is reliable
they'll be thrown out of their boat
near Cattolica, tied to weights,
81   betrayed by a bloodthirsty tyrant.
From Cyprus's island to Majorca
Neptune never saw such a crime,
84   not in the actions of any pirates
or Greeks. That one-eyed betrayer,
who rules land one here with me
87   wishes he'd never set eyes on,
he'll get them to parley with him;
then he'll ensure there's no need
90   for vows, prayers, at Focara's gale.'
I reply, 'Explain, and show me him
if you want news taken back of you –
93   him who regrets where he saw.'
Then he put his hand to the jaw
of a companion, opening the mouth,
96   shouting, 'He's mute, can't talk.

instigator of quarrels between the tyrants of Romagna (see note to XXVII, 37).

74 **the lush plain** etc: the boundaries of the Po valley plain are referred to here as the town of Vercelli and the castle of Marcabò, which was destroyed in 1309.

77 **Guido and Angiolello** etc: nothing is known about this incident except what Dante tells us here; as with Mohammed above, Dante has Pier 'prophesy' an actual event. The 'bloodthirsty tyrant' (l. 81) with one eye (l. 83) is Malatestino, lord of Rimini (see note to XXVII, 46); the two citizens of Fano were thrown overboard near Cattolica, ensuring that any worries they had about the notorious gales off Focara (l. 90) were redundant.

82 **From Cyprus's island** etc: i.e., such a crime had no equal in the history of the Mediterranean, with all its piracy ancient and modern.

86 **one here with me** etc: the identity of this figure, and why he wishes he'd 'never set eyes on' Rimini, is revealed below in answer to Dante's question, ll. 94–102. Caius Curio persuaded Caesar to cross into Italy over the river Rubicon near Rimini, thus ensuring the Roman civil war. See Lucan, *Pharsalia*, I, 261ff.

Exiled, he removed Caesar's doubts,
  insisting that when all's ready
  delay can only be a drawback.'   99
Ah, he was silent now all right,
  his tongue chopped off at the root –
  Curius, so eager to speak then!   102
And one with his hands sliced off
  raised his stumps in the murky air
  so that his face was all bloodied,   105
and shouted: 'Remember Mosca too,
  saying, "What's done is done with,"
  that began the Tuscans' troubles.'   108
I added: 'And the deaths of yours;'
  so that, with woe on top of woe
  he went off, maddened, miserable.   111
Now as I was watching the crowd,
  I saw something I'd be scared
  testifying, minus other witnesses;   114
but I'm backed by my conscience,
  that ally that gives a man heart
  and assurance he's in the clear.   117
I really saw – I almost see now –
  a body going by without a head,
  one among the other poor devils;   120
but it held the head by its hair,
  hand dangling it like a lantern,
  and it looked at us, moaning 'Oh . . .'   123
Yes, he lit his way with himself,
  two out of one, one out of two:
  how it's possible the Lord knows.   126

---

106 **Mosca** etc: Mosca dei Lamberti, whose laconic advice (l. 107) prompted the murder of Buondelmonte de' Buondelmonti and the beginning of the Guelph–Ghibelline conflicts in Florence. Buondelmonte was betrothed in 1215 to a member of the Amidei family, but reneged on the agreement; Mosca's urging of his murder led eventually, via the civil war, to the persecution of the Lamberti family themselves and to their expulsion from Florence in 1258 (l. 109). Mosca was one of the Florentines Dante had asked Ciacco about at VI, 80.

When he got up under our bridge
he lifted hand and head as one
129   so he wouldn't need to shout,
and said, 'Now see what pain is,
you living one, visiting the dead:
132   see if anything's worse than this.
And so you can take back my news,
know that I'm Bertran de Born,
135   evil counsellor to the young king.
I set the father and son at odds:
Achitofel was no worse with David
138   and Absolon, pricking them on.
Because I sundered those joined,
I carry my brains separately
141   from their stem in my poor body.
So the counterpass, on show in me.'

132 **see if anything's worse** etc: cf. Lamentations 1: 12.

134 **Bertran de Born** etc: lord of Hautefort (Altaforte) near Périgord, and one of the most famous troubadours of the twelfth century. His poetry celebrates the passions and violence of warfare (as in his celebrated *canzone* in the version of Ezra Pound, 'Sestina: Altaforte'). He is said to have set Prince Henry of England (the 'young king', l. 135) against his father, Henry II (also duke of Aquitaine). Bertran wrote another famous *canzone* commemorating the prince's death (also in a version by Pound: 'Planh for the young English king').

137 **Achitofel** etc: see 2 Samuel 15–17.

142 **counterpass:** this is Dante's only use of the term that expresses the concordance between sin and punishment that obtains throughout Hell. Bertran de Born's fate expresses it with a particular vividness. The term itself is taken from a medieval Latin translation of Aristotle's *Ethics*, and was often associated by commentators with the Old Testament's 'eye for eye, tooth for tooth' (Exodus 21: 24).

CANTO TWENTY-NINE

All the people, all the mutilations,
   they'd sated my eyes to overflowing
   so I wanted to stay and weep;   3
but Virgil says, 'Why keep looking?
   why indulge your sight down there
   among those sad, maimed ghosts?   6
You didn't do this in the other pits:
   if you're set on counting them all,
   think, this circles twenty-two miles.   9
The moon's already below our feet:
   not much time's allowed to us now
   to see what remains to be seen.'   12
'If you'd waited for why it was
   I looked there,' I said to him,
   'perhaps you'd have let me stay.'   15
He was already going, my leader,
   with me behind, replying to him,
   and I added: 'Inside that ditch   18
that I was studying so keenly now
   there's a soul of my own blood,
   I think, weeping his sin's costs.'   21
He says, 'Don't break your heart
   over him, while we're moving on,

---

9 **twenty-two miles**: in this and the next canto we get the first exact measurements Dante gives us of any part of Hell, leading to various critical attempts to plot the dimensions of the whole.

10 **The moon's** etc: the time is about 1 p.m.; seven hours or so have passed since the last time reference involving the moon (then on the western horizon) at XX, 124-7.

173

24   let him be, attend to other things:
   I saw him down beside the bridge
   point you out and shake his fist,
27   and heard his name, Geri del Bello.
   Then you were absorbed so totally
   in him who'd once held Altaforte,
30   you didn't look there till he'd gone.'
   'O my master, his violent murder
   that no one who shared the insult
33   has avenged yet,' I said to him,
   'this made him scornful; so he went
   without speaking to me, I reckon:
36   this made me pity him the more.'
   Meanwhile, on the rock, we're there
   where all the next pit is visible,
39   or would be, with greater light.
   When we're above this last cloister
   of Malebolge, so all its converts
42   can appear to our sight, howling
   assails me like tremendous arrows,
   their iron points tipped with pity,
45   so that my hands cover my ears.
   As much pain, as if every hospital
   in Valdichiana, Maremma, Sardinia
48   should from July to September
   spew all its patients into one pit;
   so it was here, plus that stink
51   that usually comes from ill bodies.
   We went down on the last bank

---

27 Geri del Bello: a cousin of Dante's father, named in documents between 1269 and 1276. It seems he was killed by a member of the Sacchetti family, and that his murder was in fact ultimately avenged. Dante's pity (ll. 31–6) for his unavenged (in 1300) kinsman exemplifies the belief in justified *vendetta* that prevailed in medieval Italy, unless Virgil's words 'attend to other things' (l. 24) are to be read as Dante's putting such matters behind him in his attention to the divine justice.

29 Altaforte: see XXVIII, 134 note.

47 Valdichiana etc: districts of Italy especially noted for malaria epidemics in summer.

of the long bridge, still leftwards,
   and then I had a better view   54
of the bottom, and justice unerring,
   high God's minister, as she works
   on falsifiers she noted upon earth.   57
I'm doubtful it was a sadder sight
   when all Aegina's people were sick
   and the air was full of plague,   60
when creatures to the lowest worm
   all fell, and the ancient people,
   according to the poets' claims,   63
were recreated again out of ants;
   so we saw along that dark ditch
   ghosts groaning in awful heaps.   66
They lay across each other's bellies,
   or their backs, or on all fours
   dragged their sad way onwards.   69
We walk slowly on in silence,
   watching and hearing the sick
   who seem powerless to rise up.   72
I saw two sat leaning together
   like pans warm against each other,
   dotted in scabs from head to toe;   75
and there's no horse ever combed
   by a groom late for his lordship,
   or one kept up in the evening,   78
as furiously as these two raked
   their nails down themselves, mad
   with the itch, with no other aid;   81
and their nails clawed the scabs
   like a cook skinning a bream
   with his knife, or other scaly fish.   84

---

57 **falsifiers**: the tenth *bolgia* contains in distinct groups the falsifiers of metals (alchemists), of identity, of money and of language. This canto concentrates on the first group, who lie down or crawl along the *bolgia* disease-ridden.

59 **Aegina's people** etc: the story of Juno's visiting a plague on the people of Aegina, and the island's being re-populated from ants, is told by Ovid, *Metamorphoses*, VII, 523-660.

Master says to one of them, 'O you,
unpicking yourself with your fingers
87   or using them on you as pincers,
tell us if there's anyone from Italy
inside here, so your nails endure
90   for the eternity they'll be needed.'
'We're both Italian, us you see here
so disfigured,' one says in tears;
93   'but who are you asking after us?'
And my guide: 'One who's descended
with this live man, level by level,
96   intent on showing Hell to him.'
Now they stop propping each other;
trembling, each turns towards me
99   with others who caught the words.
My good master comes up near me
and says, 'Ask them what you want;'
102   and I do as he wishes, saying,
'So your memory in the first world
doesn't vanish out of human minds,
105   so it lives on beneath many suns,
declare who you are, and your city:
don't let this hideous, awful pain
108   put you off revealing yourselves.'
'I'm from Arezzo,' one of them says,
'and Albero da Siena had me burnt;
111   but why I died didn't damn me.
It's true I said to him as a joke,
"I'm able to fly through the air":
114   at this, all whims and stupidity
he's after me to teach him the art,
and just because I'm not Daedalus
117   he has me burned by his "father".

---

109 **I'm from Arezzo** etc: Griffolino
d'Arezzo, alive in 1259, dead by
1272. In his disappointment at not
learning to fly, Albero had Griffolino
burned by the bishop of Siena, who
may have been Albero's real father
(l. 117).

116 **Daedalus**: see XVII, 109 note.

But to this tenth and final valley
  Minos, who can't mistake, damned me
  for the alchemy I used on earth.'   120
I ask the poet, 'Were ever people
  as empty-headed as the Sienese?
  Not the French, by a long way!'   123
And the other leper hears my words
  and says, 'But leave out Stricca,
  who knew how to be economical,   126
and Niccolò, who first introduced
  the expensive taste of the clove
  to the garden such seeds relish;   129
exclude Caccia d'Ascian's cronies
  who wasted his vines and timber
  and proved l'Abbagliato's wisdom.   132
But so you identify your seconder
  against Siena, sharpen your sight
  here, so my face is clear to you: 135
you'll see I'm the shade of Capocchio
  the alchemist, falsifier of metals,
  and if I see you right, you'll know   138
how well I aped things, by nature.'

120 **Minos, who can't mistake**: early commentators report that Griffolino was burned on a trumped-up charge of heresy, occasioned by the private grudge noted above; here the unerring justice of God is contrasted with the specious justice of men.

125 **leave out Stricca etc**: Dante's observation on the Sienese is ironically seconded by the new speaker, who refers to four examples of Sienese vanity. Stricca and Niccolò are usually identified as brothers of the Salimbeni family, members with the two other figures named in ll. 130–2 of a group of 'cronies' in Siena dedicated to luxurious and wasteful living (we have already met another of their number: see XIII, 120 note).

129 **the garden**: Siena itself.

136 **Capocchio**: a Florentine reputed to have been a fellow student of Dante, and a famous impersonator of others; he was burned alive as an alchemist in 1293.

CANTO THIRTY

During the period of Juno's fury
  against Thebes, because of Semele,
  as instanced on several occasions,   3
Athamas developed such a madness
  that seeing his wife and two sons
  go by, one in each of her arms,   6
he cried: 'Spread nets at the pass,
  I'll have lioness and cubs together;'
  then he reached his evil claws   9
to the one named Learchus, took him,
  swung him, smashed him on a rock
  while she drowned with her other.   12
And when Fortune turned the wheel
  on Troy's all-daring presumption,
  king and kingdom falling as one,   15
poor sad Hecuba, brought so low,
  she saw first her dead Polyxena

---

1 **During the period** etc: Juno was enraged against Thebes because of Jupiter's adultery with Semele, daughter of Cadmus, king of Thebes. Among her other acts of revenge she visited a madness on Athamas, husband of Ino (Semele's sister), who stalked his wife and two sons in the manner described. Ino and Melicertes jumped into the sea to escape the fate of Learchus and drowned (ll. 10–12). See *Metamorphoses*, IV, 512–62.

13 **And when Fortune** etc: Troy's destruction by the Greeks is seen as a just punishment for its 'all-daring' pride (l. 14), e.g., in the original abduction of Helen. Hecuba, wife of Priam, king of Troy, was made a slave by the Greeks, and later witnessed the murdered bodies of her daughter and son; she then clawed out the eyes of the latter's murderer, Polymnestor. In Ovid she is changed into a dog (*Metamorphoses*, XIII, 399–575).

18   and then came across Polydorus
   along the shore: she howled in pain,
    indeed like a dog, senseless,
21   misery had crazed her so much.
   But no lunatic of Thebes or Troy
    ever went at man or beast even
24   with the ferocity I witnessed now,
   as two souls, all pale and naked,
    raced around gnashing their teeth
27   like boars let out of their pens.
   One fastened on Capocchio's neck
    and bit tight, dragging him off
30   so his belly scraped on the floor.
   The Aretine was left there trembling
    and says, 'That devil Gianni Schicchi,
33   he goes crazy at people like that.'
   'So you don't feel the other's fangs,'
    I ask, 'pray tell us who that is,
36   before it hares off out of sight.'
   He says, 'That's the ancient spirit
    whose friendship to her own father
39   broke all bounds, the bad Myrrha.
   In order that she could sin with him
    she masqueraded as someone else,
42   just like the other, who dared,
   so he got the pick of the stable,
    to dress himself as Buoso Donati
45   and draw up and sign his will.'
   And now they'd gone their way,

22 **But no lunatic** etc: the two mythological references introduce the second type of sinner in this *bolgia*, the falsifiers of identity, reduced to rabid madness.

31 **The Aretine:** Griffolino.

32 **Gianni Schicchi:** his crime of impersonation is described below, ll. 42–5. A Florentine, he was induced by Simone de' Donati to masquerade as his father, who had already died, and sign a will ensuring that the family property was left to Simone; Gianni also willed himself the father's best horse (l. 43) as payment. Gianni had died by 1280.

39 **Myrrha** etc: who committed incest with her father by disguising herself as another woman; see *Metamorphoses*, x, 298–502.

these two rabid ones I'd watched,
   so I turned to the other sinners.   48
I saw someone almost like a lute:
   that is, if he hadn't had legs
   he'd have been lute-like exactly.   51
The heavy dropsy, deforming form
   with fluid that won't drain away,
   so the head is dwarfed by the guts,   54
it made him pant away with thirst
   like a consumptive, his lower lip
   drooling, the other lip turned up.   57
'You two who aren't being tortured
   in this dire place, I don't know why,'
   he says, 'look here and witness   60
the misery of me, Master Adam:
   alive, I had enough of everything
   and now, ah, a drop of water!   63
Those streamlets on the green hills
   of Casentino, trickling into Arno
   coldly and softly in their courses,   66
I can always see them; with reason,
   they dry me more than this sickness
   that strips the flesh off my face.   69
The absolute justice that proves me,
   it takes the region I sinned in
   to make my sighs go even faster.   72
Romena's there, where I falsified
   the coin stamped with the Baptist;
   I left a body burned for it above.   75

61 **Master Adam** etc: the representative of the falsifiers of money, he seems to have been born outside Italy, but established his forge at the castle of Romena (l. 73) in the Casentino, the hilly region of the upper Arno south-east of Florence. His being plagued by visions of the Casentino streams recalls the famous punishment of Tantalus in the classical Hell.

74 **the coin stamped** etc: i.e., the Florentine florin, decorated with an image of the city's patron, John the Baptist. Adam seems to have been burned for his crimes (l. 75) in 1281.

But if I saw Guido's sad soul here,
       or Alessandro's, or their brother's,
78   I'd swap Branda fountain for it.
One of them's here, if the lunatics
       that charge round can be trusted;
81   but what good's it to me, crippled?
But if I was slim enough to travel
       even one inch in a hundred years,
84   I'd have begun the trek already
to find him in this diseased crowd,
       even though it's eleven miles round
87   and half a mile wide, at least.
They introduced me to this family:
       through them I forged the florins
90   that had three carats base metal.'
I ask, 'Who are the two poor devils
       lying near together on your right,
93   steaming away like winter washing?'
'They were here when I dropped in,'
       he says, 'and haven't moved since –
96   I don't think they ever will move.
It's the liar who accused Joseph
       and false Sinon, the Trojan Greek:
99   they boil over from fierce fever.'
Well, one of them didn't enjoy it,
       being described like this perhaps,
102   and he punches that taut belly
making it boom out like a drum;

76 But if I saw Guido's etc: Adam explains later (ll. 88–90) that the figures he now mentions induced him to operate as a forger: the Conti Guidi brothers, rulers of Romena, of whom Guido (died 1292) had already been condemned to this same *bolgia* (the others dying after 1300).
78 Branda fountain: either the famous fountain of that name in Siena, or a spring that once rose near Ro-mena itself.

86 eleven miles round: see note to XXIX, 9.

97 It's the liar etc: the two falsifiers of language are Potiphar's wife, the accuser of Joseph (Genesis 39: 7–19) and Sinon, who pretended to swap sides in the Trojan war ('the Trojan Greek', l. 98) and persuaded the Trojans to take the wooden horse into the city (see note to XXVI, 56).

then Adam hits him with his arm
   back in the face, just as hard,   105
and tells him, 'Though I can't move
   because of the weight in my paunch,
   I've an arm free when I need it.'   108
The other says: 'It wasn't so free
   when they hauled you to the fire,
   but nimble enough for forging.'   111
And him with dropsy: 'True enough –
   shame you couldn't tell the truth
   when they asked you for it at Troy.' 114
'I faked truth as you did coins,'
   Sinon says, 'but mine was one lie,
   yours more than any other devil!'   117
'Don't give me that, you perjurer,'
   shouts big belly, 'recall the horse –
   all the world knows your crime!'   120
'And your crime cracks your tongue
   with thirst, and fills you with pus
   so your belly blocks your view!'   123
Then the forger: 'Your trap opens
   and evil comes out, as previously;
   I might be thirsty and swollen   126
but you burn with your headaches,
   and to lick at Narcissus's mirror
   you wouldn't want much inviting.'   129
I was completely absorbed in them
   when master tells me, 'Just keep on!
   Any more and I'll lose my temper.' 132
When I heard him angry with me
   I turned to him in such shame
   my memory still keeps it fresh.   135
Just as someone having a nightmare
   wishes he wasn't: dreaming already,
   he wants it all to be a dream –   138

128 **Narcissus's mirror**: water; see   *Metamorphoses*, III, 407–510.

well, this was me: I couldn't speak
to excuse myself as I wanted to,
141   but excused myself without knowing.
'Less shame washes away more crime
than you're guilty of,' says master,
144   'so off with any dismay you feel;
but understand I'm always by you
if it happens you arrive again
147   where folk are arguing like this;
wanting to hear evil is evil itself.'

CANTO THIRTY-ONE

The same tongue first stings me,
   bringing colour to both my cheeks,
   and then turns into my medicine;   3
just as I've heard of that lance
   that Achilles and his father had,
   harmful at first and then benign.   6
So we turn from that grim valley,
   crossing the bank that borders it
   and going onwards, in silence.   9
Here, it wasn't night, it wasn't day,
   so my sight didn't get very far;
   but I heard a trumpet sounding   12
so loud, any other would be faint,
   and retracing this noise's journey
   my eyes fixed on one point alone.   15
After the tragic rout of Charlemagne
   when he lost the holy company,
   Roland's call was never so terrible.   18
So I look, and seem to make out
   a lot of high towers – and I ask,

---

4 **that lance** etc: according to tradition, Peleus and later Achilles possessed a lance that could inflict wounds and then heal them; the image was a commonplace in medieval love poetry to express the power of the lady.
16 **the tragic rout** etc: in the medieval French epic *La Chanson de Ro-* *land*, Charlemagne's nephew Roland was given command of the rearguard of the Christian army, returning from fighting the Saracens in Spain. Attacked and defeated by his enemies in the pass of Roncevalles, Roland alerted Charlemagne, eight miles away, with a blast on his horn.

21   'Master, tell me, what's this city?'
      'Because you pierce these shadows
      from too far away,' he tells me,
24   'you go astray in your fashioning.
      You'll realise as you arrive there
      how much this far view tricks you,
27   so push yourself further onward.'
      But then he takes my hand kindly,
      saying, 'Before we go any closer,
30   so it seems less uncanny to you
      know these are giants, not towers,
      and they're in the well at its edge
33   sunk from their waists downwards.'
      Just like when fog starts to thin,
      your eye gradually figures things
36   the air-padding vapour hides,
      so, as I penetrated that obscurity
      and got even nearer to the brink
39   error fled and terror increased;
      because, just as round its circle
      Montereggion's crowned with towers,
42   so around that enormous well
      half their bodies are towering up,
      horrible giants, ones that Jupiter
45   threatens still, when it thunders.
      One face I'd already made out,
      shoulders, chest, much of the belly
48   and the arms hanging alongside.
      When she left designing such beings
      Nature undoubtedly did very well,
51   depriving Mars of such performers,

---

41 **Montereggion:** a castle outside
Siena, circled by a wall carrying fourteen towers, though these are now
not so high as in Dante's day. There
is a photograph of it in Singleton's
commentary on the *Inferno* (1970),
opp. p. 568.

45 **threatens still** etc: i.e., Jupiter re-
minds the giants of their defeat at his
hands at the battle of Phlegra; see
note to XIV, 58.

51 **depriving Mars** etc: referring to
the giants' propensity for violence.

and if she doesn't repent of whales
  or elephants, it seems more discreet
  to subtle thinkers, and more just: 54
because where the force of reason
  is added to malice and to power,
  there's no defence men can make.   57
The face seemed as long and wide
  as the pine-cone in St Peter's, Rome,
  with the other parts in proportion;   60
so that the bank, like his apron
  lower down, still revealed enough
  above, that three men of Friesland   63
couldn't claim they'd reach the hair:
  so thirty large palms he appeared
  to me, to where you'd tie a cloak.   66
'Raphel mai ameche zabi almi'
  the fierce mouth starts shouting,
  knowing no more tuneful psalm,   69
to which master replies: 'Idiot soul,
  stick to the trumpet – play on that
  to vent your anger, or whatever!   72
Search your neck, the strap's there
  that holds it, you muddled oaf,

---

59 **the pine cone** etc: made of bronze and over seven feet high, today displayed in the Vatican. See Singleton, opp. p. 570.

63 **men of Friesland** etc: a province of the Netherlands, noted for the height of its inhabitants. Attempts to chart the exact dimensions of the giants from the details given, like those to plot the dimensions of Hell itself (and later those of Lucifer), run into various problems; estimates of the giants' height vary between 50 and 80 feet.

67 **Raphel** etc: Virgil later identifies this giant as Nimrod (l. 77), held by patristic commentators to have presided over the attempt to build the Tower of Babel to 'reach unto heaven', an act of presumption which God thwarted by visiting a confusion of tongues on the builders, the origin of the earth's diversity of languages (see Genesis 10: 8–10, 11: 1–9). It is therefore fitting that Nimrod's own language here is gibberish. Dante follows tradition in seeing Nimrod as a giant; his horn (l. 71) derives from the description of him in the Bible as 'a mighty hunter'. In the giants (as in Lucifer) Dante is concerned to give a picture of inert, oafish and massive stupidity.

75   that stripe down your vast chest.'
He tells me: 'He's his own accuser:
it's Nimrod, through whose mad plan
78   one language isn't used on earth.
Let him be, let's not waste words:
every language is alike to him
81   as his to others – no one knows it.'
And so we move on, going left,
and a bowshot away is another,
84   only much more big and ferocious.
Who the locksmith might have been
I don't know, but he was bound
87   with a chain, left arm in front,
the other behind, from neck down
the chain twisting round his body
90   five times, over the visible part.
'He wanted to test his power out
on high Jove, this vainglorious one,'
93   my master says, 'hence this reward.
It's Ephialtes; his great push came
when the giants were striking fear
96   into the gods: the arms he flexed
then, now he never moves.' I say:
'That measureless one, Briareus,
99   I'd like to see him if it's possible.'
He replies: 'You'll see Antaeus nearby

94 **Ephialtes** etc: he and his brother (sons of Neptune) attempted to invade heaven and make war on the gods by piling Mount Pelion on top of Ossa; Apollo slew them both (see *Aen.*, VI, 580–4).
98 **Briareus**: in the *Aeneid* a monster with fifty heads and a hundred arms who also threatened Jupiter (X, 565–8); here Virgil describes him as monstrous only in stature, like Ephialtes (ll. 103–5).

100 **Antaeus**: Dante meets this giant later, at ll. 112–13. He dwelt in the valley of the Bagradas, in Libya, where Scipio later defeated Hannibal at the battle of Zama, and lived off lions (ll. 115–18). He is not chained here (l. 101) because he didn't take part in the war of the giants against the gods, a piece of good fortune for the latter (ll. 119–21). Dante takes his details from Lucan, *Pharsalia*, IV, 593–660.

who can speak and isn't in chains;
　he'll put us on the floor of Hell.　　　　102
Him you want is much further on,
　bound like this one, like him too
　to look at, only much more fierce.'　　　105
And no earthquake ever raged away
　to make a tower shift violently
　as Ephialtes was ready to shake.　　　108
I feared death more than ever then,
　death coming from the terror alone
　if I hadn't noted those chains.　　　111
Now on we go, arriving beside him,
　Antaeus, standing five good spans
　out of the well, the head apart.　　　114
'O you who, in that fateful valley
　ever glorious because of Scipio
　and Hannibal's retreat with his men,　　　117
made meals of a thousand lions;
　who, if you'd been at the epic war
　with your brothers, some men say　　　120
the sons of earth would have won;
　don't disdain to lower us down
　to where Cocytus is locked in ice.　　　123
Don't make us use Tityus or Typhon:
　what is craved here, this man gives,
　so bend, don't turn your nose up.　　　126
He's able to renew your earthly fame:
　he's alive, and expects long life
　unless Grace calls him to Him early.'　　　129
Thus master spoke; and at once
　he's taken by those hands, whose grip

123 **to where Cocytus** etc: i.e., the
floor of Hell.
124 **Tityus** etc: another of the rebel
Titans, slain by Apollo for his attempted rape of Latona, and staked
out in Tartarus with vultures eternally eating his liver (see *Aen.*, VI,
595–600). Typhon was a rebel giant
slain by Jupiter and buried under
Mount Etna; Lucan mentions the
two giants together (*Pharsalia*, IV,
593–7).

132   Hercules once felt in all its force.
   And Virgil, when he felt himself held,
    tells me, 'Here, so I can take you,'
135   and binds us close with his arms.
   As someone looking up at Garisenda
    on the side it leans, when it moves
138   or seems to, if a cloud approaches,
   so Antaeus was to me, all anxious
    to see him bend; and then it was
141   I'd have liked another way down.
   But gently on the bottom, that gorges
    Lucifer and Judas, he put us off;
144   and without delay, after leaning over
   he was up again, like a ship's mast.

132 **Hercules once felt** etc: however in Lucan's account Hercules managed to kill Antaeus by lifting him off the earth (contact with which renewed his strength) and crushing him in the air.

136 **Garisenda**: the smaller of the two leaning towers in Bologna, built in 1110.
143 **Lucifer and Judas**: see canto XXXIV.

CANTO THIRTY-TWO

If I had rough, grating verses
   that would suit the awful void
   all the other circles press on,   3
I'd squeeze the juice of my idea
   more fully; but since I haven't,
   I worry here, starting to speak: 6
it's no schoolboy lark, to describe
   the bottom of all the universe,
   no theme for a baby's prattle,   9
so may those Muses help me now
   who helped Amphion wall Thebes,
   so that my poem fits the facts.   12
O worst of creation, stuck here
   where it's so hard to describe,
   better had you been born beasts!   15
As we stood in that black basin
   lower down than the giant's feet,
   while the high wall stupefied me,   18
I heard a voice: 'Look out there,

1 **rough grating verses**: indeed Dante's Italian in this canto is conspicuous in the prevalence of hard consonants to express the asperity of the deepest part of Hell. What we are about to witness contrasts with the pause in the brutality of the action found in the previous canto.
11 **who helped Amphion** etc: Amphion was able to wall Thebes through the sheer delight of his lyre-playing (assisted by the Muses), so that stones from Mount Cithaeron drew near and composed the wall of their own accord; see Horace, *Ars poetica*, ll. 394–6. Dante's invocation here, like that at the beginning of canto II (l. 7), stresses the solemnity and arduousness of his undertaking.
13 **O worst of creation**: i.e., the traitors, the inhabitants of Cocytus.

don't kick our heads as you pass;
21   we're still brothers in our pain.'
So I turned, and saw all around
a lake under my feet, iced over
24   as if the water had become glass.
No veil as thick could ever cover
the Danube in an Austrian winter,
27   nor the Don under its cold sky
as was here; if Tambernicchi
or Pietrapana collapsed onto it
30   it wouldn't creak, even at the rim.
And like frogs poke their heads
above the pond to croak, that time
33   the country girl dreams of harvest,
so up to where we display shame
the sad, blue ghosts were iced in,
36   teeth a-chatter, sounding like storks.
They all kept their faces bent down,
mouths witnessing the cold, and eyes
39   the misery here in every heart.
I looked all round, then I saw
two so close, right at my feet,
42   their hair was knotted together.
'You two, cheek to cheek,' I say,
'who are you?' Necks straighten,
45   they lift their faces up to me,
and tears confined to eyes before

28 **Tambernicchi** etc: various identifications of this mountain have been made. It may well be Tambura, in the Apuan alps, near to which Pietrapana (now known as Pania della Croce) is situated.

34 **where we display shame**: i.e., the face. The first category of sinners, whose heads are free of the ice, are those who betrayed members of their own family. This first region of Cocytus is known as Caina (l. 59), after the first fratricide (Genesis 4: 8). It is the place referred to by Francesca (v, 107) as the destination of her murdering husband. The Cainites are able to hold their faces down so that their tears don't freeze at source, a relief not granted, it seems, to the second category of traitors, those with 'lifted faces' beginning at l. 70, and one which the third category certainly feel the lack of (see the following canto, ll. 91ff.).

trickle to their lips, freeze over
and so lock them together again.   48
No bolt ever screwed two blocks
so close, and they butt like rams,
so much anger overcomes them.   51
And another, who'd lost both ears
with frostbite, still looking down
says, 'Why gaze in us like a mirror?   54
If you want to know their names,
the valley Bisenzio drops from
was their father Alberto's, and theirs.   57
One body bore them: you'll search
all Caina, you won't find spirits
better qualified for this freezer,   60
not him with chest and shadow
holed by one thrust from Arthur,
not Focaccia; not him whose head   63
blocks my vision wholly like this,
whose name is Sassol Mascheroni;
if you're Tuscan, you'll know him.   66
And to avoid further conversation,
know that I'm Camicion de' Pazzi,

56 **Bisenzio** etc: the valley of the Bisenzio near Florence, where the two souls referred to owned much land. They are Napoleone and Alessandro, sons of Alberto degli Alberti, who killed each other in 1286 – the culmination of a long squabble over their father's property (they also took different sides in the Guelph–Ghibelline conflict). Alessandro's son later killed Napoleone's.

62 **holed by one thrust** etc: in the old French romance of *Lancelot du Lac*, Arthur's nephew Mordred tried to overthrow the king. Arthur killed him with a thrust of his lance that went right through the body, so much so that sunlight was able to

pass through the wound.

63 **Focaccia**: Vanni dei Cancellieri, a White Guelph from Pistoia who murdered his cousin.

65 **Sassol Mascheroni** etc: a Florentine who in a celebrated case killed a cousin in order to become his uncle's heir. Before being beheaded he was rolled round the streets of the city in a cask pierced with nails.

68 **Camicion de' Pazzi** etc: Alberto Camicione dei Pazzi di Valdarno, who killed a kinsman, Ubertino, in order to enjoy sole possession of their joint property. His crime will be 'mitigated' in comparison with that of another kinsman, Carlino (l. 69), who in 1302 betrayed a castle where

69   waiting my mitigation in Carlino.'
Next I saw a thousand lifted faces
purpled with cold, so I'll shiver,
72   always, at any pond with ice on.
So we headed towards the centre
that every weight converges on,
75   me frozen in the eternal dark,
and by chance, design or destiny
I don't know, but my foot struck
78   a face, hard, as I threaded them.
It screams in pain, 'Why kick me?
Unless you're adding to the penalty
81   of Montaperti, why pick on me?'
I say, 'Master, wait for me here
till I make certain of this one;
84   afterwards, I'll hurry as you wish.'
So he halted; I say to this other
who's still mouthing away like mad,
87   'Who are you, dressing me down?'
'Who are you, visiting Antenora,'
he replies, 'smashing people's jaws
90   so that I just wouldn't bear it
if I was alive?' 'I'm alive,' I say,
'and a friend if you want fame –
93   I'll put your name in my records.'
He says, 'It's the opposite I crave;
clear off, don't pester me again,
96   you'll sell nothing in this sump!'
Well, I got him then by the scruff

---

many of the White Guelphs had taken refuge from the Blacks. As a traitor of cause, or party, Carlino will be punished in the second region of Cocytus.

81 **Montaperti:** see note to X, 32.

88 **Antenora:** the second part of Cocytus, for political traitors, is named after Antenor, the Trojan who was reputed in the Middle Ages to have betrayed his city to the Greeks, and to have opened the gates to the wooden horse.

94 **It's the opposite** etc: the traitors have naturally no great relish for being commemorated on earth; they are keener in this canto to denounce and identify others rather than name themselves.

and I said, 'You name yourself
  if you want any hair left on top.'   99
And he says, 'You can scalp me,
  I won't tell you name or number,
  not if you bounced on my head.'   102
My hand was still among his hair,
  and I'd plucked a few tufts off
  as he howled, still looking down,   105
when another cries: 'What's up, Bocca?
  Aren't chattering teeth noisy enough
  without shouts? What devil has you?'   108
'Right,' I say, 'no more from you,
  you bloody traitor; to your shame
  I'll report back truly about you.'   111
'Away,' he says, 'say what you like;
  but if you get out, don't forget
  this one who blabbed just now.   114
He laments here his French money:
  you can say, "I saw him of Dovera
  among the guilty in the cooler."   117
If they ask, "Who else is there?"
  him of the Beccaria is alongside
  whose neck the Florentines axed.   120
Over there is Gianni de' Soldanier,

---

106 **Bocca**: the sinner's identity is now finally betrayed by one of his fellows, though at the mention of Montaperti (l. 81) Dante had obviously suspected who he was. Bocca degli Abati was a Ghibelline sympathiser who affected to fight on the Guelph side at Montaperti, where he attacked the Guelph standard-bearer, leading to loss of the standard and confusion of the Guelph forces. Dante's physical actions underline his loathing of such a crime here.

114 **this one who blabbed** etc: Bocca gets his own back by identifying, among others, 'him of Dovera' (l. 116), i.e., Buoso di Dovera, who betrayed Manfred in giving passage to the French forces of Charles of Anjou (see note to XXVIII, 16).

119 **him of the Beccaria**: Tesauro dei Beccaria, Pope Alexander IV's legate in Tuscany, beheaded by the Florentines in 1258 for intriguing with the exiled Ghibellines.

121 **Gianni de' Soldanier**: a Florentine Ghibelline who betrayed his party in 1266 and went over to the Guelphs.

I think, with Ganellone and Tebaldello
123   who opened Faenza while it slept.'
We'd already moved away from him
when I saw in the same ice-hole
126   one head on another, like its hat;
like a famished man savages bread,
so the upper one chewed the other
129   there, where brain meets the nape.
Tideus must have dined like this
on Menalippus's forehead, in his hate;
132   so the menu here, skull and so on.
'O you who behave like an animal
in your hatred of him you eat,'
135   I say, 'explain this situation;
if your anguish over him is just,
with your name and his crimes
138   I can yet recompense you on earth
while there's a tongue in my head.'

122 **Ganellone** etc: in the *Chanson de Roland*, the knight who betrayed Roland and the rearguard of Charlemagne's army to the Saracens; see note to XXXI, 16. Tebaldello de' Zambrasi avenged himself against the Bolognese Ghibellines by opening the city gates to the Guelph forces in November 1280.

130 **Tideus** etc: one of the seven kings who laid siege to Thebes (see note to XIV, 46). Given his death blow by Menalippus, he managed to kill his enemy in turn, and when the latter's head was brought to him savaged it as he died. See Statius, *Thebaid*, VIII, 739-62.

CANTO THIRTY-THREE

His mouth leaving that grisly snack,
  the sinner wipes it with the hair
  of the head he'd eaten at the back   3
and begins: 'You want me to renew
  the hideous grief that wounds me
  even in memory, before I speak.   6
But if I sow the seeds of disgrace
  for him, this traitor I'm chewing,
  you'll see me speak, and weep too.   9
I don't know who you are, or how
  you've come down here; Florentine,
  though, that's what your talk seems,   12
so you'll know of me, Count Ugolino,
  and this is Archbishop Ruggieri:
  hear why I'm patting his shoulder.   15

4 You want me to renew etc: cf. Aeneas's famous words to Dido prefacing his account of the fall of Troy: 'Infandum, regina, iubes renovare dolorem . . .' (*Aen.*, II, 3).

9 and weep too: the line echoes that spoken by Francesca at V, 126. The present episode, one of the most famous in the poem, is often compared with the equally celebrated canto V; the two sinners here, in their mutual hatred and betrayal, form an interesting pair to put alongside Paolo and Francesca.

13 Count Ugolino etc: the speaker identifies himself, knowing that the basic facts of his death would already be well known to anyone from Florence. Ugolino di Guelfo della Gherardesca was a Ghibelline nobleman, who worked however to secure the Guelph triumph in Pisa in 1275, the betrayal which probably led to Dante's putting him in Antenora (see note to l. 86). After several reversals he gained control of the city in 1284, but a Ghibelline uprising in 1288 led by Archbishop Ruggieri degli Ubaldini (following on Ruggieri's betraying a pact he held with Ugolino) led to his imprisonment and death the following year.

That it was through his evil plans
I was captured, after trusting him,
18   and then murdered, I needn't say –
but what you couldn't have heard
is just how cruel my death was,
21   so hear now, then judge my case.
That hunger tower named after me,
though I won't be its final inmate,
24   there's a crack in the wall there
I could see the new moon through
month by month, before that dream
27   that rent the future's veil for me.
I dreamt this man led the hunting
for wolf and cubs, on that mountain
30   that blocks Lucca from Pisan eyes.
Gualandi's, Sismondi's, Lanfranchi's,
they were all well up to the front
33   with fast dogs, trained and hungry.
It wasn't long before they flagged,
father and cubs, and their flanks
36   were ripped into by the sharp teeth.
Before morning I woke up; I heard
my lads who were with me crying,
39   and begging bread in their sleep.
You're a hard man if you don't cry,
realising what my heart forbode:

22 **That hunger-tower** etc: the Torre dei Gualandi in Pisa (no longer standing) henceforward to be known as the 'Tower of hunger' after Ugolino and his fate.
26 **month by month**: Ugolino was imprisoned from June 1288 till his death in February 1289.
29 **on that mountain** etc: Mount Pisano or San Giuliano, situated between Pisa and Lucca.
31 **Gualandi's** etc: Ghibelline families who assisted the archbishop in his attack on Ugolino; the 'hungry' dogs indicate the popular support the Ghibellines had.
38 **my lads**: Ugolino was imprisoned with two of his own sons, Gaddo and Uguiccione, and two grandsons, Nino ('Brigata', l. 89) and 'little Anselmo' (l. 50), aged about fifteen. Thus 'the pages of the most intense human pity in the entire *Comedy*' in Sapegno's words achieve their effect in part through Ugolino representing his 'lads' as younger than they actually were.

if you don't, what do you cry at?   42
They were all awake; the time came
  our food was usually given to us,
  and our dreams made us all fret;   45
and then I heard that hideous tower
  having its door below nailed up;
  and I just looked at my boys.   48
I didn't cry, I was stone inside,
  but they cried: my little Anselmo
  says, "Dad, what are you thinking?"   51
I didn't reply or shed any tears
  all that day or the following night,
  until the sun came back to us.   54
But as soon as a ray of light
  entered that awful prison, I saw
  my own face in their four faces   57
and gnawed my hands in my pain;
  they thought I did it in hunger
  and at once they all rose, saying,   60
"Father, our misery would be less
  if you ate us: you clothed us
  in this poor meat, you unclothe us."   63
I calmed down, to keep them calm;
  two more days we were all quiet;
  why didn't earth swallow us up?   66
And then when we came to day four
  Gaddo threw himself at my feet
  crying, "Dad, why can't you help?"   69
and there he died; as you see me,
  I saw three more fall one by one
  over two more days; blind by now,   72
I could only grope about for them
  and call them, two days further:
  then hunger was stronger than grief.'   75

75 **then hunger** etc: i.e., hunger finally overcame Ugolino and his grief
by killing him. There seems little
critical support for the idea that

Ugolino fed on the bodies of his dead
sons, hunger 'overcoming' grief in
that sense.

He said this, then twisted his eyes
and his teeth back to that skull,
78   crunching the poor bone like a dog.
Ah, Pisa, Pisa, you shame everyone
in the lovely lands that say 'sì';
81   as neighbours delay punishing you,
may Capraia and Gorgona uproot
and dam the mouth of the Arno
84   so that everyone inside you drowns!
Even if Count Ugolino betrayed you
over some castles, as rumour ran,
87   why torture his children for it?
They were too young to be guilty,
you new Thebes – Uguiccione, Brigata
90   and the other two recorded above.
So on we passed, and now the ice
binds another lot of people tight,
93   not vertical, but on their backs.
Their own tears prevent them crying,
grief finding a barrier in the eye
96   and returning to increase the pain,
since the first tears make a lock
like a kind of crystalline visor
99   filling all the cavity of the brow.
And although like calloused skin

80 **that say 'sì'**: i.e., in Italy.

82 **Capraia etc**: two islands near the mouth of the Arno, beside which Pisa stands.

86 **as rumour ran**: while in power in Pisa, Ugolino allayed the threat of the union of Genoa, Florence and Lucca against him by ceding to these cities some Pisan castles. Here Dante seems to be suggesting that such an action was a betrayal only in rumour, and that Ugolino's presence in Antenora is due to other factors (see note to l. 13).

89 **new Thebes**: ancient Thebes was notorious for the bloody events in its history (see e.g., XXX, 1ff., XXVI, 54); there was a tradition that Pisa itself had been founded by a daughter of the Theban royal house.

91 **on we passed etc**: into the third section of Cocytus, Tolomea (l. 124), for those who betray their guests. It is named either after Ptolemy, governor of Jericho, who invited his father-in-law Simon to a banquet with his two sons and then slew them (1 Maccabees 16: 11–17), or after Ptolemy, king of Egypt, who killed Pompey after he had taken refuge with him.

all feeling had fled from my face
  on account of that enormous cold,   102
I still thought I felt some wind:
  so I ask, 'Master, what causes this?
  There's no circulation down here?'   105
And he says, 'We'll soon be there
  where your eyes will answer that
  and see the reason for this breeze.'   108
Then a spirit from the ice crust
  shouted at us: 'You wicked pair,
  allotted the final place in Hell,   111
smash the hard veil from my eyes
  so I can relieve myself a little,
  before these tears ice over again.'   114
And I say, 'If you want any help
  tell me your name; I'll unveil you
  or go right to the ice's bottom.'   117
Then he says, 'I'm brother Alberigo
  whose fruit was from an evil garden;
  here I'm served dates for my figs.'   120
'What!' I say, 'You're already dead?'
  He tells me, 'How my body does
  up on earth, I've no knowledge.   123
It's the privilege of this Tolomea
  that souls will often plummet here
  before Atropos slices their threads.   126
And so you'll smash more willingly
  these tears that glaze my face,
  I'll tell you this too: like mine,   129

117 **or go right** etc: as it turns out, Dante himself practises treachery here, of course, since he's heading for the bottom of the ice in any case.

118 **brother Alberigo** etc: Alberigo di Ugolino dei Manfredi, a Jovial Brother (see note to XXIII, 103) from Faenza, and a leader of the Guelph party in the city. In 1285 he invited two kinsmen he was in dispute with to dine with him; the call for the fruit to be brought in was the signal to his men to appear and kill them.

120 **I'm served dates** etc: i.e., my punishment amply compensates for my crime. The date was more valued than the fig.

126 **Atropos** etc: i.e., death. Atropos was the Fate who cut the thread of life.

all traitors' bodies are taken over,
the moment they sin till they die,
132   by devils that rule their actions.
The soul drops into this ice-rink;
perhaps the body still shows above
135   of the ghost wintering behind me.
You'll know him, if you're new down:
he's Branca d'Oria; several years
138   have passed, since he was frozen.'
'You're having me on,' I tell him;
'why, Branca d'Oria's never dead,
141   he eats, drinks, sleeps and dresses.'
He says: 'Where the Malebranche are,
in that boiling pit of thick pitch,
144   Michel Zanche hadn't arrived there
before this one vacated his body
to a devil; a kinsman did the same,
147   who helped him in his treachery.
But now, reach your hand out here,
open my eyes.' Well, I wouldn't:
150   it was manners being rude to him.
Ah, you Genoese, you're all strangers
to anything decent – you rabble,
153   why isn't the earth cleared of you?
With that evil spirit from Romagna
I found one of yours, such a sinner
156   that in soul he's already in Cocytus
while in body he seems alive here.

137 **Branca d'Oria** etc: Branca, as-
piring to the governorship of Logodoro, murdered his father-in-law
Michel Zanche (see XXII, 88) after
inviting him to dinner, abetted by a
kinsman (l. 146). Alberigo reveals
that the murderer's soul arrived in
Hell even before his victim's did
(ll. 142–6), though Branca's body remains active on earth. There is uncertainty over the date of the crime
(either 1275 or 1290); Branca died
c.1325. The fact that he came from
Genoa leads to Dante's concluding
invective against the Genoese
(ll. 151–7).

154 **from Romagna**: i.e., Alberigo.

CANTO THIRTY-FOUR

'*Vexilla regis prodeunt inferni*
  towards us; if you'd see them,'
  master says, 'look forward now.'   3
As when a thick cloud blows over
  or when it's dark, imagine the look
  a windmill takes in the distance,   6
and that's what I seemed to see;
  and then I drew in behind master,
  the only windbreak I could find.   9
We were – I tremble to write it –
  where souls were fully iced over
  like splinters beneath the skin: 12
some are horizontal, some vertical,
  stood on their feet or their heads;
  others have heads and feet joining   15
in a big bow. And now we arrived
  where it pleased master to show me

1 *Vexilla* etc: 'The banners of the king of Hell advance.' The Latin is an adaptation of the opening of a hymn sung on Good Friday before the unveiling of the Cross, where 'the banners of the king' refer to the Cross itself. Here they refer to Lucifer's six wings (see ll. 46–52). The ritualistic invocation sets the tone for the awesome subject matter of this final canto.
11 **where souls** etc: i.e., in the final zone of Cocytus, Judecca (identified at l. 117), named after Judas, where those who betrayed their benefactors are found.
13 **some are horizontal** etc: the different positions doubtless represent different modes of treachery; e.g., treachery to benefactors who are equals (horizontal), superior (upsidedown), inferior (upright), and treachery to both superiors and inferiors (arched).

18   that creature, once so beautiful:
he moved aside and made me stop:
'Here is Dis,' he said, 'and here
21   you'll need every bit of courage.'
How shivery and weak I felt then,
don't ask, reader: I don't write
24   where words can only fall short.
I wasn't dead, I wasn't alive:
think, if you've the faintest idea,
27   how I felt, not one nor the other.
The emperor of that dire empire
was stuck chest deep in the ice;
30   and I'd come nearer to a giant
than a giant would to his arm,
so you see how enormous he was
33   with all of him on this scale.
If he's as ugly as he was lovely
when he stood up to his maker,
36   all pain indeed derives from him.
Oh, what a marvel followed then,
when I saw he had three faces!
39   One vermilion, looking forwards,
and another two joining this one
above the middle of each shoulder,
42   all three uniting at the crown –

18 **once so beautiful:** Lucifer was the fairest of created beings before his fall. Dante, here as elsewhere, refers to him as Dis, l. 20; see note to VIII, 68.

38 **three faces:** Lucifer is plotted in careful antithesis to the idea of the Godhead. He has already been referred to as an 'emperor', recalling the description of God at the beginning of *Hell* (see I, 124), and here the three faces on one head are a travesty of the divine Trinity. They invert the attributes of the Trinity given at III, 5–6: power is replaced by impotence (the yellow face), wisdom by ignorance (the black face), love by hate (the vermilion face). Other interpretations of the faces have been proposed. Lucifer retains his six cherub's wings, but now in an ugly, bat-like form (ll. 46–9). Modern readers have sometimes expressed disappointment in him; see for example T. S. Eliot, who believed that 'Dante made the best of a bad job' ('Dante', *Selected Essays*, 3rd ed., 1951, p. 251).

the right a sort of yellowy-white,
the left coloured like the people
who live where Nile descends.   45
Two huge wings beneath each face
stuck out, big as everything else,
bigger than the sails on a ship,   48
not feathered, more like a bat's;
these he was flapping around him
and so giving rise to three winds: 51
this is what makes Cocytus freeze.
His six eyes weep, his three chins
drip with tears and gory slaver.   54
In each mouth, his teeth grind away
at a sinner; as you'd rake flax
with a scutch, so this poor trio,   57
but to him in front this chewing
was nothing next to the clawing:
his back was regularly skinned.   60
'That soul suffering most up there,'
master tells me, 'is Judas Iscariot,
stuck inside his mouth head first.   63
The others whose heads dangle out
are Brutus, inside the black snout,
writhing in silence as you see,   66
and in the other, hefty Cassius.
But night is rising again, now
we must go – we've seen it all.'   69

---

57 **scutch:** a rake-like tool, used to
pound flax to separate out the fibres.
62 **Judas:** see Matthew 26: 14–25.
65 **Brutus** etc: Brutus and Cassius,
two of the principal conspirators
against Julius Caesar, here paralleled
with Judas in illustration of Dante's
world-view that the Empire was ordained by God as the optimum political system governing man's secular
welfare, just as the Church took care
of his spiritual state. Dante's politics
are presented in his treatise *Monarchia*, and discussed in my Introduction. The reference to Cassius as
'hefty' (l. 67) seems to show he is
confusing Caesar's assassin with the
L. Cassius mentioned by Cicero (*In
Catilinam*, III, 7).
68 **night is rising again:** twenty-four
hours have passed since the poets
began their journey at the beginning
of canto II.

He wanted me to hold round him
    as he chose his time and place:
72   when the wings opened enough
he grabbed on to those shaggy ribs
    and climbed down, tuft by tuft,
75   between the coat and the ice crust.
When we reached where the bone
    curves out, right on the hip joint,
78   master then, panting and straining,
he got his head where his legs were,
    then climbed up the skin: I thought
81   we were heading back into Hell.
'Hold tight – by stairs like these'
    – he says, gasping with the effort –
84   'it's fitting we quit so much evil.'
Then he made for a rocky cavity
    and sat me on the edge of it,
87   following after with his sure step.
I looked up, expecting to view
    Lucifer exactly as I'd left him;
90   but I saw his legs up in the air:
I leave the ignorant to imagine
    how amazed I was – they won't see
93   what that point was I'd crossed.
'Up,' says master, 'on your feet:
    the way is long, the path is wild,
96   the sun's at half-terce already.'
It wasn't like a palace ballroom
    where we were, but a real cavern
99   with a rough floor and no light.

93 **that point:** the centre of the earth, and consequently of gravity, which 'every weight falls towards' (111).
96 **half-terce:** terce is the first of the canonical hours of the day, running from 6 to 9 a.m. The time is therefore about 7.30. Dante is bewildered (l. 105) to learn that it is already morning, after having been recently told it was dusk (l. 68). Having passed to the antipodes of course he is now about ten and a half hours behind what he was (allowing about an hour and a half to climb down Satan's body).

'Before I surface from this abyss,
  please master,' I say, on my feet,
  'clear things up for me a little: 102
where's all the ice? And him there,
  how's he upside-down? The sun,
  how's it made morning so quickly?'   105
He says, 'You still think we're over
  beyond the centre, where I took
  this wicked earth-maggot's coat.   108
We were as I climbed downwards;
  but turning, we passed the point
  that every weight falls towards.   111
You're under the other hemisphere
  now, to that over all the lands
  below whose centre he was killed,   114
the man born to live without sin;
  you're standing on a little sphere
  whose opposite face is Judecca.   117
It's day here when it's night there;
  and this one, our shaggy stairway,
  he's still fixed as he first was.   120
On this side he fell from heaven;
  and land that spread here before
  he frightened away under the sea,   123
driving it to our hemisphere; perhaps
  the island over here hurried up

112 **You're under** etc: 'the other hemisphere' here is the southern celestial hemisphere, opposite the northern one that covers 'all the lands' (the northern terrestrial hemisphere was supposed to contain all the earth's dry land, the southern being all sea). Christ, 'the man born to live without sin' (l. 115), was crucified at Jerusalem, on the central point of the northern hemisphere following Ezekiel 5: 5 ('I have set [Jerusalem] in the midst of the nations . . .').

121 **On this side** etc: Dante has Lucifer fall to earth directly opposite the site of Jerusalem, and fables that land which previously existed on the surface of the southern hemisphere was frightened away by his fall to congregate in the northern.

125 **the island** etc: Mount Purgatory, which Dante will visit in the next section of the *Comedy*, and the only land 'over here', i.e., in the southern hemisphere, at the antipodes of Jerusalem. Virgil suggests it

126   away from him, leaving this cave.'
         At the farthest spot from Beelzebub
         you could reach inside that tomb,
129   you can hear but you can't see
         a little stream; it's flowed down
         through eating a hole in the rock
132   with its winding, gradual course.
         Master and I by this hidden way
         set off, back to earth and light;
135   and without any care for resting
         up we climbed, him ahead of me,
         until I saw through the tunnel
138   some beauties that stud the sky;
         and out we were, back to the stars.

was formed by the land that Lucifer displaced at the centre of the earth, as well as by the land that occupied the cavernous space where Virgil and Dante now stand (Lucifer's 'tomb', l. 128), fleeing from him.

127 **Beelzebub:** a frequent name for Lucifer in the Gospels, e.g., in Matthew 12: 24.

139 **and out we were:** i.e., just before morning on Easter Sunday. The journey through Hell has taken the twenty-four hours between the dusk of canto II (Good Friday, l. 1) and XXXIV (l. 68); in crossing the centre of the earth Dante has 'returned' to the morning of Easter Saturday (see note to l. 96); and the ascent up the passageway to the surface of the earth takes another twenty-four hours or so.